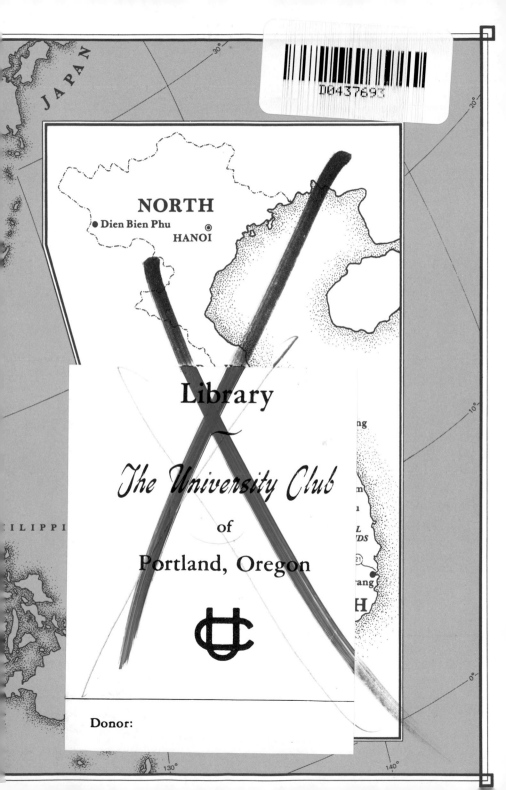

NORTH
● Dien Bien Phu   ◉
         HANOI

Library

The University Club

of

Portland, Oregon

The
Last
Ambassador

The
Last
Ambassador

A Novel by

BERNARD KALB &
MARVIN KALB

LITTLE, BROWN AND COMPANY   BOSTON · TORONTO

FIRST EDITION

Excerpts from *Great Spring Victory* by General Van Tien Dung,
chief of staff of North Viet Nam's People's Army, unofficial translation from *Nhan Dan*, the official newspaper of Viet Nam's Communist Party, April 1976, as relayed by Foreign Broadcast Information Service.

Library of Congress Cataloging in Publication Data

Kalb, Bernard.
  The last ambassador.

  1. Vietnamese Conflict, 1961–1975 — Fiction.
I. Kalb, Marvin L. II. Title.
PS3561.A41628L3   813'.54   81-8259
ISBN 0-316-48222-0   AACR2

MV

Designed by Janis Capone

*Published simultaneously in Canada
by Little, Brown & Company (Canada) Limited*

PRINTED IN THE UNITED STATES OF AMERICA

NOTE

Saigon was overrun by North Vietnamese Army units on April 30, 1975. That is a fact. The characters in this book are fiction.

For our daughters
Tanah
Marina
Deborah
Claudia
Judith
Sarinah
and their generation

Acknowledgment

Our gratitude to Phyllis Kalb
for her creative contribution

The
Last
Ambassador

Prologue

"When the decision to attack Ban Me Thuot was definitely taken . . . I hastily prepared to go to the front. . . . I promptly organized a group of cadres to accompany me. . . . The group had the code name A-75. Due to the importance of the campaign, my movements had to be kept under the strictest secrecy and everything had to be done to distract the enemy's intelligence. According to plans, after my departure, the press would carry a number of reports of my activities as if I were still in Hanoi. Daily, the Volga sedan would make the trips from my house to the General Headquarters at 7 AM and 2 PM and from the General Headquarters to my house at 12 noon and 5 PM sharp. Late in the afternoon, the troops would come to the courtyard at my house to play volleyball as usual, because I have the habit of playing volleyball after the afternoon working hours with them.

"I signed in advance the messages of greetings on the occasion of the Army Days of the USSR and GDR — February — and of Mongolia — March 1975 — to be sent out when the time came. I prepared in advance New Year gifts and cards. . . . All the preparations — beds, hammocks, clothes, and knapsacks of everyone in the A-75 group — were made at the office of the General Headquarters. . . .

"My personal secretary, who lived with his family in a community area, would pretend serious illness on the eve of the departure. An ambulance would bring him to a hospital, and the next morning he would begin his journey from the hospital. . . . In all communications, information, liaison, and discussions during this campaign, Comrade Vo Nguyen Giap would be referred to as Chien, and I as Tuan.

"On 5 February 1975, that is, the 25th day of the 12th lunar month, I went to Gia Lam airfield to take a plane for Dong Hoi. Hanoi was full of flowers at the approach of the new spring. I was in a general's uniform instead of the pajama-type clothes of the cadres going to the B region. This was to give the impression that I was going to Quang Binh to make an inspection of the troops there. . . .

"At 1030 AM sharp, the AN-24 plane took off, two hours later than scheduled. . . . Our plane landed at Dong Hoi. . . . We went to Quang Tri by car. . . . Coming to the bank of the Ben Hai River, we boarded a motor boat going upstream. It was sunny, but the weather was very cool. Late in the afternoon, we landed at a river port in the southern part of the river and went to the 559th Troop Command in western Gio Linh. . . .

"Lying in a cottage, I could not sleep, although night had long since descended, because I kept thinking about the coming campaign in which we must achieve victory in the Central Highlands . . . and, particularly, about how we were going to conduct the attack on Ban Me Thuot. We should fight hard to cause the enemy's quick collapse. My usual combat method again came to mind — launching surprise attacks against the enemy, conducting a lightning offensive, and smashing the enemy's command. However, I wondered if all this could actually be carried out. . . .

"We continued to go farther into the rear. Our vehicle's number plate was repainted and the marking TS-50 was added to it. This marking meant priority No. 1 for the Truong Son troops.

"On the strategic route, our combatants were actively building or repairing the roads. Female shock youths sang and laughed while working. . . . They said: Commander, the Lunar New Year is drawing near, yet we have not got any letters from home. We stopped and gave them a few hundred hairpins as gifts. Groups of trucks roared northward after bringing ammunition to the battlefront. The brother drivers stretched out their hands, saying: Commander, we are now on the eve of the Lunar New Year and we have no cigarettes left. We handed them some cigarettes as Tet presents.

"On the way, we met Division 316 going on a military operation. This was the first time this division had used 500 trucks to move its men and equipment to the battlefront. An order had been given to this division: From the time its men set out until the time they opened fire, they must have absolutely no radio contact, so as to keep their operation secret. We intercepted an enemy radio message saying Division 316 could no longer be seen and no one knew where it was going. . . .

"Electric lights equipped with shades for protection against enemy planes were used everywhere. On the morning of the first day of the Lunar New Year, the brothers displayed flowers, glutinous rice cakes, pork-pies, cigarettes, candy, and jams on a large table. We enjoyed the festival with them and wished them new armed exploits in the New Year. . . .

"On arrival in the Central Highlands, I established the command post west of Ban Me Thuot. . . . Our residence was in a green forest . . . the dry leaves of which covered the ground like a yellow carpet. Whenever someone walked on these dry leaves, they cracked as crisp griddle-cakes do, and the noise could be heard in every part of the forest. A small spark might set the forest afire. Combatants of signal and communications units had to work hardest here. Whenever a fire broke out and destroyed communications wires, these combatants set out to quench the fire and returned with their bodies as black as coal miners'. Another problem was caused by herds of 40 to 50 elephants which snapped communication wires, even though some of these had been hung on high tree branches. . . .

5

"Up to that moment, the enemy had not yet thought about the possibility of our organizing an offensive with large-scale forces. The enemy had not yet clearly realized that our forces were on this side of Ban Me Thuot since he could not detect our movements. In the coming days, it would be necessary to continue to make the enemy believe that our main thrust would be toward Kontum and Pleiku. . . .

"By maintaining the element of surprise concerning the target, the time and the fighting method, isolating the enemy and bringing into play a decisively superior force without the enemy's knowledge, we would insure fewer losses and quicker victory in battle. . . .

"My secretary . . . reported to me on a new incident: The Front Command reported that a group of officers of our artillery regiment had had an engagement with the enemy west of Ban Me Thuot on 5 March while on a reconnaissance mission. One of our combatants was wounded and captured with his diary. I thought: 'We will attack Ban Me Thuot within 4 days. What will the enemy do in the coming days? So far, he has misunderstood us as far as our main offensive target is concerned; but if similar incidents revealing our secrets continue to occur, the enemy will certainly reassess the situation. . . .' I telephoned Comrade Vu Lang to remind him to closely check the implementation by each soldier of all regulations on the preservation of secrecy. . . .

"On the night of 9 March we were at the command post, watching developments in the situation and awaiting D-hour. Staff officers sitting around me could not conceal their joy and emotion as the important moment drew near. For those soldiers who were braced for the fighting that night, waiting for D-hour was like waiting for New Year's Eve to come. All our soldiers, from the top brass to the rank and file, had been awaiting this 'New Year's Eve' for many years now. What a tranquil night in the Truong Son Range! But tens of thousands of men were moving to their targets.

"All commanders, some of whom had white hair, were now

checking their plans on maps for the last time. It was certain that at this moment the puppets from Saigon to the Central Highlands could not guess how we were going to act. Nor could they calculate our strength. We had led them from one mistake to another. . . ."

> — *Excerpted from "Great Spring Victory," a personal account of North Viet Nam's victory over South Viet Nam, written by General Van Tien Dung, North Viet Nam's Chief of Staff; he served as field commander of North Vietnamese forces in South Viet Nam in the fighting that led to the collapse of the Saigon regime in the spring of 1975.*

1

It was a lovely way of shutting out the war on a boring Sunday in Saigon in the spring of '75.

Tony and Suzanne, fingers touching, lay sprawled across a rattan bed covered with a six-by-nine Stars and Stripes. "My Country 'Tis of Thee" flowed softly from a tape deck. Old newspaper photographs of JFK, LBJ, and Nixon were tacked on the wall. Yet the red-white-and-blue ambience saturating Tony Catlett's room on Gia Long Street was anything but evidence of homesickness — just the opposite, a personal spoof of the Americanization of South Viet Nam.

Suzanne reached out and clicked off the tape deck.

"What's the matter?" Tony murmured. "You tired of 'our song'?"

"I can't shake off the feeling that we're a triangle. That even on Sundays your mind is still on *him.*"

Tony shook his head, turned toward Suzanne, gently stroked the curve of her thigh.

She removed his hand. "I appreciate the thought, Tony, but I'm not convinced." She made a move to leave the bed.

He pulled her toward him. They tumbled together, laughing, touching, both glistening with the humid wetness of the Saigon morning. Their bodies were streaked with slats of pale light that filtered through the bamboo blinds. A ceiling fan with wooden blades circled slowly, scarcely stirring the tropical heat.

Suzanne's fingers drummed lightly on Tony's chest. "Actually," she whispered, "I think my father's rather fond of you."

"See?" Tony smiled. "This time it's *you* who brought him up."

"Conditioning. Except for my four years in college, I've lived all my life under the spell of that giant ego. Do you know what it's like? An only child? A widowed father? And now, just as I thought that I'd found someone who could replace him, it turns out — I can hardly believe it — that you are as obsessed with him as I've always been."

For Tony and Suzanne, Hadden Walker, U.S. Ambassador to South Viet Nam, was not exactly a new subject of discussion; in fact, he increasingly dominated their agenda. They could be in a noisy Chinese restaurant in the Saigon suburb of Cholon, picking their way through a menu, and Tony would ask the waiter for an order of "sweet and sour Walker." They could be strolling through the hot streets of the capital, talking about nothing more threatening than a sudden cloudburst, and Tony would say something about "an ambassadorial thunderclap." Or they could be where they were now, at Tony's place on one of the many tree-shaded streets in Saigon, and both Tony and Suzanne would feel he was right there in bed with them.

"Sometimes I wonder . . . ," Suzanne began.

"What, my love?" Tony kissed her neck.

". . . whether you'll ever be able to separate me from him. Whether you, me, him, this damned war, are not knit together in some kind of crazy tapestry. Pull one thread and the whole picture unravels."

"The first time I saw you . . ."

"I was with him."

"You were with him. Was it only a year ago? God, by then I had already been here *four* years. The airport at Tan Son Nhut that day was a furnace, the diplomatic corps strangling in their suits and ties. I remember thinking how cool and sleek the official plane looked, landing in that blistering wasteland."

Suzanne kissed the nape of his neck where the dark hair lay

9

in damp wisps. "And then?" She had heard him tell the story many times, of his first sight of her, but she wanted to hear it again.

"And then," Tony teased, knowing what she was waiting for, "I saw *him* come down the ramp, Hadden Walker, America's finest, starched, silver-haired . . ."

"And then?"

He couldn't resist laughing. "And then . . . I saw *you.* Silhouetted against the clouds. From where I was standing, way back, I couldn't see this beautiful face, only the halo of auburn curls." He buried his face in her hair.

She pulled him closer. "Nice," she said. "I like it, so far. What about the dress? Tell me about the dress."

"Ah . . . the famous dress. A swirl of raspberry and pink. It was those buttons down the front that really got me."

"Really?"

He winked at her. "As if you didn't know. I remember how quickly, that day at Tan Son Nhut, you diverted my eyes from official business. How I kept thinking that *un*official business might have a more interesting future." He ran his hands from her thighs to her hips to her breasts to her face, where his fingers traced the contours of her cheekbones.

"You are the handsomest, most charming, funniest spook I've ever had the pleasure of loving."

"Excellent. Perfect diplomat. You haven't lived with your father for nothing."

"See — there he is *again.*"

"I remember his arrival speech, even now." Tony began to mimic the Ambassador's imperial style. " 'United States will not dishonor its word . . . Americans and Vietnamese have died side by side . . . this nation may live in freedom . . . not go back on our commitment . . . America's pledge . . . *my* pledge . . . stand by ARVN — the brave Army of the Republic of Viet Nam.' " Tony's voice relaxed. "And then the goddamned applause."

"It was a good speech, Tony. He *meant* it."

"I *know* he meant it. That's what's so fucking sad." He recalled the way Walker had saluted the flags of the two countries, then descended from the platform to shake hands with the VIPs. Walker was clearly the towering figure, commander-in-chief in mufti.

"A whole generation of ambassadors had said those same words before him," Tony went on. "They *all* meant it. Once even I meant it. But there he was, so late in the war, standing on the tarmac, meaning it all over again. Meaning to dig us in deeper instead of trying to get us out."

"Tony, is there *anybody* who has a monopoly on wisdom about this war?"

For a long moment, they lay in separate silence.

"A marvelous performance that day, your father's," Tony finally resumed. "America the invincible. But who stood behind all that rhetoric? The President? The State Department? The Pentagon? The American people? Whose commitment was it? *His alone?*"

Suzanne clapped silently, a satire of applause. "And who in God's name appointed you 'Resident Genius'? Why are you right and he's wrong?"

"Because I deal in raw data. I see it, Suzanne, like it is. Corrupt. Rotten. Irreversible. Hopeless. Want more?"

"And he?"

"*He* filters it . . . through honor . . . and power . . . and responsibility. Sentiments that turn the truth into star-spangled fantasies."

"You're beginning to sermonize." She wrapped the bedsheet around her. "Can't we have a cease-fire — a cease-talk — between us, about him?"

Tony slowly pulled the bedsheet down to her waist. "Your terms are much too generous," he murmured. "I am prepared to offer you unconditional surrender."

She reached out to him, their bodies meeting swiftly, famil-

1 1

iarly. After a while, they rolled apart, drained, staring at the ceiling. It was covered with a giant-sized map of South Viet Nam — with a blood-red circle around Saigon.

"How about a change in scenery?" Suzanne asked suddenly. "Just some place away from the KIA, WIA, MIA, Tony. We both can use a change of geography, vocabulary, faces." She propped her head up on her arm, leaned over, kissed his cheek. "Couldn't the Agency get along without you for a few days?"

"That's very flattering." He picked up a handful of darts he kept on the floor next to the bed and began pitching them at the small Viet Cong flag pinned to the wall. One after the other, the darts missed the bull's-eye: the yellow star centered in the half-blue, half-red rectangle.

"See," Suzanne said. "You really do need a break. Try. That mind of yours hasn't been trained by the CIA for nothing. Be devious. Think of a good conspiratorial reason for getting away. Out of the country. Where shall we go?"

"Maybe you're right . . . this war is forever anyway. And it's only because you are the Ambassador's daughter —"

"Cease-talk!"

"Violated it again." He laughed. "The war *is* in one of those lulls. The intelligence we're getting from the field suggests that the North Vietnamese have nothing more ambitious in mind, at least for the moment, than a few nibbling actions. Same old monotony, same old meat grinder. In go soldiers, out come casualties."

"Well then, how about . . . Bali?" Suzanne's voice filled with sudden excitement.

A rush of impressions crowded Tony's mind: terraced rice paddies climbing toward the sky, walled temples, bird-boned twelve-year-old nymphets moving sinuously to the rhythm of the gamelan. "You've never been there?" he asked.

Suzanne shook her head.

"Okay, Bali!" Tony shouted, leaping from the bed. "Last one dressed is a VC."

He caught a glimpse of his face in the mirror hanging from

a captured AK-47 that was mounted on the wall; the boyish, eager look he had brought to Saigon in 1970 had been replaced by an expression of anxiety, as though he were constantly on guard. He remembered his mother once joking that she had bought his face at Tiffany's — not during a sale, either. Well, Tony thought, if there had been any glitter at all, it was gone now; Viet Nam had siphoned off the gold.

Suzanne's face suddenly appeared, the top of her head almost on a level with his. She looked into his dark eyes and said, almost apologetically, "I'll have to stop by at the orphanage before we do anything about Bali. Thi and Thach . . . they wait for me every day. I'll need to explain to them —"

"Don't move," Tony said. Their faces were close together in the mirror, as though they were posing for a photo in a locket. They stood very still, looking into each other's reflected eyes, both conscious of a sudden need to freeze the moment. She looked marvelous, Tony thought, exciting, a mischievous glint of sex in her face, her mouth half open, lips wet, eyes glowing amber.

It was Suzanne who broke the image, with a flirtatious wink. "Love me?" she asked.

"Adore you."

" 'Love me?' is what I asked."

"Complicated word, 'love.' " He could see his arm in the mirror reaching around her neck. "Scary. Especially in Saigon. Is 'love' possible in such a crazy place — where nothing is real?"

"Love's love," Suzanne said. She threw a kiss at the mirror. "Say after me, 'I love you.' "

Tony looked at his mirrored mouth. " 'I love you,' " he repeated.

Suzanne laughed. " 'A' for pronunciation, 'B' for emotion. You'll have to practice, if you're ever going to convince me."

They turned from the mirror.

Tony plucked a stray dart from the wall. Stepping back a dozen paces, he took careful aim at the center of the VC flag —

and let go. The miniature feathered missile whirled over the tape deck, the stacked books, his pile of clothes and hers — and hit an inch from the edge of the flag.

"Off target again," Tony muttered. "Just like the U.S. in Viet Nam."

He reached down, picked up Suzanne's bra and white cotton blouse, her flowered skirt, and tossed them to her. He was just climbing into his khaki trousers and safari-style jacket when the phone rang. "Oh God," Tony groaned.

"Who can that be — Sunday morning?" Suzanne asked.

"Miss South Viet Nam?" Tony laughed. "My fellow spooks? Your omnipresent, omniscient . . . family relation?"

Suzanne laughed. "If you don't answer, it will go away."

"The White House? Telling us the war is over and we can all go home?"

The ringing persisted. Tony, frowning, picked up the phone. He nodded to Suzanne, holding his hand over the receiver. "A fellow spook it is," he whispered.

Suzanne smiled. But as she watched Tony's face coming to attention, her antennae, diplomatically fine-tuned after years of living with her father, picked up the distress signals. "Bye, bye, Bali," she murmured to herself.

"Some new stuff just in from the boonies, Tony," said the voice at the other end of the line. "Looks like 'Big Daddy' may be up to some mischief in the Central Highlands. Not far from Ban Me Thuot."

The NVA near Ban Me Thuot? Tony's eyes narrowed. ARVN, he knew, was stretched thin in that area and had very little in the way of heavy equipment there. What the hell was the NVA — the North Vietnamese Army — doing in that part of the Central Highlands? There had been no intelligence reports that "the other side" was infiltrating new units into that godforsaken region.

"Just to let you know, Tony," said the voice. "Nothing urgent. I hope."

Tony hung up and turned to Suzanne and told her that a bit

14

of a military mystery might be unfolding in the Central Highlands.

Suzanne shook her head. "And I suppose," she said, "that there's only one super-spook who can —"

Tony nodded.

"— find out what it's all about?"

Tony grinned. Until she spoke, he had not realized that he had already decided to fly up-country for a recon of Ban Me Thuot.

Minutes later, in Tony's 1969 white Fiat convertible, they were wheeling through the crowded streets of Saigon — a city that, for Tony, was always a kind of surrealistic blur of sun-sprayed fingers: manipulating fingers, delicate fingers, massaging fingers, thieving fingers, begging fingers, weary fingers, trigger-callused fingers, fingers in a corrupt cauldron that the French in their colonial heyday had called "The Pearl of the Orient."

As Tony maneuvered through the city's tangle of traffic, he could not resist telling Suzanne about the contrasts he always felt between weekend Saigon and weekday Saigon. The city was as usual enveloped in a haze of blue automobile exhaust, but the Sunday crowds were less frantic, strolling instead of running, smiling instead of scowling, individuals rather than a confetti of repetitious people. Sundays, even the pickpockets seemed to conduct their affairs with a touch of elegance, less jostling. The whores seemed less brazen; they still littered the doorways on Le Loi, Nguyen Hue, and Tu Do and still called out to every passing foreigner but they seemed to recognize that weekends required less garishness, more ladylike behavior. It was as though Saigon ached to be a "pearl" once again — except that it never worked; it was all surface, never real, and the symptoms of war were everywhere: green camouflage uniforms, M-16 rifles slung across shoulders, amputees who had left an arm or a leg on a battlefield long since forgotten. And everywhere the undercurrent of constant tension, of never knowing whether the smiling old lady with the betel-stained teeth selling you a bouquet of coral gladioli wasn't a Viet Cong agent. Or whether the gladioli were not simply the packaging of a plastique that would later explode in your bedroom.

At Tan Son Nhut, Tony jumped out of the Fiat. He waved at Suzanne and whistled the opening bars of "My Country 'Tis of Thee."

"You're off-key," Suzanne shouted, but Tony didn't hear her. By then, he was racing toward the compound operated by Air America, the "cover" for the CIA airplanes operating out of Saigon.

2

Within a half hour, Tony was airborne, flying north in a twin-engine Beechcraft in the direction of Ban Me Thuot, 150 miles north-northeast of Saigon. The pilot, Jim Barnes, an old hand in the skies over Viet Nam, struck Tony as the original air jock straight out of Captain Midnight; snub-nosed, crew-cut, just over six feet tall, he never went anywhere, not even to a Saigon bar, without a pistol on his hip and a sheathed bayonet in his left flying boot. Jim knew the South Vietnamese terrain — every mountain, every valley, every forest — better than he knew the streets of his Louisiana home-town.

Tony's eye reconnoitered the landscape below; South Viet Nam looked deceptively serene, almost sensuous, a panorama of endless green glittering in the tropical sun, with shafts of light bouncing blindingly off a thousand pockets of water, old bomb craters filled with accumulated rain. "War can be beautiful," he said through the intercom.

"Only from seven thousand feet," Jim replied.

Both men studied the landscape as they flew north toward the Highlands. The flat provinces just north of the capital slowly began to bulge, the foothills of the Chaine Annamitique looking like green hippos taking a nap. Still life, posing for a photograph.

About an hour out, the photograph caught fire.

"Over there!" Tony shouted. "To the right." Bursts of smoke — yellow, gold, orange — erupted from the ground. The plane began vibrating, shaken by artillery blasts from below.

"You see that little clump of forest off to the left?"

Tony nodded.

"Well," Jim went on, "It wasn't there yesterday. The bastards moved in during the night carrying their own trees. Damned good cover."

The forest spat out tongues of flame — big guns at work.

"What the hell is going on?" Tony called out. ARVN units shooting at each other by mistake? Crazy bastards, Tony thought. But it wouldn't be the first time. His mind instinctively produced a printout of a CIA map, back at the Embassy, with all the known NVA positions in this area. The printout showed only scattered ARVN units in the vicinity of the Darlac provincial capital of Ban Me Thuot, no NVA — *no NVA* — and if those were NVA down there, it could mean only one thing: the North Vietnamese had succeeded in outwitting Saigon and U.S. intelligence once again, infiltrating into a region where they had not yet been detected. Where they *had* been detected in any kind of strength — anything approximating the force of the artillery explosions below — was more than a hundred miles to the north, in the jungles east of Cambodia and west of the strategically situated Highlands city of Pleiku. Some unusual NVA movements had been spotted *there*. Not here.

"Can we go lower?" Tony asked, desperately hoping that, on closer inspection, the firing down there would prove to be an accidental ARVN shoot-out.

"You're my guest," replied Jim, nonchalantly. The Beech dropped from seven thousand feet to three thousand feet. The four-thousand-foot descent only made the salvos look much more threatening.

It had to be NVA, Tony thought: ARVN did not have that

kind of heavy weaponry at its disposal in this sector. The big guns were laying down a barrage of fire, blasting at targets on the far approaches to Ban Me Thuot. No, there was no mistake, and given the intensity of the firing it was obvious that the NVA had moved in a lot of heavy equipment and was positioning itself for what Tony sensed would be a major attack.

The plane suddenly shuddered.

"Whoopee!" Jim shouted. "We've taken a hit."

Tony could see Jim anxiously maneuvering to retain control of the plane. For a moment, the Beech seemed to hang in mid-air. Jim pulled the yoke back slowly — and the plane began to climb.

"Stay cool, man," shouted Jim. "It's a war." He pointed to the wing, to a small tear in the aluminum skin. "Just a lucky hit by an NVA sharpshooter, a little memo from our 'friends' suggesting that we mind our own business."

"Let's go higher," Tony said.

"Still want to watch the show?"

"If you think it's okay."

"You're my guest."

They climbed to ten thousand feet, Jim volunteering that the higher altitude should put them out of enemy reach. "Unless of course," he added, "the Russkies or the Chicoms have shipped the NVA some new long-range stuff."

Jim piloted the plane in lazy circles in the pastel sky while Tony studied the terrain below. The continued heavy firing by the NVA confirmed his original estimate: the enemy seemed to be opening up a critical new front in an area where earlier only sporadic firefights had taken place. Why?

In the distance, Tony could see the town of Ban Me Thuot, the sleepy capital of the tribal mountain people known as the Montagnards. He remembered the place as having an exotic *National Geographic* look to it: Montagnards strolling barefoot through the dusty streets or thudding into town on the backs of elephants. In their loincloths, the Montagnards were an odd, anachronistic contrast to the Chinese shopkeepers and French coffee-tea-and-rubber planters who gave Ban Me Thuot a hint of the cosmopolitan.

Ridiculous, thought Tony, for a battle to be starting up, this late in the war, in the very place where America had first slid into the conflict — brandishing butterfly nets. Those first GIs, back in the early 'sixties, had been Special Forces soldiers — on the CIA payroll — who posed as, of all things, lepidopterists. What they were actually trying to catch were the seminomadic hill people, to train them in the art of twentieth-century killing and to lead them in battle against "the other side." It was a most unlikely place to launch an "Uncle Sam Wants You" campaign, but the Montagnards — from the Rhade, Jarai, and other tribes — volunteered by the thousands. For one thing, the pay was good, more money than their civilization had ever seen; Tony remembered CIA home movies showing the Montagnards lined up on payday for piastres that had been flown in by the sackful from Saigon. But the piastres were an incidental bonus.

The Montagnards' real craving was for modern weapons with which to even the score with their old enemy, the Vietnamese. For decades, the Vietnamese, from the height of their comparative sophistication, had looked down on the mountain people as *"moi"* — savages — fully deserving to be deprived of their tribal landholdings. Armed only with crossbows, the Montagnards had no real way of resisting — that is, until the "lepidopterists" arrived with their bulging arsenals. But there was a little problem. The Montagnards had to be taught to aim their newly acquired weapons at the *right* Vietnamese — those from the North and not from the South. This subtle distinction was wasted on the Montagnards; to them, a Vietnamese was a Vietnamese.

Tony scanned the erupting landscape. Wouldn't it be the ultimate irony, he thought, the last bit of crazy comedy, if some of these very U.S.-trained Montagnards — right down there, below — were now leading NVA troops over secret mountain trails and being paid for their guide services with promises? Promises that the Montagnards would be left to rule over their own lands, once Hanoi won? Tony pressed his face against the window. Nothing had changed in this fickle fuckle war since those first GIs had arrived with their nets: the U.S. was still chasing butterflies.

By now, Tony had seen enough, enough to know that he was witnessing still another intelligence failure: disastrous for the Agency, disastrous for ARVN, disastrous for the Embassy, disastrous for the U.S. One of these days, it was going to be more than a single disaster; they were going to lose the whole fucking country.

"Let's get back — fast," he shouted. "If you were a chopper, I'd ask you to land on the Embassy roof."

Jim did a U-turn and headed the plane back toward Saigon.

"I'm a Beech, Tony," he said, "but if only that roof had a few feet of runway, I'd give it a try. You're my guest."

For Tony, the ride from Tan Son Nhut to the U.S. Embassy in downtown Saigon was an exercise in self-control. Traffic was always a mess; he drove the borrowed jeep in bursts, darting into every opening in the long chain of mammoth American V-8s, Renault *deux chevaux* left behind by the French, Honda motorcycles carrying families of five on two seats, *cyclopousses* peddled by weary Vietnamese, the endless maddening bicycles. Thirty-five minutes later, he made a left turn off Cong Ly and sped down Thong Nhat. Looming ahead was the Embassy — a six-story dazzlingly white reinforced-concrete cube that towered over the local hodgepodge of Oriental, French, and bastardized architecture.

He hurried straight past the Marine at the main gate, and a nick of history caught his eye. The nick was just to the right of the Embassy doorway: a slight crevice produced by a VC bullet during the Viet Cong's '68 Tet offensive that had penetrated the Embassy grounds. That bullet, violently multiplied by VC and NVA barrages and ground assaults on U.S. positions throughout South Viet Nam, had driven one President out of the White House and his successor to military disengagement from Viet Nam — on the installment plan, between '69 and '73. "Coitus interruptus," someone had observed about the pullout strategy at the time. Tony, rushing through the lobby toward the elevator, wondered whether Tet was reaching out of its tiny white grave to taunt him. Would the developing battle he'd seen just an hour ago at Ban Me Thuot make '68 look like a minor skirmish?

On the fifth floor, he burst into the office he shared with Hal James. "I'm just back from Ban Me Thuot. The NVA is up to something, and it's not little old nibbling. Anything in," he asked as he quickly shuffled through memos on his desk, "from our people up there?"

James, always in a shirt and tie regardless of the stifling Saigon temperatures, began reading from a typewritten page. "Some notes on a radio chat I had just a couple of hours ago," he began. "With our man in Ban Me Thuot. Says ARVN was taken by surprise by the suddenness and intensity of the NVA operation. ARVN didn't have a clue that the NVA had units — in such strength — in that area." He laughed nervously. "ARVN wasn't the only one."

"Snafu?"

"Snafu could turn out to be a charitable way of putting it," James said. "It'll all depend on to what extent the NVA is committed, and to what extent ARVN will be able to hold them. We should know in the next few days."

"Keep your fingers crossed," said Tony, walking toward the door. "I'm going to talk to His Highness. You know if he's in?"

"You mean just because it's Sunday? God may have rested on the seventh day. Not our Walker." James pointed a finger at Tony. "He's already seen a copy of my notes on Ban Me Thuot."

"And?" Tony asked eagerly.

"I have no idea how he's choosing to assess the situation. I understand he's sent a cable to Washington about Ban Me Thuot, but the bastard isn't sharing his thoughts with me." James looked up from the typewritten page and smiled. "What else is new?"

3

"Is he free, Helen?" Tony asked the Ambassador's secretary. "Urgent."

Helen had survived a thousand earlier urgents; no one could ever remember seeing her stampeded — by anyone but the Ambassador, that is. She was a huge soapbar of a woman, extremely efficient and, above all, loyal to the man who occupied the office on the other side of the thick mahogany door; in fact, she'd been loyal for so long now that Walker was her third ambassador in Saigon.

"When," she asked with a laugh, "is it non-urgent?"

"Urgent urgent." Tony mixed a little charm with his impatience. "Honest honest."

She gave him a sudsy smile and, hitting the intercom button, announced that Tony Catlett would appreciate a moment of the Ambassador's time. "He says it's very urgent, Mr. Ambassador." A second later, Tony entered the office.

The contrast in mood was striking. Tony — tense, agitated, eager to detail what he had just seen in the Central Highlands; the Ambassador — calm, dispassionate, cuddling a small Sung celadon bowl. Behind him were three crowded shelves of porcelain: plates, bowls, vases, ewers, a span of Chinese history dating from the Tang to the Ming. Tony felt he had interrupted a lover in the midst of a particularly tender moment.

"Yes, Tony," he said coolly, moving toward his desk. "What is so — urgent?"

There it was, Tony thought, that goddamned disguised sarcasm, the know-it-all quality in his voice, the aloofness in his manner. How could any American be so steely, bloodless, un-American? Was he impersonating Nixon? Calvin Coolidge? It was as though Walker had deigned to descend from the stratosphere for a moment or two, exchange a syllable with earthly mortals, and then would quickly repair to his own heaven. His physical appearance went with his personality: he struck Tony as having been put together with parts of an erector set—screws, bolts, strips of metal. Never a hint of emotion; Tony often felt that he was talking to a suit of armor. Even the Ambassador's eyes were in character: cold, depthless — like painted ceramic. An aura of unreachability radiated from Walker. How the hell could *he* be Suzanne's father?

But Tony, and everyone else in the Embassy, also knew of Walker's formidable reputation as a diplomatic troubleshooter who had scored breakthroughs in various negotiations that had seemed hopelessly deadlocked. His stature, above all with the Presidents and Secretaries of State he had served, had increased with each difficult assignment: in New Delhi, at the time the "nonaligned" Indians were flirting outrageously with the Kremlin; in Jakarta, when President Sukarno was romancing the Chinese Communists in the early 'sixties; in Prague, when the Russians burst in with their tanks in '68; in Moscow, more than a decade earlier, when the Cold War was at its iciest. The White House admired him for his professionalism, his ability to shuttle between silkiness and toughness, his readiness to play hardball diplomacy even at the risk of a host government's resentment. As South Viet Nam's anxiety grew in the wake of the U.S. military pullout in 1973, Washington turned to Walker as the ideal choice for Saigon; his reputation as a committed anti-Communist might reassure the South Vietnamese about the unshakability of the U.S. commitment. "He's a tough s.o.b. to work with, I grant you," the President had once remarked, "but he may be worth four U.S. divisions to ARVN, morale-wise. And he always makes it come out right for our side."

Walker's underlings had a less flattering view, though even they would privately, reluctantly, concede that he had a good record for promoting U.S. interests wherever he'd been posted. Walker Saigon, they argued, would be the same as Walker New Delhi, Walker Jakarta, Walker Prague, and Walker Moscow: domineering, rigid, a smoothie whose Southern manners masked the instincts of a street fighter. When word got out in mid-'74 that Walker would be named Ambassador to South Viet Nam, there was a gleeful feeling among many of the old pros at State that Walker had finally met his match in the art of the devious, the conspiratorial, the Byzantine.

"I've just come back from a quick trip to the Highlands," Tony began.

"Have you, Tony?"

Tony checked an impulse to smash one of the Ambassador's prize blue-and-white vases. Instead, he quickly described what he had seen near Ban Me Thuot: NVA units in areas where they had previously not been detected, big enemy guns where CIA intelligence showed none — the beginnings, in short, of what could be a major enemy offensive. "It's the kind of technique they've used before," Tony continued, "and before, that kind of operation produced some pretty large-scale operations in which ARVN was clobbered."

"I have the feeling," Walker replied without showing a hint of concern, "that your doomsday portrait — have I got the right word, Tony? — is slightly overdrawn."

Tony wondered whether this was a probing action or a simple put-down. He decided to try again, reconstructing every detail of the morning's aerial reconnoitering. He stressed the enemy's unanticipated position, and the heavy artillery they had brought into action. "When the NVA wants to go small-scale," Tony added, "they go small-scale. This is different. It's big."

"Tony," replied the Ambassador, rubbing his palm on the celadon bowl, "I find it difficult, at least so far, to concur with your assessment. Not that I'm dismissing what you've said. But it strikes me that your report simply tends to confirm the early intelligence that even your people have been putting out: nibbling actions, some bigger than others perhaps, but still nibbling. Nothing major."

The Ambassador leaned over his desk and picked up a copy of a cable. "I told Washington only this morning that, apart from the usual small actions, contacts here and there, the war is simply throbbing along." His voice suddenly tensed. "The thing to worry about, Tony — and I've told the same thing to Washington, more than once lately, as you know — is getting emergency funds for ARVN. Congress" — he uttered the word with contempt — "has cut the annual appropriations for military and economic aid, and, unless the cut is restored, Saigon will be in trouble. The Russians and the Chinese aren't that foolish; in fact, they are increasing their aid to Hanoi. If you want something to worry about, Tony, worry about that."

But Tony's own priority was to get his message across to the Ambassador: something serious was shaping up in the Highlands.

"If it weren't for the President, I'd be worried, too," the Ambassador continued. "But I have his personal pledge that he will find a way to triumph over the myopia of our elected officials on Capitol Hill — and to get those funds appropriated. He told me that, precisely, the day I last met with him at the White House. A bit of a hassle, the President thought, but he said he'd continue to fight, whatever the political cost, to get those funds. I have his word of honor" — the Ambassador seemed to underline that phrase — "and I have the Secretary of State's personal word, too."

It was like trying to pierce a steel wall. "If you'll allow me, sir, and if you'll pardon the expression," Tony blurted, "there seems to have been a major U.S. intelligence fuck-up."

"A fuck-up," the Ambassador replied instantly, "is in the eye of the beholder. Let me tell you, Tony, that I know best of all that Saigon has been the burial ground of ambassadors who arrived here only to find their preconceived optimistic conclusions shattered by the enemy. I haven't made that mistake. My confidence is in the President. He'll come through on the aid; ARVN will have its money. Money means weapons. Weapons are what ARVN needs. They cannot fight armed simply with ambassadorial reassurances. I hope you won't mind my being equally blunt but I think you respect bluntness, Tony. Your appetite for alarmist projections verges on the insatiable. Odd, for someone in your profession."

Tony could see the ceramic eyes aimed in his direction.

"But at the same time, Tony," the Ambassador continued, his voice suddenly softening, "let me offer a word of appreciation for your initiative in hurrying up to the Highlands to get a firsthand look at the situation." It was vintage Walker, Tony thought: first the stiletto, then a Band-Aid of charm. "It's usually just the opposite: people passing around secondhand information saturated with the conventional wisdom that the war is unwinnable. So while I may not share your conclusions — this leap of yours to a worst-case scenario — I do admire your enterprise."

"Mr. Ambassador," Tony countered, "I may be off base — it wouldn't be the first time. But I know what I've seen, and I've been around here long enough, tracking the NVA, to be suspicious about what I saw with my own eyes this morning. A fuck-up. I repeat it. A fuck-up in our intelligence."

"I'll make a note of that, Tony."

Tony recognized the signal of dismissal; he backed toward the door. "And" — Walker smiled; Tony thought he heard metal creaking — "Suzanne and I are dining at the French Embassy tonight — but why not join us for a drink before we go? About seven?"

"Thank you sir," Tony answered automatically, wondering once again just how much Suzanne had told her father about the two of them.

Once Tony was on the other side of the door, Walker picked up the copy of the cable he'd dispatched to Washington and let his eyes roam over the text. No, not a syllable needed revising: it was all there — a deft mix of specificity and ambiguity, all bases covered, both present and future.

THE WAR IS SIMPLY THROBBING ALONG, WITH THE NVA INITIATING SCATTERED CONTACTS THAT MAY OR MAY NOT ESCALATE. BUT I HASTEN TO ADD A CAUTIONARY NOTE: IN SOUTH VIET NAM, APPEARANCES CAN BE MISLEADING, HAZARDOUS, EVEN FATAL. OUR INTELLIGENCE, AS YOU KNOW, IS LESS THAN ADEQUATE; OUR ALLIES, NOT ALWAYS GALLANT; AND THE VERY LONG-RANGE UNCERTAINTY OF THE SITUATION ONLY UNDERSCORES THE URGENT NEED FOR EMERGENCY FUNDS TO BUTTRESS ARVN'S ARSENALS.

It was the kind of diplomatic cable-writing at which Walker excelled: an accurate picture of reality — coupled with a built-in alert to potential catastrophe.

Ever since his arrival in Saigon, in fact, Walker had more than ever carefully composed his cables with two sets of readers in mind: today's and tomorrow's. He wrote for the President and the Secretary of State and the Pentagon but he also wrote for history; he saw his careful phrasing as a form of insurance against being singled out in any postmortems — if South Viet Nam did collapse — as the fool on the spot who didn't know what the hell was happening. Walker sensed that the President and the Secretary, notwithstanding their promises on aid, had at least subconsciously written off South Viet Nam. They had dropped the mess in his lap and if it collapsed, well, they could always argue that even a hard-liner like Walker had not been able to salvage the situation. Yet Walker had decided to accept the challenge of the appointment in the hope that he could make the White House live up to its promise of aid. True, he was concerned about his own reputation in the history books, but he also felt that the loss of South Viet Nam — a U.S. ally — had to be prevented at all costs because it would produce an image of a weak America, one that would tempt the Soviets into new global adventures and risk a superpower confrontation.

In his cables, Walker was always careful to inform Washington of exactly what was going on in South Viet Nam, though he might choose to accent particulars that would promote his own view: with sufficient U.S. aid, ARVN should be able to hang on long enough for the Kremlin to become weary of the venture and advise Hanoi to pull back. The odds, he knew, were against it. It was a long shot — but the only strategy he could think of. He felt that it was worth pursuing.

Still, Tony's eyewitness account troubled him.

He dialed the DAO — the Defense Attaché's Office — asked to speak to General Collins, and arranged for a meeting later that night, with the General and the Director of Military Intelligence. "By the way," Walker concluded, just before hanging up, "I'd rather you didn't mention this to anyone. Keep it to the three of us."

4

It was midafternoon, the city dozing in the thick heat, when Tony opened the door to his room. Suzanne was waiting.

"He never disappoints me," Tony muttered. He collapsed onto the bed and stared at the ceiling map of Viet Nam, his eyes fixed on the Central Highlands — flat, a lovely pastel green, peaceful. Maps are liars, he thought.

Suzanne interrupted his reverie. "Do I need to ask who?"

"He who always lives up to my expectations."

Suzanne's face flushed. "I don't need three guesses," she said limply.

"Suzanne," Tony said, turning toward her, "will you be the jury? I always have the feeling when I'm talking to him that, somehow, I'm in the dock — that I must prove I'm innocent, that I haven't betrayed him."

In quick strokes, Tony reconstructed the last few hours: his flight to the Ban Me Thuot area, the surprise discovery of the NVA offensive, his dash back to the Embassy, and, finally, his frustrating encounter with the Ambassador.

"Nothing I said dented him," Tony continued. "By the time I left, I was trying to convince myself that I had seen what I had seen."

"Poor Tony. It's been quite a day for you." Suzanne stretched out beside him.

"I hoped you would be here." Tony kissed her, lightly, gratefully.

"I'm glad I waited." She looked around the room — the big bed, the VC flag on the wall, the map of South Viet Nam on the ceiling. "It's not Bali, but . . ."

"Suzanne . . . I know we agreed to a cease-talk, but you've got to hear me out. Who else can I tell it to?"

She ran her fingers gently across his face. "As the only one you can tell it to, and as the only living expert on Hadden Walker, I guess I'm stuck."

"You know, don't you, what I'm trying to say?" He searched her eyes for understanding. "We clash — my reality and his illusions. He's got some kind of ideological mind set that rejects what he regards as unpalatable and absorbs only what reinforces his position. I think that makes him dangerous. He's whispering sweet nothings into the ear of the White House, when he should be yelling 'FIRE!' "

"Tony, even you must know that he's a decent, courageous, loyal —"

"Suzanne, could you be the jury instead of a character witness?"

"I wish you wouldn't think I'm defending him because he's my father. Over the years, I've seen him tangle with his staff, tangle with Washington, but — what was that word you used — 'whispering'?" She leaned over and kissed Tony. "If he were a 'whisperer,' he wouldn't have been assigned here — to Saigon, at this time."

Tony was silent.

"In fact," she smiled, the idea suddenly striking her, "someone ought to do a Ph.D. on 'Hadden Walker, Diplomat Warrior.' "

"Cold-warrior," Tony muttered.

"Your Honor" — Suzanne looked up at an imaginary magistrate on the bench — "will you please ask the witness not to interrupt?"

Tony put his index finger across his lips.

"Thank you, Your Honor," she said, turning back to Tony. "Do you think he takes you on because he's the Ambassador and you're just a lowly spook, my love? That would be conceit, if you don't mind my saying so. He's taken on Presidents, and he's done it because of an old-fashioned sense of obligation to tell them what they don't always want to hear — the cold truth even when it clashes with their political needs."

She stood up. "Tony, do you remember Prague, 'sixty-eight? 'The Prague Spring'?"

An album of faded newspaper photographs flickered through his mind: Soviet army tanks rumbling through the cobbled streets of the Czech capital, Red Army soldiers armed with bayoneted rifles, bodies of Czechs sprawled on the sidewalks, the lean anguished face of a broken Dubček. "Prague Spring" — snuffed out.

"I was there, Tony. It was the summer between my sophomore and junior years at Duke. My father was alone; my mother had died only that winter, and I wanted to be with him. I was twenty at the time, majoring in history — and there was history unfolding before my eyes. One day, the Czechs were flirting with the idea of freedom — even controlled freedom in a Communist society — and they couldn't believe it. They went wild with joy. The next day, Soviet tanks. But the point is, Tony, all through June and July, my father had been cabling Washington that Moscow wouldn't tolerate Dubček's reforms, that Moscow was afraid that even a small spark of liberalization would spread like wildfire throughout Eastern Europe. The whole Soviet bloc would be threatened."

She sat down on the edge of the bed and looked into Tony's eyes. "Do you know what the White House was replying?" she asked.

Where was I in the summer of 'sixty-eight? Tony thought. At

3 3

the "farm" — the old-boy term of affection for the CIA training center in Virginia — learning about "covert actions," "clandestine operations," and "dirty tricks."

" *'Stop being an alarmist, Walker,'* " Suzanne's voice conveyed the irritation of LBJ's White House.

Alarmist! That was the word he'd thrown at *me* just an hour ago, Tony thought.

"It was almost a direct order from Washington," Suzanne went on. " *'Stop being an alarmist, Walker.'* You know why? Because his analysis — that the Russians would feel obligated to crush Dubček — conflicted with President Johnson's eagerness to hold a summit with Leonid Brezhnev. Diplomatic coup, right? The White House could already see the headlines: 'President Confers With Kremlin Leader.' 'Historic Rendezvous Between the U.S. and U.S.S.R.' But . . . you know what happened, Tony!"

Once again, Tony's inner eye focused on Dubček's anguished face.

"On August twentieth — on the very day that Johnson was ready to announce the summit — Brezhnev sent his tanks into Prague. The President, the State Department, even people in the Embassy had simply been unable to believe that the Russians would jeopardize the summit by moving against Czechoslovakia. My father never doubted it."

"Bravo!" Tony exploded with sarcasm. "You can enter all that as 'Exhibit A.' " He was sorry the moment the words were out of his mouth.

"Cheap shot, Tony."

They both drifted into silence.

"But that was a decade ago," Tony finally resumed, with a glance at the Central Highlands on the ceiling map. "And now it's as though he's determined to un-alarm Washington." He looked at Suzanne, but she avoided his eyes. "Since Prague, there have been summits, détente, even China — but always more and more Viet Nam. Suzanne, what I'm trying to get across is this: your father is not cabling reality back to Washington these days, the way he did from Prague. He is cabling lyrics — exactly what Washington wants to hear: that Saigon is gung-ho, that ARVN can hack it, that the antiwar people are anti-American. Your father's cables make it easier for Washington to concentrate on what's really on its mind these days: the Middle East — and oil. And what's dangerous is that his cables serve as the basis for U.S. policy toward South Viet Nam, and if he's wrong, so's the policy, and if the policy's wrong . . . not only does Viet Nam go down — but so does the U.S. Defeated! Humiliated!" He slammed his hands together for emphasis.

Suzanne stared at the Viet Cong flag, surrounded by five of Tony's darts that had missed the yellow-star target. "If anyone can extricate the U.S. from this mess," she said softly, her muted voice tinged with defiance, "in a way that leaves South Viet Nam and America in one piece, it's my father."

Tony's voice softened. "Suzanne, you love him. You've loved and admired him all your life. You see him in one dimension. Flat. A portrait of the 'Lord of the Manor.' To me, he's a puzzle. He's too smart to believe all that bullshit he's sending back. There's got to be more to it than that. If I could only slip a 'bug' into his head and tune in on his *real* thoughts."

"It's that simple, is it? You're saying that if he weren't play-acting, he'd admit that you're right. Is that it?"

Tony opted for silence. "Case rests," he said finally.

"Tony, we've got to stop this. Am I always going to be in the middle? Or am I supposed to turn on him in the interest of the Tony Catlett vision of truth and reality? Or maybe in the interest of proving I love you?"

Tony reached for Suzanne and held her tightly. "Of all the girls in the world, I had to pick you — the daughter of the 'Lord' . . ."

"Of all the guys in the world, I had to —"

He kissed her, silencing the words. "Suzanne, I'm fed up. Fed up with punching that stone wall of bureaucratic minds, egos. I want you just to hold me, to listen to me, to say, 'Yes, Tony.' 'You're right, Tony.' 'Someday they'll all know it, Tony.' . . ."

Slowly, lovingly, she stroked his hair, his face. Then she began to croon in a low light voice a lullaby she did not know she remembered. "Skeeters am a'hummin' on the honeysuckle vine," she sang. "Hush, Kentucky babe. . . ."

After a while, she could feel Tony's body loosen. He began to breathe easily like a child. He slept, and then, so did she.

Suzanne woke to a throbbing in her temples that gave warning of a full-blown headache. A deep gold late-afternoon light slanted through the bamboo blinds. Perspiration soaked her white batiste blouse; her cotton skirt was sodden, bunched between her legs. She felt Tony's weight on her shoulder.

She glanced at her watch. Five o'clock. Gently, she nudged him. "Tony . . ." She sat on the edge of the bed and slipped on her shoes.

He opened one eye. "Suzanne, you're here?"

"Not for long. I'm already late. Have to go home and get dressed. I've got a date."

"I know."

"You know?"

"His initials are H.W. He's taking my best girl to dinner at the French Embassy." •

"I talked in my sleep?"

"No, but guess who's invited for a drink before you two go off together?"

She smiled, leaned over and kissed him. As she headed for the stairway to the lobby, Tony's voice overtook her. "What's the verdict?"

Her voice filtered back. "Hung jury."

5

After she had left Tony, Suzanne, torn by the recurring tension between them, headed instinctively for the one place in Saigon where she could be sure of an uncomplicated welcome.

"Thi, Thach," she shouted on entering the courtyard. Two tots — a girl and a boy — quickly detached themselves from a circle of children and ran, arms outstretched, in Suzanne's direction. She scooped them up, kissing them both, and they wrapped their scrawny arms around her neck. Neither Thi, whose glittering black hair hung down to her waist, nor Thach, whose most distinguishing feature was a missing front tooth, understood more than a couple of words of English — but language made no difference. Their reunions were noisy and exuberant, but Suzanne was always haunted by the fear of what would happen to the children when her father's tour in Saigon ended and she left.

They had already been orphaned once, in a blinding instant, a few months earlier when a bomb hit their village not far from Pleiku in the Central Highlands; the tragedy was compounded by the fact that the bomb had originated with neither the Viet Cong nor the NVA. Rather, it was a South Vietnamese Air Force bomb; sloppy targeting had turned the village into a mound of ashes. When the smoke cleared, Thi and Thach, discovered amid the rubble, had been loaded as so much cargo onto a Saigon-bound truck and eventually dumped at the orphanage. It was par for the war but not for Suzanne; she had been on duty that morning and she was so moved by their frightened faces as they stood in the doorway, hand-in-hand, that she had unofficially adopted them on the spot.

"Sooz-zinn," Thi shouted. She was five years old, more outgoing, more demonstrative than her brother; Thach, a year younger, was shy, sad-looking, but his missing tooth endowed him with an offsetting comic touch. Suzanne held them tightly as she picked her way through a crowd of children playing *nhay lo co* — a Vietnamese version of hopscotch — and proceeded into the building, to the makeshift office that had once served as a master suite.

"Thi and Thach gave me such a glorious hello," Suzanne said to the woman seated at the only desk in the room, "that I feel guilty about not being able to spend more than a few moments here today."

Mrs. Nguyen Thi Can — the headmistress, about forty, wearing the traditional *ao dai* combination of black pantaloons and long, side-split white tunic — looked up and smiled; she always welcomed the volunteers, despite an uneasy feeling that theirs was drop-in love whereas these shattered children needed constant, nearby love. The volunteers were dabblers, she thought, but she recognized that Suzanne's connections had produced a steady flow of contributions for the orphanage from the American community in Saigon. "I'm so pleased to see you here," said Mrs. Can. "Thach has been very moody since last night, and your visit will do him good."

Suzanne hugged Thach closer to her bosom. Thach gave her a tiny smile.

The orphanage occupied what had once been the villa of a Saigon merchant — a "war profiteer," according to the South Vietnamese authorities — who had had the bad luck of being turned into an Object Lesson during one of the periodic "crackdowns" against corruption. The "crackdown" was aimed less at corruption than it was at reassuring an increasingly irritated U.S. Congress that the American dollars shipped to South Viet Nam were not ending up in private pockets. Moreover, given the anti-Chinese prejudice among the Vietnamese, it was inevitable that the "crackdown" would be against a member of the Chinese minority, guilt or innocence being a mere technicality. Indicting and jailing any wealthy Chinese was popular with the masses; it was also an effort at self-acquittal by those Vietnamese authorities with their hands in the till. It was, in short, an exercise in hypocrisy, a farce; the Object was almost always Chinese and no one learned any Lesson. But it was as good an excuse as any, so far as the Vietnamese authorities were concerned, to confiscate a bit of property for a cause that would be especially appealing to the Americans.

This grandoise three-storied villa, set back on a green lawn obscenely well manicured in a country pockmarked by war, had been turned over to a quickly put together organization called "Home for the Children of Parents Killed by the Viet Cong." The name was not accidental; the organizers expected that "Killed by the Viet Cong" would attract large donations from local foreigners. The chandeliered salons had been converted into giant rumpus rooms for children, none over the age of seven, all of whom had been found in the debris of hamlets that had been obliterated by the war.

Suzanne went back to the courtyard with Thi and Thach and watched them join in a game of *nhay lo co*; every time they managed a giant leap without falling down, they looked at her for approval. She laughed and applauded. When she turned, finally, to go, they stopped their play and ran to her, trying to prevent her from leaving. She kissed them and said goodbye, with a promise to herself to come back again tomorrow. Even as she opened the front gate, they were still clinging to her skirt.

6

The Ambassador's residence at 58 Phung Khac Khoan had once been owned by a grizzly, chainsmoking French entrepreneur; his years in Saigon, he had told the U.S. government lawyers at the time of the sale in 1965, had been *formidable*, filled with a million happy memories and even more piastres, but he had decided it was time to go, convinced that the Americans would fare no better in Viet Nam than the French had.

It was a well-proportioned old house, spacious, with cool thick walls and marble floors, situated in one of the loveliest residential quarters of Saigon. Nostalgic for the old country, the French colonialists had built two- and three-story replicas of Parisian *hôtels particuliers*; they had planted leafy trees that dappled the streets with shade against a torrid sun; they had laid down walkways — wide, bourgeois, perfect for a stroll between dinner and the evening's entertainment. For the French, old Cochinchina — despite the heat, the frustrations, and the ingratitude of the native *nha-gués* for the opportunity to be refined by France's *mission civilisatrice* — had been a golden paradise where every *fonctionnaire* could feel himself a king.

Now, Phung Khac Khoan was blocked off at both ends with concertina wire and sandbags against surprise VC attacks; armed sentries cleared all visitors. But Tony's face was familiar — he had visited the residence many times — and when he pulled up in his Fiat, he was immediately waved through.

A young Vietnamese houseboy opened the door. Tony proceeded directly to the living room. The Ambassador and Suzanne would be joining him shortly, he was informed; meantime, would he like something to drink? His eye swept the large living room furnished in a mix of bureaucratic modern and Vietnamese bric-a-brac, neither of which was Walker's style. His style was on display along one wall: glass shelves holding a small sampling of the Ambassador's Chinese porcelain collection.

The many sides of Hadden Walker, Tony reflected. To which one would he appeal this evening? It was, after all, to be a social get-together, almost a family get-together given his own relationship with Suzanne, and he'd made up his mind to avoid any kind of confrontation. The afternoon session had been a disaster. This evening, he would nod, smile, gossip, burnish the Ambassador's famous ego. He would employ a little VC strategy — the idea amused him — in his dealings with Walker; he would try to — how to put it? — *infiltrate* the Ambassador, win his confidence. It might not be a hopeless strategy, either; he remembered Suzanne's remark that her father was actually rather fond of him and the Ambassador's own praise of Tony's initiative in flying up to Ban Me Thuot. Well, he would learn in a moment whether the living room would prove to be a hot landing zone or a friendly one.

Suzanne was first down the stairway, wearing a dress he had never seen before: solid black, perfectly cut, with a tantalizing deep V neckline. Her curls had been tamed into sleek wings sweeping back from her face. She had managed, in the hour since she had left his place, to transform herself from a rumpled girl into a breathtaking, sophisticated woman. Her sidelong glance at Tony struck him as part flirtation, which he welcomed; part warning to be on his best behavior, which he found superfluous.

The Ambassador, a martini on the rocks in his hand, a cigar in his mouth, welcomed Tony with no trace of the afternoon's tension. No glint of armor, either; just his black-tie diplomatic uniform.

The three of them began by exchanging views on the weather. The conversation passed politely through an analysis of Saigon humidity versus Washington humidity, then wilted into uncomfortable silence.

"Where are you from, Tony?" the Ambassador suddenly asked.

Tony was startled. He knew that the Ambassador was familiar with the entire Anthony Catlett dossier going back to his date of birth, but he also sensed that his host was deliberately serving up an unprovocative topic of conversation.

"The South, sir. Mississippi."

"Of course," the Ambassador said as he sat down on the couch. "We're from Georgia." The Ambassador nibbled on an olive. "I've always been fascinated by the impact of geography on personality. Northerners tend to be insensitive, aggressive, single-minded while Southerners . . ." He glanced at Tony and smiled, welcoming him to the charmed territory below the Mason-Dixon line. "Well . . . you know what I mean."

The moment had arrived, Tony thought, to start implementing his strategy. "Sir, I've been wondering whether, when this is all over, whatever way it ends," he began with a glance at Suzanne, "I ought to try to switch from the Agency to the Foreign Service. The diplomatic life has an appeal for me."

The Ambassador seemed flattered to be asked for personal advice. "It certainly has for me, Tony. I've been at it now — how long? — forty years. Almost memoir time. Probably make a lot of enemies if I ever wrote what I really think of some of the people I've dealt with in the White House, State, the Pentagon." He sipped his drink. "Interesting life, I think. Won a few countries. Lost a few countries." He laughed. "Tell me, Tony, how did you ever get into the Agency in the first place?"

Suzanne had heard Tony's story more than once, but she cast

herself in the role of rapt audience, relieved that Tony and her father were on relatively neutral territory.

Tony recounted how he had been in his last year of college, a political science major uncertain of his plans after graduation, when a CIA recruiter turned up on campus one day. It was mid-'65, just at the time the U.S. was beginning to get involved in Viet Nam in a massive way.

So much for neutral territory, Suzanne thought.

Mostly on a dare from an antiwar classmate, he'd decided to accept the recruiter's invitation for a casual chat. Much to his surprise, Tony had found the description of life in the "intelligence community" attractive. The recruiter had pointed up the possibility of Tony's doing *real* graduate work in the field instead of spending his life incarcerated in the library of some New England university. "I remember his saying to me," Tony recalled, " 'The CIA will give you a chance to be one step ahead of history.' A sales pitch, sure, but irresistible all the same, the idea of getting in on the ground floor of the future."

"Cloak-and-dagger aspect have any appeal?" the Ambassador asked.

"Yes, it still does, in fact," Tony said, "but I found out once I was on the other side of the fence, how naive it was to think that the Agency could shape reality according to its own blueprints." He looked directly at the Ambassador. "Take Viet Nam, for example. The CIA was not exactly a bystander in the 'sixty-three coup that ousted Ngo Dinh Diem, but the results since then have not exactly been a triumph for U.S. policy." He paused. "All conversations, I guess, lead to Viet Nam." He glanced at Suzanne.

She looked uneasy.

The Ambassador studied Tony for a moment. Impetuous maybe, but serious, outspoken, attractive. Could be my son-in-law one day, he thought. A widening of perceptions might be in order.

"Honor," the Ambassador began very professorially, as though he were lecturing a class of undergraduates. "Do you think 'honor,' the way we learned it as children in the South, has any future as far as the U.S. commitment to Viet Nam is concerned?"

Spur-of-the-moment quiz? Tony thought. "Haven't times changed?" he replied. He tried to keep his voice free of emotion. "This is nineteen seventy-five. The 'Cold War' is over."

"No, not really," replied the Ambassador just as emotionlessly. "We're still fighting the same enemy."

There was an uncomfortable silence.

"How old are you, Tony?"

"Thirty-two."

"You may wonder what age has to do with it, Tony," said the Ambassador. "The answer is — everything. People your age, yours and Suzanne's, have no sense of a past, nothing to recall; your generation was raised on Viet Nam and is dominated by Viet Nam. It's obsessed only with the present — without any awareness that the present is simply a projection of the past and a curtain-raiser for the future. A future threatened by Communists."

"But why," said Tony reaching into an ambassadorial pause, "do we have to think of Viet Nam only in terms of the Soviet Union? Why can't we think of it as a country with its own people, its own history, and not as just a piece of real estate?"

"Because," the Ambassador continued patiently, "that limited view is all very well for scholars. Not for people who deal with the real world, with the threat of hostile powers that could destroy not only Viet Nam . . . but all of us. We have got to curb the Communist appetite."

Tony was about to say something, but Walker rolled right on.

"I know that you think we should push Saigon to negotiate with Hanoi on forming a coalition government. But that's like putting out a welcome mat, inviting the Communists to take over. I tell you, Tony, you just offer them a chance to negotiate, and they'll grab it."

Suzanne decided it was time to intercede. "You two could be here all night. It's time we got moving, Dad."

"In just a moment," Walker said. The ceramic eyes looked directly at Tony. "You disagree? Well, do you think Hanoi will opt to humiliate us? I don't. They'll need us when this is over, to rebuild their country, maybe even as a counterweight against their great friends up north, the Chinese. Anyway, I didn't accept this assignment to preside over the dissolution of South Viet Nam. We're going to find a way to turn the war *against* the Communists."

His soliloquy hung in the humid air as he glanced at his watch. They all stood up. Well, Tony thought, he'd tried — but he had walked right into the Ambassador's geopolitical trap. If the VC don't get you outside, Walker will get you inside.

"See you tomorrow," the Ambassador said cheerfully. His mind began computerizing Tony. Short on historical perspective, but ready to take on the establishment. Good; same thing I've done all my life. The computer suddenly stopped. Good God, am *I* the establishment to him? Is he the me of four decades ago? The thought at once entertained and troubled him, but there was no time to punch up his early years to determine whether there was anything to that flashing parallel between early Walker and present Tony.

Stiffly, Tony shook the hand of the Ambassador, then turned toward Suzanne. Her eyes signaled that a kiss would be unwise at this moment. Tony considered taking her cue, then suddenly changed his mind. As he reached her, she turned her head. His kiss glanced off her ear.

Tony caught the amused look on the Ambassador's face, the embarrassed look on Suzanne's.

"Good night, Tony," she said.

"Have a great time at the party," he answered.

7

Party sounds drifted through the open windows as the Ambassador and Suzanne approached the French residence, an imposing white colonial mansion built pre–World War Two as a monument to *la belle France's* belief that her flag would fly over Indochina forever. A salvo of hellos greeted them at the door. Walker smiled emptily, acknowledging one guest and then another with a ritual smoothness honed at hundreds of such dinner parties. He scanned the reception room, finally focusing on a tall, sleek woman, her face an elegant blend of Europe and Asia. His eye caught hers, and they exchanged a warm glance.

A very short pâté of a man, whose roly-poly softness made him look as though he could be smeared on toast, broke free of the cluster of guests and hurried over to Walker. Delighted, Ambassador Henri Bodard murmured, absolutely delighted that Hadden and Suzanne could make it that evening. There was always the possibility of something unexpected happening — this, after all, was Viet Nam, *n'est-ce pas?* With a sigh of relief that left him deflated, he added that he would be eternally grateful to the war for being cooperative — for once.

"Come," continued Bodard, his voice a whisper, as though he were reading top-secret cables from the Quai d'Orsay. "I want you to meet our guest of honor, a great hero of France."

He led Walker toward the crowd — about twenty men and women in all, most of them recognizable fixtures on the Saigon diplomatic circuit — and came to a stop before a tall thin man in his sixties, with a Légion d'Honneur ribbon on his lapel.

"Pierre Delmas," Bodard said. "Ambassador Walker. It is my great honor to introduce you. Hadden," he continued, looking at the Ambassador, "Pierre and Viet Nam have known each other for a long time." Walker was puzzled — but only for a moment. "Pierre was at Dien Bien Phu — at the end, in 'fifty-four."

Walker and Delmas shook hands, bowing slightly.

"An end," smiled Walker. "For others, a beginning, a new challenge."

"Perhaps, Monsieur l'Ambassadeur," replied the guest of honor. "But history is the final judge."

The two men sparred politely for a few moments. Walker glanced casually in the direction of the Eurasian woman on the far side of the crowded room. She nodded, and Delmas caught the discreet exchange. "I knew her husband, François de Clery," he said. "A young captain in the French army. Killed in the very last days of the war — at Dien Bien Phu." He shook his head. "Madame de Clery and I had a long talk earlier today." He looked toward her. "That combination — half French, half Vietnamese — can be extraordinarily tempting."

He turned, a bit reluctantly, from Madame de Clery to Walker. "This," Delmas told the Ambassador, "is my first trip to Viet Nam since 'fifty-four. Many times I have thought about Viet Nam, but it was impossible, emotionally, for me to return to . . . the scene of the crime. But Henri" — Delmas pointed to Bodard, who was then hovering over an hors d'oeuvre — "my old friend Henri has been pursuing me to revisit Viet Nam . . . before it is too late. So, since I was in the neighborhood, in Bangkok, on a few days of business, I decided to make a detour to Saigon."

The phrase "before it is too late" caught Walker's attention, but before he could begin to explore whether it was just a simple cliché or a French forecast of things to come, the circle widened and the guests began quizzing the Ambassador about new rumors being spread by "Radio Catinat."

"Radio Catinat?" Delmas asked with surprise. "It's still in business?"

"Never stopped for an instant," Walker replied. "Your favorite boulevard — 'Rue Catinat' — may have been renamed 'Tu Do,' but human nature does not change. The street is still a breeding ground of wild rumors, and the 'network' is still called 'Radio Catinet.' The same cafés, bars, bistros still pump out their daily supply of" — his voice filled with disdain — "gossip." He turned to the other guests. "Well, what have you heard today?"

"Rumors about new military moves by the North Vietnamese in the Central Highlands," said one of the guests. "Are these rumors true?"

The question surprised Walker — he had not expected the rumors to travel so swiftly — but it also gave him an opportunity to do a bit of delicate perception-shaping in his role as U.S. Ambassador. He began with a broad smile of camaraderie, as though he were about to share his entire file of classified intelligence. "If there were any kind of serious military situation," Walker asked, "do you think I would be here — eagerly awaiting the delights of Ambassador Bodard's chef?"

His remark produced, for the moment, the desired reaction — a defusing laugh. Walker tried to relax, aware that any appearance of anxiety on his part would intensify the fear in Saigon and in turn — with the help of idiotically exaggerated headlines back home — fuel the growing antiwar and anti-aid sentiment on Capitol Hill.

They sat down at the dining table, an expanse of white linen graced by candles, freshly cut crimson gladioli, and crystal goblets. The food was, as usual, delicious: tender *médaillons de veau* in a subtle sauce; *pommes vapeurs* that had actually been steamed; young *aspèrges* cooked not a moment too long; and a Château Margaux 1961. It always amazed Walker how the

French, even in wartime, even in the tropics, invariably succeeded in producing an excellent replica of Parisian cuisine.

Walker found himself engaged in chitchat with the woman on his right — Madame Bergeron, the stiffly coiffed, overanimated wife of the French political officer. Small talk was clearly not one of his strong points, but he had developed a certain tolerance for it during his years in the diplomatic service. Chitchat often served as an aperitif to more interesting discussions.

"De Gaulle?" he responded to a question about the former President of France. Yes, he had met the General once — in the 'sixties, at the Elysée, oddly enough on a visit to Paris with an eight-year-old niece, and perhaps the best way he could think of to describe de Gaulle was to tell a story involving his niece. "One day, some weeks later," he said, "my niece was attending a religious class at her school in Georgia, and the subject under discussion was God. Well, divinity is a bit complicated for youngsters — even for oldsters — but, anyway, after the teacher talked about the encompassing omniscience, the mysterious, the total, commanding power of the Supreme Being, she asked whether anyone in the class had ever *seen* God. Well, my niece's hand shot right up. The teacher was startled. 'You *have?*' the teacher asked. 'Yes,' answered my niece. 'Well, who is He?' 'General de Gaulle,' my niece replied."

The guests burst into laughter, even a round of applause. "Hadden, you've got the perfect audience for that story," Bodard said.

Walker smiled; it was an anecdote he had used more than once, and it was always a triumph regardless of the nationality of the audience: the French, he had found, saw it as a reaffirmation of their sense of superiority; those who found the French insufferable saw it as a reaffirmation of Gallic conceit.

De Gaulle as God led to de Gaulle as doomsayer on the Viet Nam war — "*la guerre sale*," he had once called it. Undoubtedly a "dirty war," most of the guests agreed, muddied further by corruption. In fact, corruption had become the titillating stuff of gossip, and the members of Saigon's inner circle of foreigners vied to outdo one another in swindle stories.

"I myself," volunteered Madame Bergeron as she leaned over the table, "heard *le dernier mot* at my Vietnamese hairdresser's the other day."

Walker's mood suddenly changed; focusing on corruption, he believed, was counterproductive, no different from giving credence to naive press accounts extolling the military capabilities of "the other side." In fact, his impatience with such damaging dinner-party chatter prompted Walker to decline most invitations in Saigon. The conversation, he had concluded long ago, was invariably repetitious and trivialized the war into a series of anecdotes, shallow diplomats seeking confirmation for their conventional wisdom, bored wives seeking refuge from the monotony of Saigon's incestuous social scene.

Now, with the onset of corruption gossip, Walker was overcome by fatigue. His eyes half-closed, he felt as though he were viewing the scene through a wide-angle lens, the guests reduced to glassy miniatures, the room suddenly transformed into the salon of a luxury liner. "PASSENGERS ENJOY CHAMPAGNE TOAST," a newspaper caption read, "MOMENTS BEFORE SHIP HITS MINE."

The high-pitched voice of Madame Bergeron roused him from his reverie.

Her hairdresser, she was saying, had told her that the wives of senior Vietnamese generals were now making more money than ever out of the war. "This is the way they do it," she continued, with an engaging smile at Walker. "The generals arrange for the sons of wealthy families to be — how you say? — *unsuitable* to fight in the war. Then the wives of the generals manage all the business. Their husbands' fingers never touch the money. That way, the generals remain" — she placed her fingertips together and lifted her eyes heavenward in an attitude of devotion — "totally innocent."

Her recital brought appreciative laughter from several of the guests. She reported that the generals' wives were now charging

150,000 piastres a head to keep the sons of the Vietnamese elite from conscription into ARVN. *"Le champ de bataille enrichit les poches bombées des généraux,"* she laughed. "The field of battle enriches the swollen pockets of the generals." The latest joke, she related, was that when the wives, who had taken to whiling away the afternoons at high-stakes poker, got together for a game last week and began upping the ante, one of the players — known as "Mme. Lieutenant-General" — called out: *"Je vais relancer un soldat."* Madame Bergeron paused. "I'll raise you a soldier," she translated with exaggerated sweetness.

Laughter trickled down the table. Walker was not amused. The voice that had so engagingly told the de Gaulle story was now tinged with barely concealed fury as he began to speak. The chitchat died.

"Corruption doesn't make or break an army," he snapped. Suzanne recognized the edged quality in his voice; she looked pleadingly at him but he ignored her. "Corruption has nothing to do with morale. Arms do. Weapons do. Corruption doesn't."

The sound of an explosion echoed through the room. Incoming? Outgoing? So close to Saigon? Silver forks and knives halted in midair.

"Sounds to me like a motorcycle backfiring," said Delmas.

The company relaxed.

"In fact," Walker resumed, pleased that some anonymous hot rod had unwittingly provided just the right sound effect, "I've lived in Asia long enough to recognize corruption as a lubricant that gets results. Results require payoffs; that's not unusual. Nor," he added, his eyes going from face to face, "is corruption confined only to the developing countries. Even in *my* country, it's an old story. Kennedy might not have been elected President in nineteen sixty if it had not been for ballot-box finagling in Cook County, Illinois. It's just that Asians are more open-minded about corruption." He smiled. "Perhaps they have advanced the state of the art, and the more 'puritanical' countries are envious."

There was an awkward moment. Suzanne made an effort to

revive the earlier mood of cozy intimacy among the guests. She talked about her work at the orphanage, about Thi and Thach, about how she had tried to avoid becoming too emotionally involved and how she was afraid now that she had not succeeded. Her effort at easing the tension was painfully obvious, but it did have the effect of stimulating a series of scattered conversations. Dinner over, everyone repaired to the high-ceilinged, massively chandeliered reception room for coffee.

Bodard looked unhappy, but he understood Walker's impatient outburst, the burdens he carried as the man caught between an increasingly desperate Saigon and an increasingly fed-up Washington; it was the empathy of one diplomatic professional for another. "Wouldn't you like something to drink, Hadden?" he asked.

Bodard's show of friendship touched Walker. "*Merci*, Henri," he said, patting the French Ambassador on the arm. "Crème de menthe with ice, please."

Bodard rolled toward the bar. His round body belied a steely intelligence, and many diplomats, much to their subsequent regret, had made the mistake of equating his contour with his mind. In fact, his packaging had over the years proved to be an asset; by the time his adversary caught the first glimmerings of Bodard's formidable intellect and diplomatic agility, the Frenchman had picked him clean. Consequently, Bodard never felt any guilt when he indulged his culinary cravings: every calorie he consumed was in the national interest, a mouthful of patriotism.

By the time Walker's drink arrived, Madame de Clery had materialized at his side.

"Monsieur l'Ambassadeur," she began, "I wanted a word with you — about porcelain."

"Ah," said Walker, with a look of mock disappointment, "I was hoping it would be something . . . more personal."

"*Here?*" She glanced around the crowded room.

"Well," Walker answered quietly, "I suppose *there* would be better."

A blush came over her face. "Will I see you . . . later?"

"I already have a midnight rendezvous —"

Her eyes widened.

"— with some generals, alas."

They both laughed. Madame Bergeron looked in their direction, then turned away.

"You know that little shop on Hong Thap Tu?" Madame de Clery asked, her voice now taking on an impersonal tone. "The Nguyen Dynasty?"

Walker nodded.

"Well, I understand that it has just acquired some new pieces" — she paused and then added — "of superior quality."

"Oh . . . tell me more. . . ."

"They are from the collection of a Saigon University professor. He was afraid that the military situation was going from bad to worse and that it was only a matter of time before South Viet Nam collapsed. He needed money to 'lubricate' " — she smiled, and Walker's face broke into an authentic grin — "local officials to obtain exit visas for his family, and so he sold off his entire collection of porcelain."

"A panic reaction," Walker said with impatience. "Saigon will not become Ho Chi Minh City this year. Or next."

"Panic or not, perhaps this is the moment to give asylum to a few deserving refugees from another age. After all, these blue-and-whites have survived for centuries. Should they be abandoned now?"

With an enchanting conspiratorial smile, Madame de Clery bowed slightly to the Ambassador, and turned away. Walker kept his eyes on her as she glided back into the crowd.

Later, as the party was breaking up, Walker called Bodard off to a corner and inquired, as casually as possible, as to whether or not he had heard anything from the French Embassy in Hanoi about a new NVA offensive strategy in the Central Highlands.

Bodard shrugged. "The signals are ambiguous," he confided. "Some minor redeployment of forces perhaps, but nothing to indicate an all-out assault." He offered Walker a cigar. "We French," he said, pointing to Delmas, "have seen it all before."

"I wonder," Walker continued, "whether you, Monsieur, in superb Bodardian fashion, might not persuade your Embassy in Hanoi to examine those 'ambiguous' signals more closely."

Bodard nodded. "Ah, but as you know, Hanoi takes no one into her confidence. Even the Russians and the Chinese, poor souls, are kept in the dark."

Walker raised his glass. "Anything you can do, discreetly, of course, would be much appreciated." He leaned toward Bodard. "Just between us."

Bodard, with a slight lift of his crystal wineglass, returned Walker's salute. "A *la santé de votre pays*," he replied. "To the good health of your country."

8

It was almost eleven o'clock by the time Walker's limousine pulled up at the main gate at the Defense Attaché's Office, six miles from downtown Saigon, on the edge of Tan Son Nhut Airport. The DAO had been known during the years of Washington's direct military involvement in the war, as MACV — Military Assistance Command Vietnam. But with the American pullout in '73, the joke among cynics was that the United States had lost an initial — and would soon lose a country. It was a joke that Walker did not appreciate.

The sentry on duty saluted, and the car moved slowly across the dimly lit grounds of the sprawling HQ complex, coming to a stop before the VIP entrance to the main building. A waiting guard escorted the Ambassador through the long, empty corridors and showed him into the "Readiness Room" — another scaled-down designation; it had been known as the "War Room" in the old days.

The generals were waiting: Harry Collins, the two-star head of the DAO, and Frank Williams, one star, the intelligence chief, ready to proceed with the latest report on the military situation in Military Region 2. Thin, about fifty-five, with a professionally worried look he'd acquired during the Korean War, Collins was seated at the oval-shaped conference table; Williams, who bore a striking resemblance to Collins in size, age, and worry, was standing, pointer in hand, before a large map of Viet Nam. The walls were covered with top-secret charts that had been designed to reduce the complexity of the war to statistics, graphs, and indicators: NVA infiltration figures, ARVN arms capability, "NVA-controlled areas," and "ARVN-controlled areas," among other calculations. There were no charts, top-secret or otherwise, dealing with such aspects of the war as ARVN morale, motivation, and officer corruption. The overhead fluorescent tubes had been dimmed, so that the map of Viet Nam, brightly illuminated, dominated the spacious room. Walker sat down in a swivel chair next to Collins and nodded at Williams.

"Sir," Williams began — he was an old hand at briefings, his voice carefully reflecting neither hope nor despair — "the latest development in MR Two during the past twelve hours is an increase in NVA activity, mostly in the area around Ban Me Thuot."

"Significant increase?" Walker leaned forward.

"Difficult to say, sir," Williams replied. "You know the problem. Our intelligence assets have been cut back drastically ever since we pulled our troops and advisers out of all four of the MRs. We're working with Air America and VNAF recon photos — not very good. Also with ARVN intelligence, which is even worse. Its reports are tailored, I don't have to tell you, to accommodate the anxieties of the President of South Viet Nam." He circled Ban Me Thuot with a pointer. "The ARVN boys always tell him everything is coming along nicely."

None of this information was exactly news to Walker, but he concealed his impatience in an effort to draw whatever substance he could from Williams's cautious, self-protective recital.

"Sir," Williams continued, pointing to the Central Highlands sector on the map, "I've got to say the NVA activity around Ban Me Thuot is something of a surprise. That's because we had picked up some enemy activity to the north in the last few days — about a hundred miles to the north, around Pleiku, and even to the north of Pleiku, around Kontum."

"Pleiku," the Ambassador repeated. He needed no reminder that Pleiku, much bigger and more strategic than Ban Me Thuot, was a periodic target for the North Vietnamese; seizing Pleiku, situated about forty miles in from the Ho Chi Minh Trail in Cambodia, would remove a major South Vietnamese block against NVA infiltration and would put the NVA in an ideal launch position to strike for the coast, less than a hundred miles to the east — thus cutting South Viet Nam in half.

"Yes," Williams said. "Pleiku it is. We've spotted some NVA troops in the area, some trucks, some tanks. Even intercepted some NVA radio traffic."

"Have they made the spotting easy for you?" Walker's controlled impatience contrasted with Williams's unhurried, methodical approach.

"I was just getting to that, Mr. Ambassador. The answer is yes — and no."

Just like the goddamned idiots in the State Department, Walker thought. A to Z positions, always taking evasive action, never getting caught with a forecast in their mouths. The only difference between the bureaucrats at State and at the Pentagon was the haberdashery: pin-stripes versus khaki. His eyes going from face to face, from Collins's to Williams's, Walker could not resist comparing these two generals with their enthusiastic predecessors in Saigon just a few years earlier — at the peak of the U.S. military involvement. He recalled the earlier eager-beaver faces he'd seen on a quick private trip to MACV in '67, the generals bombarding each other with triumphant reports of "body counts" and "enemy weapons captured" and "search-and-destroy operations." What difference did it make whether the seventeenth parallel separating the two Viet Nams ran from east to west or north to south; we'd be home by Christmas! The sense of invincibility was so overwhelming that no one then would have been surprised to hear a general announce one day that the United States had decided to air-condition the war. Even later, Walker remembered, when doubt first began to infiltrate the euphoria, the generals had maintained their military machismo: "Don't knock it; it's the only war we've got." There were still reputations to establish, careers to be made, stars to be won. But after the final pullout of U.S. combat troops in '73, it had all changed; generals, unwilling to be interred prematurely in a professional graveyard, resisted assignment to the Attaché's Office in Saigon. After a while, only second-rate brass turned up at the DAO, mostly men at the end of their military careers; the younger officers on the rise, concerned that identification with Viet Nam might jeopardize their chances of making general one day, avoided a DAO tour of duty. Walker understood all this, but it didn't make his job of holding off a South Vietnamese defeat any easier.

"I say yes and no," Williams repeated, "because we simply can't be sure whether the NVA is 'posing' for us, or whether we've caught them red-handed, so to speak."

"What's been done by way of counteraction so far?" Collins asked. "By way of a response?" It was obvious that he was offering his intelligence chief an opportunity to lay out the latest military countermoves by ARVN.

"Well, what's been done so far," Williams explained, grateful for the cue, "is that, on the basis of detected enemy activity, ARVN has moved one regiment of the Twenty-third Division from Ban Me Thuot to Pleiku. Also, some Ranger battalions have been moved to Pleiku."

"What does that leave in Ban Me Thuot?" asked Walker.

"That leaves only one regiment in Ban Me Thuot," Williams replied. "The Fifty-third."

"Could the enemy activity you've spotted around Pleiku be a feint? Could they be thinking about hitting Ban Me Thuot?"

"That brings us back to square one," Williams blurted in exasperation. "We just don't know what NVA intentions are. We simply don't have the intelligence assets to make any educated estimates." He looked, first, at Collins, then at Walker, then at the map. "It's also possible that the new activity around Ban Me Thuot is designed to draw ARVN into reinforcing its positions in that area — and thinning them out in Pleiku — and then striking at Pleiku itself." His pointer went from Pleiku to Ban Me Thuot and then back to Pleiku.

"In other words," Walker probed, trying to dig out Williams's best estimate, "there's some new enemy activity around Ban Me Thuot; some sudden, even obvious, spotting of enemy activity around Pleiku. But we're not clear on what it all means: whether it's all nibbling activity around Ban Me Thuot; whether the NVA activity around Pleiku is a diversion; whether Ban Me Thuot or Pleiku, or both, are the real targets; whether it's just more of the same?"

"Exactly," exclaimed Williams. "I couldn't have put it better myself."

"I'm sure," Walker replied, aware that the sarcasm of his response was lost on the Generals.

An enlisted man brought in a tray of coffee, placed it on the table, and departed.

"Who's the MR Two commander?" Walker inquired.

"Lam. Major General Nguyen Van Lam."

A portrait of Lam flashed through Walker's mind; the Ambassador recalled meeting him at a reception given by the President of South Viet Nam: round-faced, short, distinguished mostly by a heavy cough. In civilian clothes, Lam might have been mistaken for a waiter in a second-class restaurant.

"How do we rate him?" Walker asked.

"Not too high," replied Williams. "Lacks imagination, initiative, aggressiveness. The most interesting thing about him is that he was taken prisoner by the Viet Minh in 'fifty-four at Dien Bien Phu when he was fighting with the French. He was a lieutenant at the time."

"How did he get the MR Two post?"

"He's a favorite of the President's," Williams replied.

"Corrupt?"

"Well," Williams smiled, "I may not be able to make a case strong enough for the Supreme Court, but . . ."

"What about the order of battle in MR Two?"

"ARVN is not all that strong there," Williams warned. "Only

two divisions. The Twenty-second, mostly in the lowland provinces of Phu Yen and Binh Dinh." His pointer picked out the two coastal provinces on the map. "Heavily populated, both of them, and of course Binh Dinh has always been something of a Communist stronghold." The pointer moved inland — to Kontum City; then it began inching south along Highway Fourteen, through Pleiku in Pleiku Province, to Ban Me Thuot, a span of one hundred and twenty-five miles in four seconds. "Now for the Twenty-third division," Williams continued. "Three regiments: two in divisional headquarters at Pleiku, the third in the Ban Me Thuot region. As for the NVA, it has more divisions in MR Two than ARVN. In short, ARVN's best defense lies in accurate intelligence — so that its limited forces can be airlifted quickly to any potential trouble spot."

Williams placed the pointer on the ledge beneath the map. "Let me sum it up this way, Mr. Ambassador," he said. "If Lam reinforces Ban Me Thuot, he weakens Pleiku. If he reinforces Pleiku, he weakens Ban Me Thuot. It's his dilemma. His decisions must be based on intelligence, and his intelligence is shaky."

Walker turned to Collins. "General, anything you want to add?"

"I think General Williams has given you the best picture we have," Collins said. "It's unclear, but I must say we've seen this all before: enemy activity that flares up and then disappears."

"But the NVA has not been spotted around Ban Me Thuot before," Walker interjected. "That's what worries me."

"Well, I keep thinking of the point that General Williams just made," Collins continued. "A surprise NVA appearance around Ban Me Thuot aimed, perhaps, at sucking ARVN troops into that area, prior to an attack on Pleiku. Or Kontum. Or nothing. That's what makes all this so goddamned frustrating for us. We've become military bookkeepers, checking credits and debits, without really knowing what the hell is going on. Lousy way to watch a war." He threw up his hands in disgust. "Anyway, it's all up to ARVN — these days."

For Walker, Collins's almost throwaway line pointed up the irony of the shift in the U.S. attitude toward ARVN. Once upon a time, when the GIs first began arriving in '65, the South Vietnamese military had been just about the last thing on the Pentagon's mind. In fact, ARVN was then regarded as more of a hindrance than an asset, and Americans pushed the Vietnamese soldiers aside in their headlong pursuit of the VC and the NVA. In fact, the war had become so Americanized that, if a tidal wave had floated the entire South Vietnamese population out to sea, MACV wouldn't have noticed until somebody discovered that the laundry was overdue. America would handle the "gooks." Well, it turned out that the "gooks" had handled America, and America dropped the war in ARVN's flabby lap.

Walker found himself scanning various charts on the wall dealing with ARVN: number of divisions, deployment of heavy weapons, desertion rates. It struck him once again that ARVN, representing the critical difference between Saigon's survival and collapse, had not been tested in any major battle since the final U.S. pullout in '73. What would happen when it was?

"General Collins, General Williams, I have the President's word that the emergency funds ARVN needs will be forthcoming." Walker spoke with a clinical evenness of tone, subconsciously reassuring himself as well as his military colleagues. "His word. To me personally. When the test comes — whenever, wherever, however — the South Vietnamese will have the hardware they need."

"I hope so," said Collins, without much conviction. Williams nodded.

It was midnight by now. Walker, flanked by Collins and Williams, headed for the main entrance; their footsteps echoed through the silent corridors that had once reverberated with self-congratulatory talk of air strikes, napalm attacks, and enemy KIA. Battalions of generals, war-intoxicated, had marched briskly through these very halls, through MACV's prefabricated steel buildings, to the PX, movie theaters, bowling alleys, tennis courts, to mess halls that featured filet mignon and baked Idaho potatoes shipped in from the States; like colonizers on the moon, they had brought their own distant and separate military civilization, complete with Mom's apple pie. Now there was an eerie emptiness, a haunted quality.

It was only after his limousine began to move toward the main gate, as he turned to catch a farewell glimpse of Collins and Williams, twin figures waving goodbye, that the image suddenly struck Walker: Stonehenge — with two survivors.

9

"The residence, sir?" Walker's driver asked as he steered the limousine along the bumpy main road leading into Saigon.

Walker glanced at the luminous hands on his watch: 12:15. That meant it was 11:15 in the morning in Washington, thirteen hours earlier. He caught the driver's eye in the rearview mirror. "No, the Embassy, please." Walker leaned back in his seat, sorting out the DAO briefing.

What had come out of it? Clearly the overriding urgency was to strengthen ARVN so it could stand up against the NVA. That meant money, and money meant Washington, without money, hell, you might just as well pack your bags and hand over the house keys to Ho Chi Minh's boys. Walker couldn't resist wondering whether Moscow's ambassador to Hanoi was facing the same problem. *Nyet!* The NVA, now more than ever before, had enormous stockpiles of military hardware — small arms, artillery, tanks, trucks, antiaircraft guns, rockets — everything you could think of, and more en route. And a lot of it — *a lot of it* — was already south of the seventeenth parallel, inside South Viet Nam, ready to go.

The ride to the Embassy was quick — the all-night curfew kept the streets clear except for some diplomatic and military traffic — and the limousine soon pulled to a stop alongside the giant tamarind tree inside the compound. Walker's postmidnight arrival produced a salute but no surprise, from either the Marine guard on duty at the gate or the Marine guard at the lobby desk; everyone in the Embassy knew that the boss often turned up at odd hours.

The moment he was at his desk, Walker picked up the military phone, dialed the DAO's communications center, and asked to be put through — on the secure line — to the Secretary of State in Washington. One minute later, the familiar voice was on the phone. Walker wondered how long it would take, this time, before their conversation reflected the true state of their relationship. Thirty seconds? A minute? Two minutes?

"You're up late, Hadden," the Secretary began. "I hope it was worthwhile."

"I'm afraid not," Walker replied dryly. "It's just that war has made me an insomniac."

A small laugh — from ten thousand miles away — echoed in Walker's ear. "Good," the Secretary joshed. "That gives us two ambassadors for the price of one."

"Well," Walker replied, "since you're saving all that money on me, how about using some of it to rescue your 'ally'?"

"Now, Hadden . . ." The Secretary's voice quickly lost its humor.

"Let me start with the obvious," Walker continued. "Does the U.S. commitment to South Viet Nam still stand?"

"Of course." The Secretary's voice was painfully patient.

"Since the commitment still stands, how are we doing on the question of more funds for ARVN?"

"We are leaning on Congress to come up with the money."

"How's the 'leaning' progressing?"

"Slowly." The Secretary's voice signaled irritation.

"It's got to go faster."

The line was silent.

"I take it you've seen my cable about a little flare-up of NVA activity around Ban Me Thuot," Walker said flatly.

6 4

"Yes. Seems like small stuff." The Secretary sounded as though he wanted confirmation.

"Did I make it *that* small? Or are you all trying to miniaturize Viet Nam so it will be out of your line of sight? That new clash I referred to underlines the desperate need here for more military equipment for the South Vietnamese."

"Hadden" — the Secretary's voice projected a sense of fellowship — "I am doing everything I can to ensure that Congress appreciates your point of view and provides additional funds for ARVN on an urgent basis."

Your point of view. Next thing you know, Walker thought, he'll be telling me it's *my war*.

"The President is doing everything he can," the Secretary persisted. "His liaison people on the Hill are doing everything they can. You won't be left empty-handed."

"Can you guarantee that?" Walker interjected sharply.

A tone of exasperation seeped into the Secretary's voice. "I don't think that I need to remind a personal representative of the President of the United States that the American system of government is not a dictatorship, do I?"

Walker glanced at his watch: it had taken a minute fifteen.

"It is precisely because I *do* regard myself as a personal representative of the President of the United States," he shot back, "that I can be blunt, even to you, in the interests of the President of the United States."

The sonofabitch, Walker thought. I'm the man on the spot, he's back in Washington, and he is lecturing me halfway across the world about Viet Nam. As far as Walker was concerned, the Secretary's leap from obscurity to prominence had produced instant megalomania; he had been concentrating ever since his appointment on solving the easy issues on the diplomatic agenda, fudging the difficult ones, and putting as much distance as possible between himself and Viet Nam. Walker was convinced that the Secretary, behind the barricade of his publicly stated commitment to the Saigon regime, believed that South

Viet Nam was a terminal case and had no intention of being identified as one of the pallbearers.

Yet in Walker's view the Secretary was unassailable, for an obvious reason: the President's weakness. The Secretary served as the President's indispensable crutch. It had been one of those blunders of democracy, this President's ending up in the White House. All his political life, he'd been a number-two man — just short of making it as his party's majority leader in the Senate, serving later as deputy secretary of this department and that department; he had always felt comfortable in the knowledge that it was the man just one notch above him who made the final decision. Well, there was no one above him now, *he was it*, Number One. Walker had sensed that even the titles — President of the United States, "leader of the free world" — overawed him. He needed the Secretary's quick brain to provide the theories and the vocabulary with which to face the world each morning. Walker's only consolation was that the Founding Fathers had had the foresight to write a Constitution that called for new presidential elections every four years. Still one more year to go with this crowd, Walker thought, before the President and the Secretary were reduced to portraits on the walls of the White House and the State Department. It was going to be a long twelve months.

Walker needed no one to remind him that his own low estimate of both the President and the Secretary was a luxury that South Viet Nam could not afford, not if ARVN was going to get those funds. He regarded it as a personal challenge to pressure both men to live up to their promise that the funds would be forthcoming, that South Viet Nam would be helped.

"You do remember our last conversation, Mr. Secretary?" Walker said, controlling his anger. "When we met with the President? His assurance that military funds would be made available?"

"Look, Hadden," the Secretary cut in. "I simply don't have the time for a replay of our usual conversation. Let me just tell you that I'll convey your feelings to the President."

"The Russians and the Chinese have been pouring in equipment and —"

"I'm sorry, Hadden, really I am," the Secretary again cut in. "But —"

"I also wanted to raise the question of B-fifty-twos — in the event Congress stalls on money and ARVN should need a bit of help."

"B-fifty-twos?" the Secretary exclaimed impatiently. "Listen, Hadden, I'd love to continue this conversation — but I am even now keeping the Saudi Ambassador waiting. . . ."

The other end of the line, half a world away, clicked dead. Walker slammed the receiver back into its cradle.

He then picked up the phone that linked the Embassy with the city of Saigon, and called Madame de Clery. Their conversation was brief.

Walker went directly to his waiting limousine. When he reached the residence, he told the driver that he would not be needing him until 6:45 in the morning.

10

It was not exactly what the semanticists at the CIA had in mind when they originally concocted that bit of ambiguity known as a "CA." A "covert action," to the agents in the field, had to do with such acts as macho as destabilizing governments, overthrowing uncooperative dictators, and hatching clandestine plots, all designed to promote the influence of the United States around the world. Dirty tricks, in short — and none of them romantic. Well, the boys back at Langley would have been amused to know that Walker felt he was embarking on a "CA" of his own every time he slipped quietly out the side entrance of the residence at 58 Phung Khac Khoan and headed for 52, four houses away. It was one of those happy coincidences — something that U.S. and French property leases had given the Ambassador and Madame de Clery gratis — that they found themselves only a couple of hundred feet apart any time after midnight.

By prearrangement, Walker entered Madame de Clery's house through the unlocked back door. Always there was that moment of hesitation on the creaky landing midway up the stairs to her bedroom when he saw himself in a double image: Walker the impenetrable diplomat, gray-suited, unsentimental, protected from passion by job and country, and Hadden the boy he had never been, overcome, past sixty, by an adolescent craving for this morsel of a woman.

She welcomed him tonight, true to their ritual, in black satin pantaloons and blouse, Vietnamese peasant-style. She had worn this chaste pajama uniform the first time he had come to her bedroom — and on every visit since. The very thought of that black satin sliding smoothly under his hands triggered images of garters and black lace, moist hidden thighs, nipples, breasts, touchable through a film of gauze. At odd moments — signing papers at his desk, meeting with the generals, at diplomatic receptions — he would suddenly feel himself begin to sweat; each time, something had caught his eye — a bit of black, or a bit of satin.

As usual, alone with her, he felt ill at ease, his own powerful desire an embarrassment. So as usual he started with a little joke, a bit of flipness, a light teasing about her costume.

"Ma petite VC . . . ," he began tonight.

She smiled, to please him, and came toward him, holding out her arms. "Hadden, you treat me as though I were just another girl in your life." It was a favorite line of hers, part of the repartee of their relationship; it always gave Walker a feeling of sudden youthfulness.

Awkwardly, still not comfortable in this lover's role, he pulled her in, embraced her. The touch of the cloth released his longing. His hands glided slowly over the black satin, postponing the touch of her skin. He bent and kissed the arc of her neck.

As always, he sensed her waiting, allowing him to drink in the rich scent of her. She smelled to him like spice, a mix of cloves and wintergreen, of vanilla, of lemongrass. Sometimes he tried to remember what Louise, Suzanne's mother, had smelled like. But there was nothing — a void, no recallable fragrance.

He walked Jeanne, slowly, toward the big Oriental canopied bed, its deep red-lacquered wood ingrained in gold with dragons and clouds. She leaned against him and his hand caressed a small breast through the black satin. He thought of a tallow-smooth, perfectly formed celadon bowl.

Gently, he lifted her. Her Asian-boned body, so perfectly balanced, and her total willingness made her nearly weightless. Kissing her on the forehead, he lowered her onto the bed. She had pulled down the covers, neatly.

As he undressed, she turned on her side, watching. In the beginning, he had tried to hide, in an alcove of the bedroom, out of her sight. But she had insisted that his privacy was an insult to her, a deprivation. For however long they were together, she had told him, there must be a completeness to it.

"You Americans!" she had laughed. "You have so much to learn!"

He slipped in beside her. Her hands feathered over his body as he undid the familiar frog closings of her blouse. His tongue roamed the silky globes of her freed breasts, crisscrossing as if following a maze, as if searching for the central core. She had taught him that too — the art of teasing, of holding back. "Not so fast," she had laughed, their first night together, as she had pushed his hands away. "Americans make love the same way they make foreign policy."

He ran his left hand to the string of the pajama bottoms, untied them, slid them down as she lifted slightly. Her skin was cool but not dry. He felt the roundness of her hips. Suddenly, mischievously, she reached for him.

"*Pas mauvais*," she laughed. "Not bad, for an amateur."

The thought crossed his mind that she was really a mix of competing humors: the French mind, dispassionate, marking his report card; the Vietnamese body, seductive, generous, uncalculating.

She opened herself to him, draining from him every drop of tension, anger, frustration.

Then she laid her head on his shoulder. "You are not a mouse," he whispered.

"You are not . . . ?" she repeated. "And who *is* a mouse?"

"A joke among the Americans," he explained. "You've never heard it?"

She shook her head.

"Forgive the undiplomatic language, Jeanne, but it goes this way: 'Fucking Vietnamese women is like fucking mice.' "

Walker could feel her shuddering. "It should give you an idea of the esteem in which some Americans hold the Vietnamese." He pulled her close. "You, Jeanne, are a tiger, a lion, a cougar."

"Merci beaucoup, Monsieur l'Ambassadeur."

His fingers touched her eyelids. "Close them," he said. "Rest with me. We have a little while."

She moved into the hollow of his body. "All right . . . a little while. . . ."

How long had it been, he wondered, since that maddening conversation with the Secretary? Forty-five minutes? An hour? A year?

Walker and Madame de Clery had met a month after his arrival in Saigon, at one of Bodard's dinner parties; they had found themselves seated next to each other. If it was matchmaking on the part of the French Ambassador, the American Ambassador was grateful. Jeanne de Clery was beautiful and sophisticated, full-bodied, with café-au-lait coloring, and she told lively stories about her upbringing in Hanoi. Her father — a diplomat from Paris — had served in the French Embassy there in the 'twenties and had married the daughter of a wealthy Vietnamese businessman. Jeanne's girlhood had been spent shuttling between two cultures; she was proud of her French connection, but had always felt drawn to Viet Nam, especially its drive for independence. She had married a newly arrived young French captain in 1953; he was killed less than a year later during France's final spasm in Indochina. Somehow she had found herself caught up in the French exodus to Paris, where she quickly got a job at the Quai d'Orsay. But her knowledge of Viet Nam — its language, culture, and history — inevitably destined her for service in the land of her birth. She had been living in Saigon now for more than a decade, as the cultural officer at the French Embassy, and had easily managed to attract a series of highly discreet lovers.

Walker was her latest. It was his sense of power, his aura of invincibility, that had attracted Madame de Clery, and he was flattered by her attention. In fact, she was the first — and only — woman with whom he had established a liaison since his wife's death seven years earlier.

For Walker, Jeanne was a delicious refuge. She had driven a wedge of sex between his obsession with Viet Nam and his frustrations with Washington, and he had reached out hungrily for her, much to his own surprise. It was she, not he, who had taken the lead in initiating their affair. She'd playfully told him once that there was more to life than simply carrying out State Department assignments, that there was a time for diplomacy and a time for passion. He had been drawn more and more deeply into the relationship; he had rediscovered the comfort of sharing confidences with a woman. But even his bursts of passion did not dissolve his instinctive caution about divulging any information that he regarded as sensitive. He always had a lingering feeling that Jeanne, even at forty-five, was still agonizing about her ultimate loyalties — whether to France or to the Vietnamese.

"You're too secretive, Hadden," he remembered her once telling him. "It's tied you into a knot. I'm going to unravel you."

He had cherished that line — she had said it during their first night together — and she'd been unraveling him ever since.

"A mouse or a cougar," Jeanne whispered, interrupting his reverie, "the Vietnamese woman is quite different from the Frenchwoman."

Walker listened contentedly to her chatter.

"The Frenchwoman can be promiscuous," Jeanne explained. "Not so the Vietnamese woman. The Vietnamese woman is extremely jealous — and her jealousy can take violent form." She ran her fingers through his hair. "But at what cost!"

"You're being *too* Vietnamese for me."

"Ah, but that is your problem, *cheri*. You live American, you think American, you have American tunnel-vision. You should try to learn a little about the Vietnamese you are trying to save."

The human side of foreign policy, he thought. Never seemed to be time for that.

"The Vietnamese have a charming cultural tradition," Jeanne went on. "When a woman discovers that her man has been carrying on with another woman, she can go berserk with shame, humiliation, rage. Viet Nam is an intimate society, no secrets, and the betrayed woman stands exposed. So she can be driven to a terrible act of vengeance. The Vietnamese have a slang phrase for it," she murmured. " *'Em cat chim anh.'* "

" *'Em cat chim anh'*?" Walker repeated.

"I would hate for it to happen to you "

"So would I," Walker said, his hands moving up her thighs. "What does it mean?"

"Em cat chim anh," she whispered. "Literally, it means 'I cut off your *bird.'* "

Walker burst out laughing.

"Yes, you can laugh, but there's more than one Vietnamese Don Juan who didn't find it funny," Jeanne continued. "You can read about it in the newspapers every now and then. A woman discovers that she has been cheated on by her man. She must reclaim her honor. So she picks up a sharp knife and while he is asleep . . . *Em cat chim anh.*"

"You telling the truth?" Walker was incredulous.

"As much truth as a Vietnamese can tell a foreigner," Jeanne laughed. "Legend has it that even Emperors have not been exempt. Gia Long? Tu Duc? Minh Mang? I forget which Emperor it was, but one of them is supposed to have lost his *chim.*"

Walker smiled. "I knew there must be a precedent for the Vietnamese love of violence," he said.

They embraced, and he suddenly heard an odd sound. It was Jeanne — sniffing in short bursts, as though she were trying to inhale him.

"Is this another Vietnamese cultural trait?" he asked.

She smiled. "As a matter of fact, it is," she replied. "I've been going through some old books in the cultural library at the French Embassy, and I came across one particular volume dealing with the way the French struck the Vietnamese when they had their first extensive contacts more than a century ago."

Walker smiled tolerantly.

"The Vietnamese were shocked by the behavior of the foreigners," she explained. "They found them crude. They were offended by their tempers, by hair that wasn't black, by faces that were white, and — you won't believe this, Hadden — by their conviction that the body odor of a foreigner was different from their own."

"Breathe deeply," he said with a laugh.

They could hear nighttime sounds outside: birds whistling, lizards croaking, frogs gurgling. An occasional echo of faraway artillery fire filtered into the room.

"Hadden." It sounded like a summons, the playfulness suddenly gone from her voice; it made him feel fully clothed. "You're a man of many masks, but the one you were wearing at Bodard's tonight — the charming raconteur, telling stories about *le grand Charles* — did not fool me." She paused, but Walker chose to remain quiet. "I'm not Washington," she finally said. "Just how bad is it at Ban Me Thuot?"

Walker laughed. "Not serious."

"No masks, Hadden."

"I thought I was naked."

"Physically, yes. Strategically, no."

"Well," Walker said, reluctantly, "I suppose there could be a problem at Ban Me Thuot — but I'm convinced of two things: one, ARVN will be able to handle any military challenge, *if* one should develop; and two, Hanoi will not go for a grand slam right now."

"Risky assumptions, Hadden."

"Well," he replied tolerantly, "I've been known to be wrong before — but not often."

"That's what makes you so irresistible." She leaned over and kissed him. "Would you like me to read you something?" she asked, picking up a book from the night table.

"Not really."

"Written by a Frenchman," she continued, ignoring his remark, "in eighteen sixty-four. It's a description of Vietnamese women by a man called de Grammont."

Walker sighed. "I guess I'm in for a history lesson."

" 'The Annamite women in general are small but well built,' " she read. " 'The shape of their faces resembles the oval of the Europeans; their eyes are straight and not slit like the Chinese; their teeth are beautiful but, unfortunately, blackened by the use of betel. They wear their incomparably black hair on the back of their neck, bound together with a studied negligence not devoid of charm. Their complexion varies from brownish yellow to yellowish white. The latter is in highest esteem. The Annamite woman walks with her head high, her breasts pointing forward.' "

"Keen observer, your de Grammont," Walker said. He reached over to the night table and glanced at his watch. It was two-thirty.

As he was leaving the semidarkened room, she called out, "Hadden, you know that, with me, you must be a one-woman man."

He smiled. Just as he was closing the door, he heard her voice once again. "Don't ever forget what happened to the Emperor."

It was the nicest compliment he had had in years.

Two minutes later, Walker was in his own bed.

11

The next morning, at a few minutes before seven, Walker arrived at the Embassy. Two totally unrelated reasons had brought him in earlier than usual.

The first had top priority: to check the military situation in MR 2. His bedside phone had not rung even once during the night — an indication that nothing dramatic had occurred. But Walker had discovered years earlier that intelligence people were often the last to recognize intelligence.

The Ambassador dialed the DAO. "General Collins?"

"You're in early, Mr. Ambassador."

Walker ignored the greeting. "What do you hear from MR Two?"

Collins turned serious, his voice deepening. "Still some contact south of Ban Me Thuot, same as yesterday, but nothing's come in that would confirm that the NVA is thinking about some kind of bang-bang. . . ." A hesitant silence hung in midair.

"Yes?" Walker prodded.

"It's just that, as I've already told you, our intelligence up there is not the best." Another throat-clearing filled Walker's ear. "Neither is ARVN's."

A minute later, Walker dialed John Sommers, the CIA station chief, an old pro who gave the impression of not having slept since joining the Agency a quarter of a century earlier. Sommers echoed Collins's report, including the caveat.

For a few minutes, Walker didn't budge. He was uneasy, but he could recall previous experiences with panicky field reports that later turned out to be exaggerated. At this moment, without any hard information from the military or the Agency, there was nothing more he could do. He began to feel the tug of the other — the private — reason for his early wake-up. He looked at his watch, figured he could be back in an hour, and left the office.

Walker headed for his limousine, parked in the shade of the giant tamarind tree — eighty feet tall, its trunk more than eight feet across, a colossus looming against the morning sky. He took a deep breath to catch its fragrance, pungent in the overnight dew. This tree, he thought, has already survived the colonialism of the French and the occupation of the Japanese. Even the U.S. Embassy architects had deferred to its aristocratic grandeur; they had laid out the chancery and the smaller buildings in a respectful design around the towering tamarind while the other trees on the lot had been routinely chopped down, discardable as used toothpicks. Long after the war is over, Walker thought, that magnificent tree will still be standing.

Just as Walker stepped into his limousine, he spotted Tony's Fiat entering the Embassy parking lot. They waved to each other. What's he doing in so early? Walker thought. Where the hell's the old sonofabitch going this time of the morning? Tony wondered.

A five-minute drive later, Walker parted a set of doorway curtains and was welcomed into another world: the Nguyen Dynasty shop.

"Ah, Your Excellency," cracked a voice as fragile as any of the antiques on the shelves.

Walker, still dazzled by the outdoor light, adjusted to the dim interior of the shop and focused on Pham Van Hoan, the proprietor. Hoan bowed in Walker's direction; bowed or erect, he was no more than half the Ambassador's height, with a spray of gray hair and a face so thin and dry the cheekbones almost cut through the pale skin. He seemed a refugee from an earlier century.

"Professor Hoan," the Ambassador began, "so good to see you again. I had a few free minutes" — his eyes quickly reconnoitered the porcelain landscape, searching for newcomers among the many familiar pieces he knew from previous visits to the shop — "and I'd heard that you recently came into possession of a 'new' collection."

"Ah yes, Your Excellency," Hoan murmured, waving his hand in the direction of the shelves. "The availability of 'new' pieces for my shop . . . seems to be in direct proportion to the state of nerves in Saigon. Sad," he added, his eyes never quite making contact with Walker's, "but a proved equation."

"And the nerves these days?"

"Good for porcelain," Hoan said with a smile that quickly vanished. "I would prefer if it were bad for porcelain. It would then be better for my country."

Walker was not in the mood to deliver a pep talk on the future of South Viet Nam. Indeed, his relationship with Hoan had always remained mercifully neutral, its tensions confined to ritualistic bargaining for the items on the shelves. The fact that one man's apprehension could enrich another man's collection — well, that's what it was: a fact. He said nothing, his eyes busily searching.

"I am sure I will not have to point out the new pieces, Your Excellency," Hoan said. "You of all people will not fail to discover them." A smile fluttered across his ancient face. "Please. Look around. The Nguyen Dynasty is yours. Would you like a cup of tea?"

Walker nodded, and Hoan disappeared behind a second set of curtains leading to the rear of the shop. The Nguyen Dynasty had always struck Walker as a rather extravagant name for an establishment that measured, at best, twenty steps in one direction and ten in the other, a hodgepodge of porcelain, bronzes, wooden carvings, some old, some new, some of uncertain vintage, some even intact. In New York or London or Paris, the Nguyen Dynasty would have had difficulty qualifying for flea-market status. In Saigon, it rivaled the Louvre. For Walker, this miniature bazaar where he could search for treasures among the vases, plates, and bowls served as a welcome refuge from the constant challenges of Viet Nam.

Walker's romance with porcelain was legend. He had encountered his first Ming a decade earlier in Jakarta, a repository for Chinese export porcelain shipped down over the centuries. He then began acquiring Tang, Sung, Yuan, and Ming pieces, although not as many as he would have liked; his ambassadorial salary could not finance the dimensions of his increasingly voracious appetite. At first, his shelves were filled mostly with enthusiasm; cracks, chips, even minor restorations did not deter him so long as the pieces sparked a response of inner excitement. But gradually his taste became more discriminating; he acquired a passion for perfection. He began to choose his pieces as though he were choosing friends, reaching out to them through the veil of history. The shelves in his office had been custom-built for his collection, and only his most intimate "friends" had been placed there on display. His lust for porcelain was the butt of jokes in the Embassy corridors. The gag was that, for Walker, porcelain had long ago replaced sex, that he preferred the cool touch of a blue-and-white to the warmer touch of a woman.

Hoan reappeared with the tea as Walker's eye suddenly hit an unexpected contour: a vase almost hidden behind a badly chipped urn. Hoan's experienced antennae caught Walker's concentration on the vase. It was an old trick of the trade: to half-conceal an interesting piece in the shadows — allowing the customer the thrill of discovery. Hoan set the tea tray on the marble top of a carved blackwood table. "That *is* an unusual piece," he observed quietly.

Walker carefully extricated the vase, and he could tell at a glance that it was a Swatow, dating back to the sixteenth century and distinguished by its raw spontaneity. Old ivory in color, decorated with a charmingly drawn *kylin* — a mythical Chinese dragon — the vase was about fifteen inches high, heavily potted. Its throat, an inch high and four inches in diameter, blossomed out into graceful shoulders, with four loop handles, called "ears," before tapering into a base that was six inches across. Walker rubbed his palm across the bottom; yes, the confirming evidence was there: the rough, embedded sand, a circle of corroboration acquired late in the Ming period, when pieces that came to be known as "Swatows" — for the port from which they were shipped — were taken hot from the kiln and cooled directly on the earth. This was an authentic piece, enchanting, and Walker felt himself succumbing.

"You know, Professor Hoan," he said, sharing an observation he had made more than once, "we are clay in the presence of porcelain."

Hoan beamed. "Yes, yes," he responded eagerly.

Walker's fingers slid back and forth across the glaze, searching for camouflaged repairs, restorations not obvious to the naked eye. He tapped the vase smartly with his knuckles; the *ping!* bounced back whole. He reached into his pocket, took out a coin, and ran it over the body of the Swatow; this enabled the ear to compensate for what the eye could not always see: metal against intact porcelain sounded quick and vibrant whereas porcelain that had been repaired gave off a flat, dead tone. He moved the coin toward the loops — a vase with original loops that had survived four centuries was unusual but not unheard of — when he was interrupted by Hoan's anxious whisper.

"I should tell you, Your Excellency, that one of the loops, alas, has been restored."

Within an instant Walker had discovered the restoration; when he ran the coin against the loop, there was not a trace of resonance. He ran the coin against the other three loops; they sang beautifully.

"A 'factory defect,' Your Excellency," Hoan said with a laugh.

Walker sighed. "A shame. It's a piece that's so easy to love, but . . ."

"Your Excellency, this piece was born long ago," Hoan continued with quiet persistence. "It has lived through upheavals, revolutions, wars — and who knows, it may be more intact, even with this little restoration, than most people." He studied Walker's face for a reaction.

"You know, Professor Hoan," Walker began, "that my usual practice is not to buy pieces that are damaged."

Hoan quickly moved in with a proposal. "Let's arrange the matter as we have before," he said. "Take it with you. Live with it a few weeks. No obligation. If it captivates you, then we'll talk. If not — well, we are both slaves to the same passion." He smiled. "I will not be unhappy to take it back again." His hands caressed the vase. "It is not often that I have the pleasure of offering you such a piece." He smiled again. "And it's only because of Saigon's nerves."

Walker still hesitated. He ran the coin once again along the restored loop; the sound — dull, leaden — confirmed the flaw. He held the vase at arm's length; it surged with vitality, and he found himself wondering who, four hundred years ago, had shaped it. Who had first owned it? How had it made the long journey south from China? When? How had it survived the violence of Viet Nam's history? The vase was filled with intriguing questions, and Walker realized that he had just about overcome his reluctance to buy anything but a perfect piece.

A wry smile of surrender crossed his face. "Done," he said finally. "I'll take your offer and live with the vase for a few weeks."

"It will get into your blood," Hoan responded excitedly. "You will see."

Hoan escorted Walker into the street. He watched the Ambassador carefully place the vase on the back seat of the limousine, move in next to it, and hold it steady as the car disappeared into the traffic. Only then did Hoan reenter the shop and carefully lock the front door. He hurried past the porcelain-filled shelves and burst through the curtains leading to the rear of the shop.

An elderly Vietnamese, lean, bony, as though he were made of bamboo poles, was seated at a small wooden table in a haze of cigarette smoke. He looked up, very slowly, his face expressionless.

Hoan stared at him, eyes questioning.

The elderly man began stroking a wisp of hair on his chin. Finally, he stood up. He looked directly at Hoan — and grinned.

12

"What the hell are you doing in so early?"

It was Hal James's welcome as Tony entered the CIA's top-secret radio room, the Agency's shortwave link to its outposts from the seventeenth parallel south to the Camau Peninsula. "It's only" — Hal looked at the clock on the wall — "seven-forty. I was lucky enough to draw night duty. But you? What are you trying to do? Win the war single-handed?"

Tony laughed, out of courtesy; Hal was a decent, dedicated guy, but humor was not exactly his forte. Tony saw him as a kind of middle-aged vacuum cleaner, plugged into the battery of CIA radios on the Embassy's sixth floor, sucking up details without ever being able to translate them into a coherent analysis, a basis for policy. He had already served seven years in Saigon and was the Agency's record-holder for time spent in South Viet Nam. Hal would be able to tell you the exact dates and casualty figures of every battle ever fought without really understanding what went wrong. Great at wheres and whens, not whys.

"Hell, I'm late," Tony said. "I just saw Walker leaving the Embassy a moment ago. Probably on his way to his favorite fortune-teller to find out what's going on." He poured a cup of coffee. "Fact is, I couldn't sleep."

"Love?" Hal asked with a wink.

"War," replied Tony.

"Ban Me Thuot?"

Tony nodded.

"Odd," Hal said as he worked the dials of the radio receiver. "Nothing's come in from 'Subway.' Even missed the zero-seven-hundred check-in."

"Subway" was the code-name for Ban Me Thuot, dating back to the early 'sixties arrival of the "lepidopterists" in that Montagnard city; one of the butterfly catchers, a jokester from Brooklyn, had code-named Ban Me Thuot in honor of the BMT — the Brooklyn–Manhattan Transit line. "Subway" had stuck; its underground connotation had appealed to the old-boy network at Langley. Those were the good old days of the war, when Viet Nam was seen as child's play — home by Christmas, coonskin on the wall, and all that.

"What do you make of it?" Tony asked. Silence from Ban Me Thuot could mean only one thing.

"Trouble," Hal said. "Trouble is what I make of it."

"Did you try calling 'Subway'?" Tony knew it was a pointless question.

Hal nodded. "No response."

Tony knew from experience that, in Viet Nam, silence shouts. Silence in this case shouted that the NVA attack he'd seen from the air yesterday had simply been phase one of a new, still puzzling strategy that the NVA had adopted for the Central Highlands. By now, the NVA must have fought its way closer to Ban Me Thuot, if not into it, thereby threatening not only "Subway" but the city itself. "Subway" had apparently opted for radio silence so as not to expose its presence to the NVA radios monitoring U.S. frequencies. Worse yet, "Subway" might have been hit.

Tony poured another cup of coffee. Hal riffled through an old copy of *Playboy*. The minutes ticked by.

" 'Subway' calling, 'Subway' calling." The voice that burst loud and desperate into the radio room belonged to Joe Peterson, CIA man in Ban Me Thuot. Tony and Hal hunched over the receiver.

"Shit's hit the fan here," the voice blared. "Got to talk fast, no interruptions, please. It's my nickel."

Some people can joke at the strangest times, Tony thought.

"Zero-seven-hundred miss was not due to a blown tube, anything like that. It's a blown city, man. Whole town's been overrun. Attack began zero-five-two-zero. Artillery, mortars, the works. Can see big Russian 'mothers' rolling by our living room right now. T-fifty-fours, one tank after another. Outlook bleak, very bleak."

Tony turned up the volume — as if he were trying to pull Peterson through the receiver, to rescue him from Ban Me Thuot.

"Where's ARVN?" Hal asked. "Over."

"You tell me. Over."

"Fucking ARVN," Tony blurted.

"Right on," Peterson said, cool as ever. "Over."

"How many with you?" Hal asked. "Over."

"Ten. Me, my wife, and two kids. Also five missionaries who've been selling God to the Montagnards. They rushed here when our 'friends' began to enter the town. Also, one scholar from Harvard had to interrupt his study of the local dialects, poor chap. Over."

"Should we send a chopper to get you out?" Hal asked. A pro forma question, Tony thought. The answer was obvious. "Over."

"I'd give all of South Viet Nam for the sight of a chopper — but all you'd be doing is offering target practice for our 'friends.' Situation here is hopeless. Over."

"Anything we can do?" asked Hal. "Over."

"Wish I could think of something. I delayed calling, didn't want to pinpoint our presence, thought maybe ARVN would show up. They haven't. Our 'friends' are going to pick us up sooner or later, radio silence makes no difference now. If *they* don't get us, VNAF will. They'll bomb the hell out of Ban Me Thuot — and us."

How long, Tony thought, before I see Peterson again?

"I've got a pillowcase tied to a pole. A white flag, dammit. Those fellows can have itchy fingers." A burst of static drowned out Peterson for a moment. ". . . some uninvited callers in our compound now . . . four of them — with AK-forty-sevens. . . ." Static filled the room. "Don't forget to write."

" 'SUBWAY!' 'SUBWAY!' "

"Care of the 'Hanoi Hilton.' " Click. The receiver went dead.

"Sonofabitch!" Hal shouted.

"Fucking ARVN!" Tony hit the desk. "Fucking NVA!"

"Poor fucking Peterson."

"Poor fucking intelligence." Tony's outburst produced a sharp glance from Hal. "That's right," Tony said. "Poor fucking intelligence."

Tony went to the window and looked down at the broad boulevard, a tangle of 9 A.M. traffic and people. It all seemed so normal, just another morning in Saigon.

Suddenly, Tony dashed toward the door.

"Where the hell are you going?" Hal asked.

"To consult God!"

Instead of waiting for the elevator, Tony raced down the stairs. He almost collided with two Vietnamese porters who were dusting the banisters.

The Ambassador's secretary was at her desk, serenely filing her fingernails.

"Is he in?" Tony bellowed.

Helen smiled. "Urgent urgent?" she asked playfully.

"Triple urgent."

"Well, he just returned a moment ago," Helen said as she lifted the intercom phone. "Let me tell him you're here."

Walker was relaxing in his ambassadorial chair, his arms folded across his chest, his eyes fixed on his latest acquisition: the Swatow vase. He'd repositioned the pieces on his three display shelves so that the new vase would be stage center, all the surrounding porcelain encircling the gleaming Swatow. A Sung celadon plate he'd bought years ago in Manila, a Wan Li blue-and-white bowl he'd picked up from a *tukang* in Jakarta, a greenish-blue Sawankhalok dish he'd found in the little antique shop on New Road in Bangkok — all faded in contrast to the Swatow. The Swatow was vibrant, alive, exhilarating. On the drive from the Nguyen Dynasty just a few minutes earlier, he'd considered keeping the vase at home; but he wanted it nearby, within sight, during the long hours he spent at the Embassy — perhaps the final hours of his diplomatic career.

The thought had crossed his mind more than once: that this — Viet Nam — would be the last diplomatic assignment he'd accept. At sixty-two, he was tired of being a fireman, the man the White House turned to every time a five-alarm blaze erupted overseas. Enough of Washington's fear of its own power, its readiness to compromise integrity, its inability to read the future. Maybe he would write an intimate reminiscence of Presidents as he had known them, not as served up by their public relations and media manipulators. Maybe he would teach; the Viet Nam generation could do with a bit of education about the world as it was, not as the State Department bureaucrats chose to color it. Maybe he would even open an antique shop. Or maybe run off to a desert isle with Jeanne. Maybe —

The buzzer on his desk broke into his fantasies. It was Helen: "Tony Catlett is in the waiting room and says he must see you. Says it's very urgent."

"Send him in." Relentless, that young man, Walker thought. If only his energy, his doggedness, his youth could be harnessed to an accurate perception of reality. Might even make a good diplomat one day. Might even make a good son-in-law.

Tony charged into the room, more agitated than usual. Walker's eyes widened.

"Morning, Tony," Walker said. "What is so urgent?"

"Ban Me Thuot, sir." Even Tony was surprised to find himself raising his voice.

"Anything new?" Walker asked. "I checked about an hour ago."

"It's all happened within the last few minutes," Tony said. "The NVA's taken Ban Me Thuot." He paused to see what impact that bombshell would have on the Ambassador, whether he would remember his mocking assessment of the initial report Tony had brought back from the Highlands.

Walker leaned forward, resting his elbows on the desk, his eyes fixed on Tony unblinkingly. Tony, trying to keep his own fury under control, gave the Ambassador a swift account of the radio contact with Joe Peterson, how Peterson had provided a running report of his own capture, how the NVA had come crashing into Ban Me Thuot without meeting any resistance from ARVN, how the loss of Ban Me Thuot . . .

Walker half-listened, half-wondered how he would handle this new development — and Tony. Heading off a sense of panic in the Embassy was almost as important as dealing with the news about Ban Me Thuot. The corridors already reeked with a smell of despair.

"The *temporary* loss of Ban Me Thuot, Tony," the Ambassador said. "ARVN may have bugged out, yes, but it isn't the first time, and it won't be the first time, either, that ARVN will launch a counterattack. It's happened before — during the enemy's Tet offensive in 'sixty-eight, during the enemy's spring offensive in 'seventy-two. Hue lost, Hue retaken. The ebb and flow of war, Tony. Don't ever forget that. Another thing, very important" — Walker tapped his finger on the top of his desk — "this is what we've been waiting for, Tony, the enemy finally coming out of the jungle and standing up and fighting. Once they show themselves, we can mow them down. For heaven's sake, don't look on this as the end of the world, will you? It's one battle, that's what it is, one battle — in a bigger battle that our side will ultimately win. Absolutely. It's just a question of tactics, strategy, time. About these new POWs? Well, Congress and the American public will go into a rage but . . ."

Walker stopped short, a thought flashing through his mind:

the loss of Ban Me Thuot, even the temporary loss of Ban Me Thuot, could be a godsend, a disaster turned into a dividend. It could — just could, if properly exploited — get the White House and Congress off their asses and frighten them into finally authorizing emergency funds for ARVN. An eyes-only cable, the instant Tony leaves: Watch out, Mr. President, it could all come tumbling down, with you and your political future at the bottom of the heap.

"Temporary loss, Tony," the Ambassador repeated. *"Temporary."*

Tony listened, with a growing sense of incredulity. Reality again bouncing off Walker's armor. When the NVA puts the torch to Saigon one day, Tony thought, Walker'll still be sitting here, all alone with his goddamned porcelain, wearing his old seersucker suit, Princeton '35, spouting the same mumbo-jumbo.

The eyes were on him again. "Well, Tony, what do *you* think we should do?" Walker asked.

To Tony, the Ambassador's voice suggested impatient courtesy rather than a search for genuine recommendations. "May I be very frank, Mr. Ambassador?"

A thin smile creased Walker's face. "I have always encouraged people on my staff to be very frank," he said dryly. "Wisdom is usually in short supply."

Tony ignored the cut. "Two things," he began swiftly. "One, immediate — military; two, almost immediate — political." He tried to avoid the cold stare. "On the military side, a judgment will have to be made about the real objectives of the new NVA strategy. Will they stop at Ban Me Thuot? Or is Ban Me Thuot a trap to suck in ARVN units so the NVA can then attack the more important — but more thinly defended — objective of Pleiku?"

It sounded to Walker like a replay of last night's intelligence briefing at the DAO.

Walker leaned back in his chair. "It would appear, as you

said yesterday, that there has been a botch in our intelligence with respect to the NVA and Ban Me Thuot. That's your department, isn't it, Tony?"

"Yes, but —"

"Let's put all that aside for the moment," Walker continued, unyieldingly. "There'll be plenty of time for postmortems."

Tony leaned over the desk. "Mr. Ambassador," he said, "I —"

"Not now," Walker said, his voice icy. "What I want to hear from you now is what you think we should do to meet this threat."

It was the question Tony had been anticipating; he tried to concentrate on the Ambassador's forehead so he wouldn't have the feeling of being imprisoned by his eyes.

"I think that ARVN should do whatever it can on the military front, but" — Tony paused, carefully measuring his next phrase — "our emphasis should be on the political front."

So predictable, the Ambassador thought, so predictable: Tony using Ban Me Thuot as an argument to promote his pet theory that negotiations will lead to a coalition government with the Communists. I will use Ban Me Thuot as an argument to get emergency funds from Washington to *prevent* a coalition.

"Given my view, Mr. Ambassador," Tony rushed on, determined to lay out his scenario, "that ARVN, no matter how much additional equipment it gets, won't be able to stand up against the NVA, the U.S. should start pushing for talks now with 'the other side,' with a view toward creating a coalition — a government of the South Vietnamese and the Communists."

"You're back to your 'doomsday' projections," Walker interrupted.

"Otherwise, the U.S. will end up with less than a coalition. The U.S. will end up with nothing, the Communists with everything — with all of the South gobbled up by the North. The French made just that mistake; they tried to keep it all for themselves, no deal with Ho Chi Minh, and all they succeeded in doing was losing it all at Dien Bien Phu."

Ironic, Walker thought, ironic that he, half my age, is the one who's ready to call it quits. Entrust the world to Catletts?

"Your analysis is — how shall I put it?" Walker got up from his desk. "Well articulated?" Sarcasm soaked his words. "But it contains a variety of flaws. Will you do me the courtesy of hearing my rebuttal?"

Walker didn't bother to wait for Tony's reply. "One," he went on, "it equates the U.S. with France. Wrong. Two, it sees the loss of Ban Me Thuot — the temporary loss — as fatal. Wrong. ARVN will now redouble its efforts. Three, it makes no distinction between the world of 'fifty-four and the world of 'seventy-five. Wrong. The cold war has been replaced by détente, and if the Soviets and the Chinese want détente with the U.S. to continue, they're going to have to lean on their client to knock it off in South Viet Nam. Four, it suggests that Washington will do nothing about Ban Me Thuot. Wrong. Ban Me Thuot, coupled with the NVA's taking of Americans as prisoners, could be just the thing to force Washington to come up with more money for ARVN. And, five, you talk about negotiations with 'the other side' *now* on the grounds that the opportunity for negotiations may be lost later. Wrong, wrong, wrong! 'The other side' will always be ready to negotiate, if we give them half a chance. I know the Asian mentality."

The buzzer on the Ambassador's desk sounded. It was just as well, Tony thought; another confrontation, another standoff. Walker picked up the phone. "Yes, by all means." The Ambassador had softened his tone.

As soon as she came through the door, Suzanne could tell she had walked onto a battlefield. Walker's face was impassive, Tony's flushed. She caught sight of the Swatow. "Lovely," she murmured in an obvious effort to ease the tension. "New, isn't it, Dad?"

"Yes," said Walker, deliberately shifting gears. "A little something that came my way and that I could not resist."

She ran her palm down the cool smoothness of the vase. "But isn't this a risky spot, on such a narrow shelf?"

Walker smiled indulgently. "The only way it could fall off," he replied, "is if the North Vietnamese were just outside the window, rocketing Saigon."

Tony moved toward the door.

"Thanks for stopping by." Walker's voice could have cut into stone. Suzanne caught the look of anger on Tony's face as he left.

"That young man, my dear, seems to think he has an exclusive insight into the Asian mind." With a quick glance at Suzanne, Walker returned to his desk. "As though he were the discoverer of the East, America's Marco Polo."

"That's unkind," Suzanne said quietly, heading for the door. "I've something to tell Tony. I'll be back."

"No, please stay," Walker called out. But by then Suzanne had closed the door behind her.

She overtook Tony at the stairway.

"I've got to get out of here," he told her tersely. He raced down the stairs, Suzanne trying to catch up with him. They sped through the lobby, past the Marine guard on duty at the reception desk, past the crowds of Vietnamese lined up before the consular office, desperate to obtain visas to the United States. Tony sprinted toward his car, Suzanne one step behind.

"Wait a minute! Please wait, Tony!" Suzanne grabbed his arm. Fighting back tears, she said hoarsely, "When I'm with you, what you say makes sense. When I'm with him . . . Tony, maybe he does see more of the overall picture than you do. Maybe he does know something you don't . . ."

"*Knowing* isn't the problem. *Interpreting* is the problem."

"And then when I'm with both of you," she continued, "I'm really torn apart. I don't know where the truth is anymore."

Tony looked at her sharply. "*He* doesn't believe me. *You* trust him. Okay, you want the truth?" He pushed her into the car. "I'll show you where the truth is!"

"Just a minute!" Suzanne, startled by Tony's unexpected

roughness, reached for the door handle. "What do you think you're doing? Where are you taking me?"

Tony slammed his foot down on the accelerator and the Fiat shot through the main gate, in the direction of Tan Son Nhut. "Where the hell else?" he shouted over the noise of the traffic.

13

South Viet Nam below was green velvet.

"The war's just like the Vietnamese," Jim Barnes bellowed over the intercom. "Taking a siesta." He glanced at Tony and Suzanne, huddled together in the cockpit of the C-47, then looked through the small plastic window and saw nothing but a landscape he had flown over hundreds of times — stretches of rice paddies, clusters of jungle, empty roads that linked the countryside together. "Looks like Louisiana on a Sunday."

"Just keep flying toward MR Two," Tony shouted.

"You're my guest," Jim shouted back. The two-engine plane, a survivor of World War Two and the Korean War, chugged through the sky of its third war.

Tony smiled weakly at Suzanne. Her face was a mixture of excitement and anxiety. What the hell am I doing? he thought. Risking her life, just to win an argument with her father? Flying her into a war zone, just to convince her that I'm right and he's wrong? An act of recklessness, insisting that she witness the eruption in the Highlands, the new turn in the war. Do I really think they can somehow communicate by blood, that what the daughter sees can reach the brain of the father, alter his perception, confront him with a reality he wishes to avoid?

He slipped his arm around Suzanne's waist and gave her a hug of reassurance. Her smile barely surfaced.

Getting the flight north had been a stroke of luck. Obsessed with the need to prove his point to Suzanne, to show her the war, Tony had taken a chance that he would find a plane at Tan Son Nhut. There were always private charters, hired by the American TV networks, landing and taking off in search of a flare-up of bang-bang that would be good for a minute fifteen on the nightly news back home; there were always Air America Volpars, Porters, and Beeches flying off to the various far corners of South Viet Nam. Tony had more than once hitched a ride; it made no difference in which direction you flew, the war was everywhere. Hell, you could sometimes even run into it on the outskirts of Saigon. You could have an espresso on the veranda of the Continental, jump into a taxi and tell the driver to follow the nearest tank, and in no time at all you'd be hearing rat-tat-tat. It was that kind of war.

But it was even easier to get a lift this time. Tony and Suzanne had pulled into the Air America compound just as Jim Barnes, his trusty pistol on his hip and his trusty bayonet in his left flying boot, was strolling across the tarmac. Jim was, in fact, about to head northeast to Nha Trang, midway up the coast, to pick up the U.S. Consul General and fly him back to Saigon for a conference with the Ambassador. The plane was empty, Jim told them, only a co-pilot, a couple of gunners, himself. But he hesitated. Nha Trang was a milk run, but still — the Ambassador's daughter? Tony, darting a glance at Suzanne, quickly assured him that Suzanne had been cleared for a quick look around, nothing dangerous, Nha Trang was perfect. "The Red Baroness," Tony said with a smile at Suzanne. Suzanne looked sharply at Tony, but Jim missed the exchange, and they all climbed into a C-47 and rolled down Tan Son Nhut and were away.

Tony waited until they were a half-hour out — after they'd flown over the provinces of Bien Hoa, Long Khanh, and Lam Dong, all running northeast of Saigon in the direction of Nha Trang — before he raised the question of a detour.

"Unbelievable, what we saw yesterday," he said to Jim.

9 5

Jim nodded.

"Think we could kind of swing by the Ban Me Thuot area on the way to Nha Trang?" Tony asked. "Just to get a peek from up here?"

Jim glanced at his chronometer — a gold Rolex, the standard status symbol of Air America's hot-rod pilots in Viet Nam. "Now let's see," he calculated out loud. "Ban Me Thuot is more north than northeast, and going that way would add another twenty minutes or so to our flying time." He checked his instrument panel. "That would mean we'll be a little late for the ConGen."

"Hell, this war's behind schedule already," Tony bantered. He looked at Suzanne; she did not seem to be amused.

"You're my guest," Jim said. "Okay, the old ConGen will have to wait." He laughed. "I'll tell him we had a flat tire." Jim headed the plane toward Darlac Province.

Tony tapped Suzanne on the shoulder. She pulled away. He could feel the tension building between them.

Just as the plane crossed into Darlac Province, about twenty miles south of Ban Me Thuot, near the hamlet of Lac Thien, the ground below suddenly lit up in jagged streaks. Now what the hell was that? As they flew closer, the streaks focused on five lines of cars, trucks, jeeps, tanks, all kinds of vehicles — motionless, dead on the road. At first glance, it looked like a Sunday traffic jam back home, families returning from a day at the beach trapped on the highway.

The radio in the cockpit crackled. "Can you hear me? Can you hear me?" Even the static could not drown out the wild panic in the Vietnamese voice. It sounded like a voice out of hell.

Jim began turning the dials, hoping to fine-tune the reception.

"I'm a colonel. Colonel Tran Van Binh. Fifty-third Regiment, Twenty-third Division. I can see you. Can you see me?"

"The guy's got to be nuts," Jim yelled at Tony. Jim looked through the window and all he could see were the vehicles, little squares of metal, and thousands of dots of people. "Yeah, I can see you," he shouted. What difference did it make?

"It's crazy here," the frantic voice radioed from the ground, two miles below. "All these vehicles running from Ban Me Thuot. Also people. When the NVA came, everyone started to run, to get out. No order. Only panic. Men, women, children, everybody running, running, running. Must be ten thousand people. Even more. Refugees. NVA artillery hitting us. People dying in front of my eyes. Help us. Help us. We are all being killed."

At ten thousand feet, they felt safe; down there, *Viet Nam.* Tony glanced at Suzanne; her face was taut, her eyes filled with fear. In all his years in-country, he had never seen anything like this: a highway of horror. The "doomsday" portrait he had drawn for the Ambassador now seemed like a field of spring flowers.

"We are trapped here," the voice screamed. "The bridge is blown up. No way to cross the river. NVA shelling us from all sides!"

"Any ARVN around?" asked Jim. He could spot flashes of artillery fire.

"No ARVN." The voice was desperate. "Just disorganized units. Soldiers running away as fast as anyone else. You must help us. I trained in the U.S. Fort Leavenworth. 'Sixty-seven. Tell Saigon. We've already told Saigon but so far no help. We are being killed here. Please don't abandon us. Please don't go away." The anguish in the voice echoed through the cockpit.

"I'm radioing your report directly to Saigon," Jim said. He immediately switched frequencies and relayed the details to Air America at Tan Son Nhut.

The voice at the other end was calm, an eerie contrast to the Vietnamese Colonel's. "Yes," said the voice, "we're getting the same report directly from the last remnants of ARVN in Ban Me Thuot. You should know that the NVA has also launched simultaneous attacks on Kontum and Pleiku. Nothing really much we can do. We're just relaying these reports to the Embassy, and the Embassy's relaying them to the ARVN Joint Chiefs. Maybe they'll get moving — but I wouldn't bet on it."

Tony looked at Suzanne; she was staring at the gunners who flanked the door of the plane.

"Still want me to go to Nha Trang?" Jim asked Tan Son Nhut.

"Yes, but the mission's changed," the voice said. "This word's just in from the Embassy: they want you to pick up not only the ConGen but also the other Americans stationed there. The Ambassador says this is not, repeat *not*, an evacuation but only a temporary drawdown." Suzanne's eyes avoided Tony's. "Bit of a problem there — which you'll see for yourself soon enough," the voice added. "Bye, bye. . . ."

Jim switched radio frequencies. His eyes swept the scene of panic. "Good luck, Colonel," he said softly. "If you can still hear me." He headed the plane east, in the direction of Nha Trang, on the coast.

As they flew toward the city, they began to see more chaos below: streams of refugees pouring down Route 21, heading south in the direction of Saigon, more than a hundred miles away. Hundreds of sampans were putting out to sea; the magnificent white beach — once the playground of the Vietnamese elite — had become a Dunkirk.

Jim flew the plane low over the airport at Nha Trang. They had a clear view of the tarmac jammed with people, goats, bicycles, motorcycles, jeeps, trucks. "We'll never be able to land down here," he shouted. He pointed the plane back into the sky. "Chaos down there."

Tony smiled weakly at Suzanne; she said nothing. Her face was drained, her fingernails digging into her palms.

"Can you hear me?" It was an American voice booming in over the cockpit radio. "ConGen here, working a hand-held radio. Panic in Nha Trang. The NVA hasn't even hit the city. Panic — because of what's happened at Ban Me Thuot. VC agents here have been spreading the word. An hour ago, all calm. Now — you take a look. Everyone here wants out. The place is about to explode."

"Keep talking," said Jim. "Hear you fine."

"Let's try this plan," radioed the ConGen. "We are now standing by at the terminal building. You put down at the runway at the far end of the field. We have jeeps. Maybe we can get to you before the crowds do. We'll have to take the chance. Otherwise, we're sitting ducks. The Vietnamese here, the ARVN, they'll turn on us. They'll tear us apart."

Jim looked down at the crowds at the airport. "Going to be close, all right," he finally said, "but there's no choice. Tell you what, sir. I'll put down on Runway Four, left corner of the field. Minute you see me lower my landing gear, you take off for that spot. We'll do a quick evac and clear out."

"Thanks," said the ConGen.

"Moment," said Jim. "How many are you?"

"Thirty-four."

Jim whistled. "Well, double-time then," he said. "See you in a couple of minutes."

Jim circled the field once and then aimed the plane toward Runway Four. He lowered the landing gear. Tony could see six crowded jeeps suddenly spurt from the terminal area and race in the direction of the plane. The C-47's wheels hit the ground. Jim slammed on the brakes; the plane shuddered and came to a quick stop. He kept the props turning over. One of the gunners opened the side door, and swiftly lowered the drop-ramp steps to the ground. There were the jeeps, almost upon them. So far, so good.

Tony stood in the door frame, Suzanne just off to the side. "Quick," he shouted. The Americans piled out of the jeeps and raced up the steps into the plane.

Suddenly the runway was swept by a tidal wave of Vietnamese — a mass of men, women, and children hurtling toward the C-47. They ignored the whirling props. They stampeded toward the open door. Tony saw an ARVN soldier swing his rifle to clear three old women from his path so that he could push his way up the stairs; he was thrown forward into the plane by a crush of screaming Vietnamese right behind him. They knocked down the gunner. He stood up and fired a warning shot into the sky but it had no effect; the crowd kept surging toward the plane.

For Suzanne, the war up to now had been remote: television, mimeographed communiqués, cocktail-party strategy, her father's talk at dinner. This was the war close up, and she turned away, sickened, terrified.

"Put this on, quick," said one of the gunners as he handed her a flak jacket. "You never can tell about these 'gooks,' even the ones on your own side."

Tony was now blocking the open door; the Vietnamese crowds surged against him. He looked into a melee of faces, arms, eyes — eyes frantic with terror, eyes pleading for life. An old man's anguished face suddenly confronted him — the eyes slitted with fear, the mouth a black hole. Tony could feel himself being pushed backward, in danger of being toppled, crushed by the crowds fighting their way into the plane.

Suddenly, Tony spotted a small bundle hurtling toward him from below. Automatically he reached out and grabbed it. It was a baby, wrapped in a white cloth from head to toe, a trace of black hair sticking out at one end. The mother, her arms outstretched, screamed to him, her cries piercing the pandemonium.

Tony stood frozen, the baby in his arms. Suzanne tugged at his shirt.

"Give me the baby!" she shrieked. An image of Thi and Thach flashed before her eyes. "Give me the baby!"

Tony, blank-faced, pushed her aside and dropped the baby into the open arms of the woman below.

"You bastard! How could you?" Suzanne screamed hysterically. She began pummeling Tony with her fists; he looked at her, as though he were in a trance, and shoved her back. A powerful arm suddenly encircled her waist; the gunner who had given her the flak jacket pulled her out of the door frame.

"This ain't no time to fight with each other," he shouted. "We may be having a *real* fight on our hands." He spun his mounted machine gun in the direction of the Vietnamese on the tarmac. "I'm going to give these motherfuckers the scare of their lives." His finger hit the trigger, and a volley of bullets sprayed above the mob. The Vietnamese halted in their tracks but, a moment later, rushed the plane.

"We're never going to get this baby off the ground if you let any more of them on board." It was Jim's frantic voice, shouting over the plane's PA system. "This plane can hold sixty, tops. There are now more than a hundred."

Tony reached for one of the M-16s stacked inside the plane, near the door. He lifted the rifle, then slammed the butt down hard on the Vietnamese hands that darted out of the crowd to clutch at the plane. He could feel bones being broken, the crunch vibrating through the rifle stock into his own hands. He heard sudden screams. The plane began racing down the runway. Some hands were still clinging to the door frame. Tony whacked away wildly with the M-16. Fingers suddenly let go in a bloody spray. The fingers of Saigon came into focus before his eyes, but these fingers were clawing for a way out of Nha Trang, an exit from horror.

"No more people," blared over the PA.

Again, Tony slammed the rifle butt on hands that were still clinging. He could see bodies whirl away as the C-47 picked up speed and lifted slowly off the ground. He leaned back from the open door and looked up. Suzanne — dress torn, her body trembling — was staring at him, her face filled with loathing.

The last glimpse Tony had of the panic below, of the hundreds of Vietnamese still on the runway, of heaps of bodies strewn on the ground, of ARVN rifles firing at the plane, was of the sun's rays glinting off the lens of a television camera pointed in the direction of the retreating C-47.

14

The big iron gates leading to Doc Lap, the presidential palace, swung open on the arrival of Walker's limousine. "Independence Palace" — its very name producing cynical titters among the Americans — was a heavy pile of glass and concrete, a modernistic fortress surrounded by sandbag fortifications, antiaircraft guns, heavily armed troops. The mass of hardware guarded not only against a surprise Communist attack, but also, given the President's own route to power, against a coup attempt. There was a saying in Saigon: Only one thing could penetrate Doc Lap and that was a phone call — and even then you could never be sure that you'd get an answer.

Washington, in the last few hours, had been firing off frantic cables demanding that Walker find out how the hell the President planned to deal with the NVA attacks in MR 2 and the other MRs. Walker had cabled back in soothing Ambassadorese that he was "confident" the President would soon reveal his counterstrategy. The truth was, the Ambassador had not been able to get through to the President since the shock of the rout in MR 2. Doc Lap had been broodingly silent. There were reports that the President had been overtaken by *immobilisme*, that he had lapsed into a state of paralysis. Was he seeing his astrologer again?

Finally, the call had come from the Palace, requesting Walker's presence. He had responded immediately.

The limousine came to a stop in front of the VIP entrance. A Vietnamese aide-de-camp greeted Walker and escorted him through the echoing halls to the presidential office on the third floor, just below the rooftop helicopter pad. South Viet Nam's leader, in his early fifties, short, round, with a smooth, deceptively childlike face, was seated behind a mahogany desk. He nodded, his eyes as blankly unrevealing as usual.

Walker would have loved to approach him directly, in straightforward American fashion. But he knew he would have to follow the traditional Vietnamese route, to ritualize the meeting before settling down to business. The difference in metabolism between the two allies was maddening; while the Vietnamese sipped tea, the Americans developed ulcers.

"How are you, Mr. Ambassador?" The President's precise English was accented by a mixture of Vietnamese and French.

Walker said he was fine. He asked how the President was.

The President was fine, too.

"How is your daughter, Mr. Ambassador?"

Walker said his daughter was fine. He asked the President how his family was.

The President's family was fine, too.

It had been only a few days since the two men had last met, but Walker knew there could be no variation in the minuet of salutation. He tried to relax but it took too much effort. It was more relaxing to remain tense.

Almost soundlessly, the heavy carved doors to the room opened. A servant entered, carrying a silver tea service. He set the tray on a polished blackwood table inlaid with mother-of-pearl. He was about to pour when the President waved him away, indicating that he preferred to do the honors himself. They waited, Walker and the President, while the tea steeped.

Walker's eyes roamed the huge room. Its opulent furnishings, imitations of the richness that had once filled the palaces of the Vietnamese emperors, contrasted oddly with the stark lines of

1 0 3

the modern building. Every chair was covered with heavy embroidered satins in brilliant reds and golds. Massive polished dark wood furniture stood on Oriental carpets. One corner was dominated by a mammoth set of elephant tusks mounted in hand-tooled silver holders. Brocaded draperies hung from the ceiling, covering walls but no windows. All of Saigon knew that, for security reasons, the room had been constructed windowless. Walker also knew — courtesy of the CIA — that one set of curtains hid a secret door to an underground tunnel that surfaced in the nearby zoo. Just in case. The room had an airless quality, always giving Walker the sense that echoes of old conversations still clung to the walls and the ceiling, trapped.

Finally, the tea was ready. The President's first words, as he poured, took the Ambassador by surprise.

"Problems in Washington?" he asked.

"Washington is not without its problems," Walker replied with a short laugh. "Neither is Hanoi, I'd venture to say." The stab at the North produced no reaction.

"What are you hearing from MR Two?"

"Not any more than you're hearing, Mr. President." Walker glanced at his watch; it had taken seven minutes to get to the point.

"I've just received a cable from Nguyen Van Hoang," the President said. Hoang was South Viet Nam's Ambassador to Washington. "Not very reassuring."

"Which means?"

"In fact," the President went on, as though Walker hadn't said a word, "Nguyen Van Hoang says more aid for South Viet Nam looks hopeless. What is more, he tells me that the antiwar movement has now attained such political strength that Washington seems ready to abandon its commitment to stand by South Viet Nam against our common enemy."

The Ambassador leaned forward in his chair; never before had he heard the President offer so blunt an assessment of U.S.–Vietnamese relations. Regardless of how close the gloomy assessment might be to the truth, Walker realized that he had to try to ease the President's anxiety.

"Your information, Mr. President," Walker began slowly, each word carefully chosen, meant to undercut Nguyen Van Hoang, "does not correspond to my own top-secret information. I am in constant communication with the President of the United States and with the Secretary of State — through various channels — and they emphasize that the U.S. commitment is unshakable, that the emergency funds for ARVN will in fact be authorized."

One small muscle twitched on the otherwise impassive face of the President of South Viet Nam. "Do you really think that your President and your Secretary will be able to stand up against Congress and public opinion?" he asked. "Do you really?"

No, I don't, Walker thought. "Yes, I do," he said.

"What about U.S. air support?" the President persisted. "You know what is now happening in the country. Don't you think Watergate grounded the B-fifty-twos?"

Yes, I do, Walker thought. "No, I don't," he said.

An ache of a smile came over the President's face. "I am glad to hear what you say," he responded wearily, "but you will excuse me if I repeat that I do not see any evidence to support that view."

It was, Walker realized, the elliptical Vietnamese way of calling him a liar — not only him but, by extension, also the President of the United States, the Secretary of State, and the U.S.A. itself. Walker's first instinct was to reiterate what he had just said, in the hope that a more forceful presentation might give it the semblance of truth. But his emotions suddenly got the best of him, and he surprised himself — and the President — with an outburst of passion.

"Look, Mr. President, I speak to you directly from the heart. I am positive that the United States — despite the problems Washington is now facing — will stand by South Viet Nam and that the U.S. will not abandon a commitment just because there is noise in the streets of America. The U.S. is a super-power and will behave in the honorable way befitting a super-power."

The President kept stirring his tea.

Walker's voice escalated. "For the United States — in its dealings with the Communist world — Viet Nam is a crucial test." His eyes fixed on the President's face.

The President sipped his tea. Then, slowly and deliberately he reached into his desk and took out a writing pad and one piece of carbon paper. He inserted the carbon into the pad, picked up a pen and began writing, his hand moving swiftly across the paper. "Give me a few minutes, please, Mr. Ambassador," he said.

Walker felt he had no choice but to comply. He leaned back in his chair, his eyes fixed on the President. A rush of adjectives came to mind to describe the man bent over the desk: cautious, aloof, conspiratorial, cunning, scheming, devious. Corrupt? The President had always — predictably — denied it, but everyone knew that the key source of his power, apart from the Americans, was his toleration of corruption among the generals; the corrupt were then in his debt. And even if he didn't take any direct payoffs, it was no secret that his wife was known throughout Saigon as "Madame Moneybags," with one of the largest collections of diamonds east of the Place Vendôme. People said she never took off her diamonds, even slept with them, wore them not only on her fingers but on her toes as well — in case the family had to make a quick escape.

Walker, studying the President, reflected that the Vietnamese leader's haughty style contrasted sharply with his origins in a Central Viet Nam hamlet unmarked on any map. His mother, he was fond of telling American interviewers — but only after he had become President — carried baskets of vegetables to the village market while his father eked out a living as a farmer. He had decided that, in a country run by France, the only way up for a poor boy was to learn the language of the colonial masters;

his contact with the French served to sharpen his suspicion of foreigners, but his study of their language opened doors. While he was still in his teens he joined the military — that was French, too, but there was no choice — and after the creation of an independent South Viet Nam in the mid-'fifties, he won a series of quick promotions to general. But it was his wife, the daughter of a prosperous Delta family, as ambitious as she was buxom, who encouraged him to use the stars on his collar as an entrée to the world of political power, of wealth. South Viet Nam, she told him, was not only a nation, it was also a cash box. He took her advice. When the senior generals fell to squabbling among themselves in the mid-'sixties about who should take over after the next coup, they chose him as the least dangerous. That was their fatal mistake; with the prodding of Madame President, he promptly purged his rivals. His quick rise to the top was given a veneer of legitimacy by an election in 1971 in which he was the only candidate.

Walker suppressed a smile as he recalled a true story that had made the rounds just before the presidential balloting. The future President had shared his concern with an American journalist that the world might suspect the elections of having been rigged. "Such a perception," the uniformed candidate remarked, "would be very embarrassing for South Viet Nam's image in the United States." "Well," said the journalist, "there is one way in which you could demonstrate to the world that the elections are honest, *mon général.*" "How?" "*Lose!*" answered the journalist. The future President felt that would be going a bit too far. Instead, he had pulled a paratroop battalion out of MR 2 to beef up the security forces around Doc Lap.

Walker glanced at his watch. Five minutes had now gone by, and the President gave no sign that he was about to stop. He was writing quickly.

"Mr. President?" Walker ventured. The President did not even bother to look up.

Walker had encountered, in his years of dealings with foreign leaders, all kinds of undiplomatic conduct: outright anger, sy-

cophancy, blackmailing smoothness, overheartiness. This deliberate noncommunication, this *rudeness*, was unfamiliar. Particularly non-Asian. Walker decided against challenging it.

A few minutes later, the President finally raised his head. He
put the pen to one side. He made two neat piles of the handwritten pages: top copy and carbon copy. He reached across the
desk and handed the top-copy pile to Walker.

"Read it to me," the President ordered. His forehead glis-
tened with perspiration.

Walker hesitated.

"Read it to me," the President persisted.

Walker reflected that there weren't any State Department regulations to cover *this* one. He looked from the pages in front of
him to the President's face. Then, his eyes returned to the doc-
ument and he began reading: " 'To my fellow countrymen . . .' "

"Louder," the President ordered.

Walker cleared his throat. " 'I speak to you tonight at a time
of crisis. I have had only one objective ever since I became
President: to bring peace to our beloved country. But the Communists preferred war. So we have had no choice but to defend
ourselves against such aggression. The toll has been terrible.
Every Vietnamese now listening to me knows the cost of this
war . . . sons and husbands, thousands, hundreds of thousands, military personnel, innocent civilians, men, women,
children, in the South and in the North, killed. Our land has
been devastated. And the United States — the leader of the
"Free World" — has always promised us support, weapons, loyalty, peace, freedom. But no longer.' "

Walker looked up sharply.

"Keep reading, please," the President said.

" 'America has proved it cannot be trusted. It has betrayed its
promises. The White House, at the time we were forced to sign
the so-called Paris Peace Agreement in nineteen seventy-three,
assured us that if the North Vietnamese were to break the agree-

ment and renew their aggression against the South, the United States would not hesitate to intervene. But then America got caught up in a trauma of its own. Watergate weakened America and made *us* the victim. The United States slashed its military aid to South Viet Nam. In the past year, the NVA attacked on many fronts but America did nothing. So the NVA intensified its attacks, and we have all seen the chaos of the last few days.

" 'America must be forced to keep its promise. We need more military aid, if ARVN is to fight. We need the B-fifty-twos, if South Viet Nam is to live on. But, my fellow countrymen, Washington has become deaf to our appeals. We have been abandoned. Washington's priority now is to become friends with Russia and China, and if that friendship should require South Viet Nam's being thrown to the Communist vultures, Washington seems ready to pay the price — *pay with our blood.* But South Viet Nam will not allow itself to become America's down payment on détente with Communism. South Viet Nam will fight on — but not with me.' "

Walker paused, looked up, surprised.

The President's eyes were fixed on him. "Please keep reading. I will regard it as a special favor to me. I do not intend it to be a humiliation of you personally."

" 'Your President has been accused by the Americans, even by some of our own countrymen, of being corrupt, repressive, dictatorial,' " Walker resumed. " 'These accusations are wrong. But I do not want to be an obstacle in the way of our country's future. So, for the sake of our beloved nation, I am prepared to sacrifice myself. I hereby resign as President of South Viet Nam in the hope that the United States — with my departure — will now provide the military aid it has solemnly promised. With this aid, all true patriots will rise as one and defeat our common enemy and create in South Viet Nam a country of peace and freedom. Farewell, goodbye to you all.' "

Walker, stunned, placed the pages on the end table next to

his chair. He was about to ask a question — a hundred questions came to mind — but the President held up his right hand, motioning for silence.

"I have, as you see, made two copies," he said. "One is for you. You take your copy with you. The other copy" — he left his chair to open a wall safe behind a brocaded curtain — "will stay here. You will transmit your copy to Washington. You will tell Washington that if the emergency aid is not approved and on its way by special airlift within the next seventy-two hours, I will broadcast this speech over the Vietnamese national television." He locked his copy inside the safe and returned to the desk.

"I don't think, Mr. Ambassador, that I need to explain to you the implications of such a speech," the President continued. "The United States will be seen by all freedom-loving countries as unreliable, its treaties worthless. As a nation that will allow a loyal ally to be overrun by the Communists. Your foreign policy will be reduced to shambles. This will tempt the Kremlin and Peking into new aggressive adventures. It will lead to further international instability. And in your own country, it will touch off a political bloodbath between the right and the left." He paused. "And all for a few hundred million dollars in emergency aid."

Walker remained silent.

"Your country cannot simply play with the lives of other countries, embrace them one day and discard them the next." The President leaned across the desk, staring full-face at Walker. "The choice is yours."

Walker sat motionless in his chair. What was this? High-risk gamble? Diplomatic theater? Ultimatum diplomacy? He had thought that he'd be calling on the President to carry out, as usual, a little hand-holding at a time of crisis. Now *this!* The "puppet" — trying to manipulate the string-puller? Using the power of his weakness to launch a counterattack not against the NVA but the U.S.?

Walker tried to make a quick assessment. The President's

either-or strategy was not unfamiliar to him. He had used it himself, in moments of desperation. What's more, he was sympathetic to this beleaguered head of state who felt himself betrayed. Particularly after his own last maddening conversation with Washington. As Ambassador he felt duty-bound to double-juggle. To keep pushing the American President for the money, to keep *this* President from resigning and causing a riot of chaos.

All right, Walker told himself, start juggling.

"Mr. President," Walker finally responded, "let me ask you, with all due respect, whether these pages are meant to shock Washington into acting or is this something that you really plan to carry —"

The President interrupted him. "I expected that question," he said, "and it deserves a serious reply. This is no instant decision; I have been thinking about it for many weeks as I have watched ARVN fighting with its bare hands against NVA units supplied by the Russians and the Chinese. I know you Americans see me as an ambitious tyrant, determined to stay in power over the bodies of my countrymen. You are wrong. I mean every word I say on the pages. You have just seventy-two hours to act. If *you* don't, *I* will."

Walker stared at the President. "Mr. President," he began anxiously, "the United States —"

"There is nothing more to say, Mr. Ambassador."

"My country —"

"Nothing."

Slowly Walker picked up the pages on the end table, folded them lengthwise, slid them into his inside jacket pocket; then he stood up.

"Good day, Mr. President," the Ambassador said.

"Good day, Mr. Ambassador," the President replied. He did not rise from his chair.

With the aide-de-camp escorting him toward the main gate, Walker tried to analyze the President's threat. Quit? Voluntarily? This had to be one of the master ploys of all time. He'd been fighting for years to remain in power, exiling generals, imprisoning opponents, sleeping in a different bed every night to avoid any assassination attempt. Give up Doc Lap? *Bluff!* IT WAS A BLUFF! It *had* to be a bluff!

Far down the corridor, Walker could make out a silhouette in uniform heading in his direction. It had a familiar quality: a tall lean bayonet of a man moving forward swiftly, despite a limp in the left leg.

"General Dinh!" Walker said eagerly, trying to camouflage his sense of embarrassment. Dinh, the one man in ARVN with whom Walker felt he had established any bond of personal trust, was the last man in ARVN Walker wanted to see just now.

Dinh, bony-faced, with a battle scar on his right cheek, reached out and clutched Walker's hand in his own two hands. "Mr. Ambassador! I am so glad to see you." He glanced down the hallway in the direction of the President's office. "I hope you brought him some good news."

A weak smile flitted across Walker's face.

"I've been summoned from division headquarters to give the President an account of the situation in the field," Dinh continued. "He knows what is happening but he wants to hear it first-hand." He shook his head. The dim light in the hallway illuminated the slash on his face.

Dinh was unique. With this spare, courageous man, Walker had developed a sense of mutual reliance. Each fought the war in his own way: Walker battling with Washington to get arms for the South Vietnamese military; Dinh, directly with the enemy in the field. Dinh's reputation was well known within ARVN: aggressive, inspiring, incorruptible, always where the shooting was. He had been wounded a dozen times. Walker remembered once visiting him in MR 1, the morning after Dinh and his men had beaten back an NVA attack and suffered heavy casualties. "My friend," Dinh had said quietly that morning, "you just see that the weapons keep coming from America, and my troops and I will see that the enemy is stopped. Please don't let us down." Walker had reassured him that the weapons would keep coming.

"You don't want to keep the President waiting," Walker said softly. "Good luck."

Dinh smiled, brought his right hand up his forehead in an affectionate salute, and continued down the hallway.

Walker watched him limp away. Then he hurried to his waiting limousine and drove to the Embassy.

Saigon's blazing sun slashed through the half-curtained windows of Walker's office, carving the room into lights and darks, golden rays bouncing off the Swatow, shadows enveloping his desk. He pressed the buzzer on his desk; Helen floated in. "I've got," he began, reaching into his jacket, "a very urgent cable I want to dictate . . ."

Suddenly he stopped. Dictate? Why not? This woman was leak-proof. The whole bloody war had moved through her fingers. But why tempt her? Or anyone? Send the cable through regular channels and you might just as well publish it in *The New York Times*; once the antiwar types at the State Department got their hands on it, they'd leak it straightaway as proof that Saigon was in its death throes and not worth another nickel.

The trick was to keep the number of persons who would see the cable to an absolute minimum. He'd type it himself. Personally deliver it to the code clerk in the communications room for transmission to Washington. "EYES ONLY" — for the President and for the Secretary of State. Then Walker would reclaim his original copy.

"Never mind, Helen," Walker said with a smile.

She turned and headed back to the anteroom.

The moment the door closed behind her, Walker quickly began to type.

VIA SPECIAL AMBASSADOR CHANNELS
IMMEDIATE
SECRET-SENSITIVE
TO PRESIDENT WHITE HOUSE
COPY SECSTATE
FROM AMEMBASSY SAIGON.

MET WITH PRESIDENT AT DOC LAP IN WHAT MUST BE MOST EXTRAORDINARY U.S.—VIETNAM ENCOUNTER IN COURSE THIS LONG WAR. HE RELAYED NGUYEN VAN HOANG'S ASSESSMENT THAT OUTLOOK FOR EMERGENCY AID FOR ARVN NOW HOPELESS. EYE TRIED DISSUADE HIM ON BASIS YOUR ASSURANCES TO ME BUT HE REMAINED SKEPTICAL. HE THEN ASKED ME TO REMAIN SEATED WHILE HE WROTE IN LONGHAND WHAT TURNED OUT TO BE DRAFT OF SPEECH. AFTER EIGHT MINUTES, HE HANDED ME COPY WITH REQUEST, FIRST, THAT EYE READ IT ALOUD AND, SECOND, THAT COPY BE TRANSMITTED TO WASHINGTON. FULL TEXT FOLLOWS:

Walker then copied the President's speech word for word.

PRESIDENT INSISTED EYE CONVEY WASHINGTON THAT IF EMERGENCY AID IS NOT APPROVED AND ENROUTE SAIGON NEXT QUOTE SEVENTY-TWO HOURS RPT SEVENTY-TWO HOURS UNQUOTE HE PLANS DELIVER ABOVE SPEECH ON VN TELEVISION.

APPRECIATE GUIDANCE URGENTLY.

WALKER

He leaned back in his chair and looked at his watch. Three-thirty P.M.; Washington time was thirteen hours earlier — 2:30 A.M. Probably the President and the Secretary would be wakened immediately by the Sitroom in the White House. If not, they'd find a copy of the cable on their breakfast trays. Either way, Walker thought, it would be one hell of an eye-opener.

15

By five in the afternoon, the office had become a prison. Walker felt walled in by the President's threat to resign; he needed desperately to break out. But his choices were limited.

One, he did not frequent the Cercle Sportif, the in-town country club that the French had built decades earlier and that was now awash with their American successors; the bikinis, the tennis racquets, the Vietnamese *nouveaux riches* aiming their faces at the sun — all of it, to Walker, seemed a mockery of the war. Two, he avoided the endless round of cocktail parties floating on scotch bought at cut-rate prices at the PX; the habitués struck him as air-conditioned warriors, exchanging simplistic formulas on how the conflict could be brought to a quick end. And three, a casual call to any of the large number of resident American correspondents was out of the question; to Walker, most of them were die-hard "doves," always ready to understand, even to admire, "the other side" while ridiculing ARVN as corrupt, demoralized, ineffectual. The war for them, Walker believed, was either an adventure or a rung in a journalistic career; they struck him as too young and too naive, or too old and too cynical, so obsessed with ideological catchwords that they failed to recognize the implications of a Communist triumph and a U.S.–Saigon defeat in Viet Nam.

Which left only Phan Thanh Giang.

Ten minutes later, Walker's limousine came to a stop in front of a small villa on Mac Dinh Chi, a broad street near the center of town. A slender, gray-haired Vietnamese, in a T-shirt, cotton slacks, and sandals, was sweeping the leaves off the driveway. He was surprised — but seemed very pleased — to see the Ambassador.

"Giang, I hope I haven't come at an awkward moment," Walker smiled.

"Not at all." Giang quickly ushered Walker into the living room. "Five o'clock is always open-house in Saigon. When I was teaching history and philosophy at Saigon University a few years ago — before I retired — my students would congregate here every afternoon." He motioned Walker toward a chair. "No, my friend, you are most welcome."

Walker and Giang had met at the Nguyen Dynasty not long after the Ambassador's arrival in Saigon. Their mutual passion for antiques led inevitably to conversation — and to an invitation from Giang to stop by for a look at his most recent acquisitions. One visit had led to another, and Walker was always grateful for the opportunity to get out of the official orbit and relax with a fellow collector.

"In fact," Giang continued, "I have been thinking of taking the liberty of telephoning you."

"Oh?"

Giang's voice, always muted, dropped to a whisper, as though he himself did not want to hear what he was about to say. "I'm worried about the way things are going."

A servant entered and set a kettle and two cups on the polished teakwood table in the center of the room.

"Very worried," Giang added. He watched the servant leave.

Giang, too? Walker poured the tea.

"Of course, I will not leave, not even if the North Vietnamese come to my doorstep," Giang went on. "I have run away once before . . . from my ancestral home in Hanoi. That was in nineteen fifty-four, after the Geneva Conference . . . in all

116

its wisdom . . . divided Viet Nam in two. I have nowhere to run to — now. But it is my destiny to safeguard the genius of the Vietnamese, not at making war" — he smiled sadly — "but at creating beauty." He stood up. "Come, let's have a look."

He escorted Walker to the back room that the Ambassador had visited several times in recent months: Giang's private museum, the shelves filled with the handiwork of Vietnamese artists over the centuries. Ancient pottery from the kilns of Binh Dinh in Central Viet Nam and Thanh Hoa in the north, a ritual bronze oil lamp dating back to the Dong Son culture that had flourished two thousand years before, terra-cotta tomb figures that had been excavated a century earlier near the Vietnamese–Chinese border, a variety of magnificent mother-of-pearl inlay boxes, an assortment of lacquerware. Altogether, Giang's treasured pieces comprised an extraordinary private collection of the art of the Vietnamese people.

"My hope is to get all these treasures out of the country before they too are turned into debris," Giang whispered.

Walker turned away, unwilling to witness the anguish on Giang's face.

"Too pessimistic am I, my friend?" Giang asked.

"Perhaps you are."

"No, I don't think so. We have always talked to each other honestly. Let me take you into the mystery of Viet Nam, try to explain what the French and now the Americans have, in their frustration, called the 'enigma' of Viet Nam." Giang began to pace the room. "Your country sees the war in terms of weapons; I see it in terms of Vietnamese psychology. The Vietnamese in power today are in a state of abdication. They have allowed Viet Nam's way of life to be supplanted by yours — and in the process they have become corrupt."

Walker shook his head.

"Yes, they have prostituted their nation's integrity in return for a moment of American power and wealth," Giang persisted. "They have sinned. They know it in their souls. They feel they have become unworthy of winning."

In a year's worth of endless conversations in Viet Nam, Walker had never before been offered such an analysis of the Vietnamese predicament. Inadequate arms? Yes. Bad leadership? Yes. Poor morale? Yes. But the Vietnamese as *sinners?* *Unworthy* of victory?

"Even a deluge of American weapons would make no difference," Giang added. "How else can you explain Ban Me Thuot, Nha Trang, the other disasters? The Vietnamese are running, not fighting anymore, and it is now only a question of time before the North fills the vacuum."

The depth of Giang's hopelessness left Walker without an answer. He retreated, for the moment, to an easier agenda. "Have you by any chance sold several *Chinese* pieces during the last few days?"

"No," Giang replied, puzzled. "Why do you ask?"

"For no special reason," Walker answered quickly. He knew that while his friend's passion focused exclusively on Vietnamese *objets d'art*, Giang would occasionally, though reluctantly, deal in Chinese objects as well. A thousand years after the Vietnamese had expelled the Chinese and thereby ended centuries of foreign domination, he still carried in his blood a deep nationalistic suspicion of the giant neighbor to the north. Make a little profit on the sale of a Chinese vase, that was business; mix a Chinese piece in with the Vietnamese treasures on his shelves, that was heresy.

Giang turned to face a faded painting of an elderly gentleman, in traditional Vietnamese turban and gown, a long white beard spilling down his chest, the cheekbones prominent, the eyes serene. "Did you know that I am an imposter?" he said with a smile. *"That"* — he pointed to the painting on the wall — "is the real Phan Thanh Giang."

The face struck Walker as having a kind of incorruptible nobility about it.

"You know who 'Phan Thanh Giang' was?" Giang continued quickly to save Walker any embarrassment. "My real name is Tran Van Dinh. But after I began studying Vietnamese history as a young man at the university in Hanoi, I renamed myself 'Phan Thanh Giang.' My hope was that I might somehow inherit even a fraction of his integrity." He smiled. "I doubt that I have, but he" — Giang waved his hand in the direction of the portrait — "has always been my inspiration."

The old history and philosophy professor was emerging, for a class of one.

"Let me first tell you *his* story," Giang said, "and then I will explain to you why I am, for what might now strike you as no apparent reason, explaining all this." He paused. "Do you have time?"

Walker nodded. He glanced at his watch. Five-twenty. Still the middle of the night in Washington. He settled back and sipped his tea.

"Phan Thanh Giang lived in the nineteenth century," Giang began, "at a time when the French were turning us into a colony. In the eighteen sixties — he was more than seventy years old, a highly respected mandarin of the court — he was sent by the Emperor Tu Duc to Paris on a sacred mission: to offer the French vast amounts of money if only they would return several of the provinces they had already seized. The French agreed, at first, but they then reneged and demanded even more land. It was, as Phan Thanh Giang put it, a contest between a tiger and a fawn. When he returned to Hanoi, he used the only weapon he had left: his life. He took an overdose of opium soaked in vinegar. On his deathbed, he extracted a promise from his sons: to resist all foreigners, even if it meant risking their lives."

Giang's eyes returned to the drawing. "In every Vietnamese there's a little bit of Phan Thanh Giang," he went on. "He's a national hero. Right here in Saigon, there's a street named for him. Just a block or two from your own house."

Walker was silent, uneasily reflecting on the moral of Giang's story.

Giang sensed Walker's discomfort. "No, my foreign friend," he said reassuringly, "I am not equating America with France. You have given us money, arms, even hundreds of thousands

119

of your young men, many of whom have died here in Viet Nam. But your generosity has been our curse. We have reached out for the material, ignoring the spiritual. We have stripped ourselves of our own inner strength, preferring instead to depend on you. Inadvertently, without meaning to, you have tempted us away from ourselves; your 'generosity' — well, you could almost call it an unwitting ally of the North. South Viet Nam has turned itself into a beggar, a whore, unworthy of its legacy and therefore, as I say, unworthy of winning." He sighed. "Not that the North Vietnamese are any more worthy. But *they* are an indoctrinated, dehumanized war machine."

Walker was surprised to find himself depleted, unable, for the moment, to counter Giang's argument.

"Despair makes me talk," Giang went on. "I cannot help myself. Please forgive me, dear friend."

He opened a closet in the corner of the room and removed a long box covered with gold brocade. Almost reverently, he lifted the cover off the box, revealing a scroll. As Giang unrolled it, Walker recognized the tightly written script as *quoc ngu*, the romanized version of Vietnamese first introduced by the Jesuit missionaries in the seventeenth century.

"Every Vietnamese, from the most illiterate to the most sophisticated, knows some of the verses here," Giang explained, his fingers gently gliding across the scroll. "It is a poem, our national poem, the anthem of our emotions. 'Kim Van Kieu' is its title. It was written by Nguyen Du some two hundred years ago. The story tells of a young girl who must give up the man she loves and sell herself to another man, in order to earn money for her impoverished family. 'It is better that I should sacrifice myself alone,' she says. 'It matters little if a flower falls, so long as the tree keeps its leaves green.' Millions of our people turn to 'Kim Van Kieu' for strength and prophecy, for comfort in time of stress, for omens about the future."

Giang was unrolling the scroll as he talked; Walker estimated its length at over seven feet.

"This," exclaimed Giang, "is only *half* of the poem."

"Half?" Walker reacted with astonishment.

"The other half is in Hanoi," Giang said. "With my brother. When I joined the exodus to the South, my older brother and I cut this scroll in two. We wept; it was a family heirloom. But our hope was that one day we would reunite the poem — when Viet Nam itself would reunite — in peace." He began rerolling the scroll. "That was our dream. . . . Do you know of any other country that is united by a poem? And divided by war?"

Tears shone in his eyes. Walker could think of no words to console him.

"I have not heard from my brother for more than twenty years now," Giang continued relentlessly, "but I have not given up trying to find him." He reached into his trouser pocket and took out a handful of postage-stamp-size photographs. "Some of my former students, now in the army, know my life story, and when they are in Saigon, they sometimes bring these little 'souvenirs' from the battlefield." He flashed them one at a time, a kind of nickelodeon of faces, before Walker's eyes. A little boy, smiling. Two children. A woman. An elderly man, the edge of the picture smeared with dried blood. Two men. A man smoking a pipe. "Where do they find them? In the wallets of soldiers from the North who have been killed in the fighting. The intelligence people look through the wallets first, in search of military information, then discard them. My former students then pick up the wallets, thinking about me. I look through these 'souvenirs,' wondering whether I will find my brother and his family. He had six sons when I left Hanoi. They all must be in the army now. I remember their faces."

Walker was overwhelmed by Giang's revelation. He had always known that Viet Nam was a war in which families fought families, but he had never been so intimately drawn into the conflict.

"That is why," Giang interrupted Walker's thoughts, "I want my collection to leave the country. Something must survive that will proclaim to the world that Viet Nam is a nation not only of violence but of beauty. That the Vietnamese can create works of art that are delicate, exquisite, tender. That the genius of the Vietnamese is no less than that of other people."

Walker nodded. "The world knows that," he murmured.

"The world," Giang replied, shaking his head, "sees us as beggars, taking charity from the Americans."

"That's not true," Walker protested, but he knew that his voice lacked conviction.

"I am now so desperate about the fate of these pieces that I feel I must put aside all inhibitions and ask you directly, dear friend: Can you find a way to transport my collection out of the country, before these pieces are reduced to rubble?"

Again, Walker felt as though he were imprisoned. First, the President, at Doc Lap a few hours earlier. Now Giang.

"It is not as hopeless as you think, Giang." Walker struggled to find words that would cut through his friend's gloom. "South Viet Nam has been in equally difficult situations in the past, and pulled through."

"Your faith is in weapons," Giang replied softly, "but our souls have been disarmed — and so we will lose. It is only a question of time."

"Don't you see, Giang," Walker said, standing up and pacing the floor, "that if I were to say yes to you, it would be like saying, 'Yes, it's all over.' There are no secrets in Viet Nam. Word would get out. People would see it as the start of an evacuation. Then it would really be all over, and I don't believe that that is going to happen."

"But these are not people I'm talking about," Giang interjected. "These are *things*."

"Yes, but even so, for *me* to send out these *things* would be to concede that the war is finished, South Viet Nam defeated."

"I do not expect a reply — now," Giang said. "As I confessed earlier, I was planning to get in touch with you — but then, suddenly, you were here. *Please*," Giang begged. "Please think about it."

"You of all people should recognize," Walker said, trying to phrase his rebuttal as gently as possible, "that these pieces must remain here to serve as an inspiration to the Vietnamese to continue the struggle, not to end it."

"I know the Vietnamese, dear friend."

Giang walked silently at Walker's side as the Ambassador returned to his limousine. As Walker drove off, he heard Giang's cry: "Think about it. *Please.*"

The limousine, suddenly trapped in rush-hour traffic within sight of Doc Lap, had now become his newest prison. Walker's brief excursion from the Embassy had produced no relief, only a terrible reaffirmation of despair.

Goddammit, do I have to prop up everybody? Walker thought. Phan Thanh Giang? The President? *Two* Presidents? The Secretary of State? South Viet Nam? The United States? Me? Single-handedly? With what? With *mirrors?*

16

I'm on the witness stand. Where have I seen these people before?

"Name?"

"Anthony Catlett."

"Nationality?"

"American."

The jury hisses.

"Tell the defendant to speak up."

"American."

"Louder."

"AMERICAN."

"Address?"

"Twenty-three Gia Long, Saigon."

"Profession?"

"Employee of the U.S. Government."

The blur of faces . . . where have I seen them . . . ?

"Mr. Catlett, we have now heard the testimony of these eye-witnesses — and survivors. Do you have anything to say in your own defense?"

I look at the walls, the floor, the windows, anything to avoid their eyes. I look at the ceiling. Ho Chi Minh, from a giant portrait, stares back.

"Your Honor, will you please instruct the defendant to reply to all the questions."
I look up at the judge. He is Vietnamese. The prosecuting attorney, Vietnamese. The jury, Vietnamese.
"I will try again. Do you have anything to say in your own defense, Mr. Catlett?"
I look at my hands.
"NOTHING? You . . . saved your life. . . ." He points to coffins covered with the gold-and-scarlet flag of South Viet Nam.
"How do you plead?"
I shake my head.
". . . jury . . ."
". . . guilty on all counts."
The hisses turn to cheers. Disembodied fingers tear at me . . . wet, sticky, bloody, mangled. Fingers cling to my legs, my chest, my face.
". . . my duty to sentence you as follows: one, you lose your American identity; two, you become a Vietnamese refugee; three, you are abandoned in Nha Trang; and four . . ."
I try to break free.
The judge is screaming. "STAND UP."
I stand. Fingers leap from the floor to form a ring around my neck.
"Proceed to 'Exhibit A.' "
I see something whirling. . . . A fan? PROPELLERS! Oh no no no no.
"Defendant! Proceed to the C-forty-seven!"
The fingers pull me toward the plane.
"PLACE YOUR HANDS ON THE BOTTOM EDGE OF THE DOOR FRAME."
I hide my hands — in my pockets, under my shirt, behind my back.
"PLACE YOUR HANDS . . ."
No escape. I watch my hands move to the edge of the doorway. The Vietnamese are now standing inside the door frame. I

look up. They are grinning. An M-16 comes crashing down on my —

The telephone, jangling, rescued Tony from his nightmare. Waking, he slapped his hands together, fingers anxiously feeling fingers. He touched his knuckles, the backs of his hands, his palms. He made fists, relaxed his hands, made fists again. Only then, with a sigh of relief, did he pick up the receiver.

The voice of the all-night duty officer at the Embassy: "The Ambassador wants to see you. *Pronto.*"

"*Pronto?*" Tony glanced at the luminous dial on his watch. "At five-thirty in the morning? What's happening? NVA finally reach the Embassy?"

"The Ambassador did not take me into his confidence. Maybe you will have better luck. All I know is that he sounded as though he's in one of those moods."

"Okay," Tony said wearily. "God calls. Mortals, and spooks, run." He put the receiver on the hook, snapped on the light, dressed quickly, and raced down the stairs to his Fiat.

As Tony drove toward the Embassy, the sun was just beginning to slam into Saigon, the overnight curfew just ending, the city just waking up: old ladies in white blouses and black pantaloons were arranging colorful bouquets in the flower market on Nguyen Hue; black marketeers were restocking their open-air stalls of stolen GI boots, ponchos, and the other haberdashery of war; iron shutters were being raised, stores opening for business; whores in tight denim jeans and spike heels were strolling home, having made their nightly contribution to the war effort. Some of the girls cheerfully waved at Tony as he sped toward Thong Nhat.

He drove under cloth banners stretched overhead, hanging from trees and covered with handwritten slogans in English: "THE UNITED STATES AND VIET NAM FOREVER," "THE PEOPLE OF VIET NAM SALUTE OUR AMERICAN ALLIES," "WE WILL NEVER FORGET YOU." The Aterbea restaurant suddenly appeared in his rearview mirror. At 6 A.M., the Aterbea was closed; last night it had been a field of combat for Tony and Suzanne.

They hadn't said a word to each other during the return flight from Nha Trang, not a word during the drive from Tan Son Nhut into Saigon, not a word as Tony drove aimlessly through the city. It wasn't so much a case of their still being in a state of shock after the trauma at Nha Trang; it was something more numbing, more devastating, more personal. Tony had been totally unprepared for his reaction to panic. Without Suzanne as a witness, he might even now doubt that it had happened, that he had cracked down on those desperate hands with the barrel of an M-16. Suzanne. He had taken her up north to show her her father's blindness. And what had he shown her? His own weakness.

After driving around town for fifteen minutes in agonizing silence, Tony and Suzanne headed toward the Aterbea, a popular bistro for Saigon's foreign colony. The Aterbea could always be counted on for noise, and noise, Tony had decided, was what they both needed to break the tense wordlessness between them.

The moment they entered, Tony realized that the Aterbea was the worst place he could have chosen. Too many people they both knew. Too much nonstop chatter, pernod and scotch, *crème caramele*. Too much of the easy side of the war. Any other night, the Aterbea would have been fun. Tonight, its noisy jollity clashed with their own silent anguish, sharpening their already heightened sense of estrangement.

But it was too late, once they were inside.

"Hey, Tony, Suzanne," boomed a voice from the overpopulated bar. "What the devil's wrong? You both look as though you've been to hell and back. Come on over. Buy you a drink." It was one of the civilian contractors, a beer-bellied, back-slapping, Hawaiian-shirted bore who was making the kind of fortune in Saigon he would never have dreamed of at home.

Tony shook his head. Just then, the French maître d', who always managed to seat Tony no matter how jammed the restaurant, spotted him and quickly cleared a table in the corner. *"Bon appétit,"* he said cheerfully.

A Vietnamese waiter was at their side a moment later. Suzanne, without looking up, motioned him away. Tony indicated they would need a few more minutes before ordering. The waiter left.

Suzanne, her voice hoarse, spoke her first words since Nha Trang. "I can't look into his eyes," she finally said. "I see *their* eyes."

Tony stared vacantly around the room; the place was even more crowded than usual, and the bar was surrounded by old and new Indochina hands in safari suits reminiscing about their exploits, both real and imagined. But Tony might just as well have been alone in a pew. His face was ashen, stony. Suzanne could not bring herself to comfort him.

"People talk about 'Killed in Action,' 'Wounded in Action,' 'Missing in Action,' " she began. "What about 'Dehumanized in Action'?" Her eyes searched Tony's eyes. "What about you, Tony? Are you unscathed?"

He picked up the menu and hid his face behind the listings of filet mignon, bouillabaisse, and couscous. "I don't believe it . . . I couldn't have. . . ."

"What about me?" Suzanne was saying as though talking to herself. "What if this place does go up in smoke? How will I behave? What will I do . . . about Thi and Thach?"

"All of us in Viet Nam," Tony said, "face the test eventually." His voice now was barely audible. "I faced mine this afternoon."

"Yes," Suzanne said flatly. "You did."

Tony winced.

"I'm thinking about my own test — whenever it comes," she said.

Tony looked toward the bar, Suzanne toward the swinging kitchen door. They lapsed into silence.

"Feeling any better?" a voice boomed. A landscape of palm trees and flamingos protruded over their table.

"Much," Tony answered.

"Well, don't let the war get you down, buddy." The Hawaiian scene moved on.

Tony looked at Suzanne. "Somebody once compared Viet Nam to an X-ray," he said. "Supposed to give you a pretty good idea of your insides. I thought it was crazy the first time I heard it. Now I'm not so sure."

"I'm not sure either. Of anything. But I think . . . maybe we're no use to each other. Neither of us has the healing words." She reached down for her bag, made a move to leave the table.

Tony clutched her hand. "Suzanne . . . please. Don't leave me now. After Nha Trang, you have every right to. There's no reason for you to stay. Except one. I love you."

She leaned across the table, took both of Tony's hands in hers. "I've often wondered how I'd feel when you said those words without any coaxing. But somehow — now — they don't reach me. The words just hang in the air — like one of those banners in the street. And they have as much impact."

"Can't you believe that I mean it?" Tony pleaded.

"I can't, Tony, but please don't misunderstand me," Suzanne said softly. "It's your — what? — your shame, your panic that's talking. You've got a need to convince yourself that you're still human, that you can feel something like love — after all that happened. But you can't. Not now." She felt his hands tighten. "It will take time. It can happen to anyone. Me, too. No one is exempt. Heroes . . . or cowards . . . are made on the spot."

"I guess I deserve that."

The waiter returned to the table. Suzanne, looking down, asked whether they could have a few more moments.

"*Oui*, mademoiselle," he said and disappeared in the crowd.

"The war, Tony," Suzanne went on, "has numbed us all. It's been going on for so long now that it's grown a culture of its own. It contaminates everything it touches — you, me, everyone. And what troubles me, Tony, is whether the damage is temporary — or permanent. Can you wash it off with a shower? Or are you dirtied forever? When this war is over, we may not be able to recognize ourselves." She looked at Tony; his face was tense. "How can anything survive here? Love? Even tenderness?"

Her eyes filled with tears, and she pushed herself up. "Don't follow me, Tony," she said. "Please."

Tony watched her as she picked her way among the tables and vanished through the front door.

"Dinner for one now, monsieur?" the waiter asked. He was back at the table for a third time.

"Dinner for none," Tony replied. He stood up with some effort and headed blindly for the street.

As Tony opened the door to Walker's office, all it took was one glance to see that the Ambassador was in his chain-mail-and-spiked-mace mood.

"Congratulations!" Walker snarled, waving a piece of paper. "You are now a television star, with a public of more than thirty million Americans. 'Anthony Catlett, the all-American boy, brought to you, by satellite, direct from the war.' "

Tony was puzzled — but only for an instant; then he remembered the glint of a lens in the midst of the terrified crowd at the Nha Trang airport, the TV camera pointing at the open door of the C-47.

"You know what you've done?" Walker was shouting now. He crumpled the paper and flung it across the room. "What you've done is given ammunition to the goddamned doves on Capitol Hill to shoot down the emergency funds for ARVN. 'More money for Saigon?' they'll say. 'When even the *Americans* are fleeing?' "

Walker stopped to catch his breath. It's all piling up at the same time, he thought, the debris of disintegration. The President's threat to resign. Giang's forecast of imminent collapse.

The runaround from Washington. The disastrous reports coming in from all the MRs. Now this.

"And you're not the only one, either!" he exploded. "The President, the Secretary, Congress . . . they're all racing for the exits, hoping that South Viet Nam will hang in there. They don't want this place to go down the drain, not while they're still in office." He slammed the desk. " 'Not now!' they're all screaming back there. 'Don't let it happen now! NOT ON MY SHIFT!' " Angrily, Walker strode across the room and picked up the crumpled ball of paper from the floor. "Know what this is, Tony?" he demanded.

Tony did not answer.

"It's a cable. From the Secretary. LISTEN." Walker smoothed out the paper. " 'TV news today dominated by satellite film of one of your staff members clubbing Vietnamese off U.S. rescue airplane at Nha Trang. Are you all crazy out there? Film has stunned the nation and refueled antiwar sentiment. Don't have to tell you this disgraceful incident complicates continuing effort to obtain additional funds for ARVN.' "

As he glared at Tony, Walker thought that the Secretary now had what he wanted. An "incident" that would allow him to wash his hands of Saigon once and for all and to blame Walker for destroying his own "continuing effort" to prod Congress into authorizing emergency aid.

"Too bad I can't give you a copy of this cable for your scrapbook," Walker added contemptuously.

Tony finally spoke. "Mr. Ambassador, I know it was inexcusable. . . ."

The words bounced off Walker's armor. "Tony," he snapped, clipping the syllables, "if you live long enough, you'll peel away even more layers of that Boy Scout uniform. But not while you're on my staff!" He slipped the cable into his desk drawer. "I'm going to have you reassigned, Catlett. *Out* of Viet Nam."

Tony's voice was louder than he intended. "Mr. Ambassador, *will you please listen?* I've spent five years in Viet Nam, five *committed* years. A big chunk of my life. What I did was crazy, okay, but it was one of those moments. An aberration. I lost control. I panicked."

"I can't afford aberrations," Walker shot back. "Viet Nam itself is an aberration, but I can't make it go away. You I can — and I will."

Wildly, knowing he had nothing to lose, Tony spit out his words. "Okay, suppose I'm nothing but what you think I am: a yellow-bellied little shit. That still doesn't change the rest. The NVA is on the attack. You're fighting back with shadows. If you don't begin negotiating with 'the other side' now, you'll have nothing to negotiate with later. You'll have an empty hand. Do you think the North Vietnamese will have the slightest interest in polite conversation when they're on the edge of Saigon?"

Walker stared at Tony with disdain. "Conventional wisdom," he sneered. " 'The other side' will *always* be ready to talk. I've cabled Washington not to be stampeded by the hyped-up dispatches of the media. Saigon will hack it. I believe that. I am ready to stake my reputation on it."

The same old ARVN-can-hack-it shit EVEN NOW, Tony thought. "But —" he began.

"But nothing," Walker cut in. "I'm giving you ten days to clear up your personal affairs. I'll recommend that the Agency assign you to an area where they can use a man with your . . . courage."

Tony felt Walker's eyes, glacier blue, fixed on him. He knew that nothing he could say to Walker would have any effect on his thinking about Viet Nam. Neither would a punch in the jaw, though he ached to let him have one. The only hope was to expose Walker's duplicity. An idea began to form in Tony's mind.

"The best of luck to you," Walker said icily, "in all your future endeavors."

"The same, Mr. Ambassador," Tony said, suppressing a smile, "to you."

17

Tony's eyes swept the blood-red circle around Saigon on the ceiling map in his room. He had raced from the Embassy, his head pounding, to his own place. The trick was to implement the idea without delay.

This would be his only chance. *Now* — before even more ARVN soldiers retreated in panic, before the NVA ran up its flag over Doc Lap; *now* — while Washington could still snatch an alternative from the jaws of imminent defeat. The idea, he knew, was despicable. A "CA" carried out against the Ambassador by none other than the Ambassador's daughter, at the instigation of her loving spook. The old saying "All's fair in love and war" flitted through Tony's mind. Well, war had the priority now. And it wouldn't be the first time that Mrs. Catlett's sonny boy had involved himself in dirty tricks; moreover, the whole fucking war was nothing but one gigantic dirty trick.

He had a feeling of revulsion as he dialed the residence, and nearly hung up before the houseboy answered. Suzanne, Tony was told, had left an hour earlier. There was only one place she could have gone. For a moment, Tony wished he did not know where to find her. But the idea had taken hold. He dialed the orphanage.

Suzanne, at the other end of the line, sounded cool, impersonal, Nha Trang still a wedge.

"How are you feeling today, Tony?"

"Better than last night," he replied. It was not going to be that easy. What did they teach you at Langley about how to ingratiate yourself, how to lay a psychological trap from which no escape was possible? He realized that he would have to break through her defenses if he were ever going to revive her feelings toward him; otherwise, his strategy was foredoomed. "In fact," he added quickly, "I'm in awful shape. Nha Trang. Our talk last night." He paused, hoping that the Aterbea reference would produce a note of sympathy.

The telephone line was silent.

"Walking wounded, that's me," he said — and waited.

"I had to come here first thing in the morning to see Thi and Thach," Suzanne finally said, ignoring his unstated appeal. "They're fine, but that doesn't ease my own anxiety." A tinge of warmth had begun to creep into her voice.

"I understand," Tony said, trying to be comforting.

Twenty seconds went by.

"Suzanne, I'm calling from my place. I really must see you. Something happened this morning. I want to tell you about it."

"Anything to do with . . . yesterday?"

He tried to heighten her curiosity by avoiding a direct reply. "Couldn't you come over as soon as you're through at the orphanage?"

"I'm not sure that's a good idea, Tony. I think we ought to —"

Tony cut in quickly. "Please. I know the impact that Nha Trang had on you, but let's not get caught in resentment, hostility, accusations." His voice took on a note of urgency. "I must see you."

"I'm not sure, Tony."

He felt she was slipping away, resisting their earlier relationship when a word from him would send her racing across town. "Suzanne, we left so many things unsaid last night."

"Please," she said, without yielding. "Let's not . . . exhume yesterday. There's only so much I can take."

"I need to talk to you."

"Anything . . . special?"

"Yes, yes," he said quickly.

"All right. But only for a few minutes."

"Thanks, Suzanne," he said, suppressing his relief. "I'll be waiting." He put down the receiver and quickly reviewed the strategy he would follow: play on her emotions, get her to see the logic of his reasoning, and then — *assuming* he had succeeded to that point — spring the trap. His mind whirled with questions and answers.

How could you even think of asking me to do such a thing, Tony?

Because, Suzanne, you have always talked about the need for honesty, that's why.

But for me, his daughter, to join in a scheme that would destroy my father?

Just the opposite; you would be helping your father.

By ruining his reputation?

Not at all; there might be some anguish in it for him but it'll be much worse for him the other way — if we just stand by as spectators.

What about later — if I did it? I couldn't live with myself, I'd never be able to look at my father again.

And what if you do nothing? Could you live with that? The choices are all bad, but doing nothing is the worst.

Once Tony had rehearsed the script, his hesitation over the morality of what he was about to attempt faded away; he now was more concerned about whether it would work, whether he could convince Suzanne.

A knock interrupted his thoughts. Suzanne, framed in the doorway, had an unfamiliar air of hesitancy about her. The yellow Liberty print dress, usually so becoming to her, today seemed to drain the color from her face.

"I'm so glad you're here," Tony said. He reached out to take her hand but she resisted. She scanned the room as though she were a stranger. Deliberately avoiding the bed, she sat down in the room's only chair, perching herself uneasily on the edge.

"Nha Trang kept me awake all night," Suzanne finally said. She placed her brown canvas handbag on the bed.

"I'm in even worse shape than you are," Tony said. He poured two cups of coffee from an electric percolator. He sat down on the corner of the bed directly opposite Suzanne. "I had a terrible blow-up with your father this morning."

"Oh, not that, too," she murmured, her voice scarcely audible.

Quickly, Tony told her about the five-thirty telephone call, his dash to the Embassy, his meeting with her father, the cable from Washington, and the Ambassador's ordering him to leave Saigon in ten days. "Ten days," Tony said bitterly, "to clear up five years of my life here, to say goodbye to . . . to . . . ." His eyes tried to find Suzanne's but she kept looking away.

Suzanne shook her head.

"He said that he'd recommend that the Agency assign me to a country where they needed a man with my . . . 'courage,' " Tony said.

"I can't believe it," she mumbled.

Tony, his eyes never leaving her face, found that he had two responses: relief that her feelings toward him were not totally destroyed by Nha Trang, and guilt that these feelings might now be tapped to advance his grand strategy. He forced himself to see her as an automaton whom he could program to carry out *the* critical job.

"Tony, what happened at Nha Trang can't be undone," Suzanne said, finally looking at him. "But I think it's important for my father to know that even though things got chaotic" — she forced a weak smile — "you saved my life." She stood up. "Maybe I ought to talk to him." She walked toward the door.

This was precisely the moment Tony had been hoping for: Suzanne's emotional pendulum swinging back in his direction. "Too late for that now," he said. "Please sit down."

Suzanne returned to the chair. "Too late?"

"Look, let me be frank. This has to do with me and your

father, and the inevitable blow-up. If Nha Trang hadn't sparked it, something else would have. I think the military situation is irreversible and if we don't negotiate for a coalition government, we're going to lose it all to the Communists. Your father thinks Saigon will be able to pull itself out of the current mess, and therefore no negotiations — and no reason to give the Communists a coalition role."

"But we've been over all this before. What makes him wrong and you right?" she asked. "In any case, Washington has faith in him."

"*Which* Washington?" Tony shot back. "One Washington — the guys who've served here before — tell me they think your father has reached the point of instability, that he's out of touch with reality, that his cables are museum pieces even as they come off the teleprinter."

"Oh, come on, Tony," she said.

Tony ignored her obvious irritation. "But unfortunately *that* Washington doesn't count," he raced on. "Those guys are so fed up with Viet Nam, feel themselves so unable to shape Viet Nam policy, that many of them have volunteered to go off into the most esoteric areas of specialization — Tierra del Fuego, the Seychelles, Antarctica, anything so long as it isn't Viet Nam. It's the *other* Washington *you* mean, the Washington that makes policy. The President. The Secretary of State. Congress. *Your* Washington does have faith in your father, yes, but it's a cynical faith. What do I mean? I mean he's telling them exactly what they want to hear. That Saigon, by God, will be able to hack it. 'Hey, see Walker's latest cable?' they say to each other. 'Terrific. Nothing to worry about.' He frees them of guilt, so they can devote their time to what's really plaguing them these days: the Middle East and oil. Viet Nam is passé."

"All right, Tony, so what's the problem?" Impatience had crept into her voice.

"The problem, Suzanne, is that Washington is basing U.S. policy on your father's upbeat cables — and that's fatal. It's going to boomerang. Instead of pushing for negotiations now while there still may be a chance, the U.S. is heading for disaster. Exactly what your father has been trying to prevent will take place: the absolute defeat of ARVN, a complete NVA triumph, the final humiliation of the United States."

"Tony, forgive me, but what's *new* about what you're saying now?"

"It needn't be new to be horrifying. Picture it, Suzanne: with defeat and humiliation come the big guns of the North, the savage retaliation of Hanoi. More than a few mashed fingers, Suzanne. Thousands of mashed *bodies*."

Suzanne looked away.

Tony waited a moment, then pressed on with his plan. "I'm convinced your father doesn't believe a word of what he tells Washington."

She stared at him. "Tony! Enough! Stop!"

"Not before you hear me out. I tell you your father wants those emergency funds for ARVN so desperately that he's willing to say anything, do anything, sacrifice anything. I tell you, Suzanne" — he paused, waiting until she looked directly into his eyes — "I don't think he's rational anymore."

"For God's sake, Tony, *you're* the one who sounds crazy."

"Okay, Suzanne, but just listen. I sometimes have the eerie feeling that there are *two* Hadden Walkers. The surface, the public Hadden Walker, controlled by some inner ventriloquist, mouthing a torrent of words designed to camouflage the other, the real, the hidden Hadden Walker. I spent part of the morning with both of them. One Walker — the *public* Walker — drew a scenario of ARVN's pulling itself out of its present fix. The other Walker — the *hidden* Walker — didn't say a thing." He stared at Suzanne. "And I'll tell you something else."

"What?" She sounded defiant.

"I'm convinced the *hidden* Walker doesn't believe a word of what the *public* Walker says."

"Ridiculous!" Suzanne answered sharply. "How can you prove it?"

The moment had arrived. "That's where you come in, Suzanne," Tony said quietly.

"Me?" She was startled. "That's where *I* come in?"

"Yes, you," Tony said, carefully choosing his words, knowing that the slightest misstep now could abort his plan. "If Washington knew what your father really believes — that ARVN *is* finished — then a command decision would be made instantly to initiate negotiations with 'the other side.' It would be a major change in policy, but it is the only way for the U.S. to salvage anything out of this mess."

"Just what are you getting at, Tony?"

Tony went to his desk and picked up a black metal object about the same width and thickness as a deck of cards but slightly longer.

"What's that?" she asked.

"A micro-recorder," he said, slipping it into the brown canvas handbag on the bed. "Voice-activated. It automatically begins taping in the presence of sound. And it's so small and sensitive that it can operate out of, say, a handbag."

He reached into Suzanne's handbag, retrieved the recorder, and pressed the "rewind" button for an instant. Then he pressed the "play" button.

" 'Voice-activated,' " the recorder played back. " 'It automatically begins taping in the presence of sound. And it's so small and sensitive that it can operate out of, say, a handbag.' "

"You can't be serious, Tony," she exclaimed angrily. She leaped out of her chair. She grabbed the handbag and held it close to her, protectively, out of Tony's reach.

"Look, Suzanne, when the NVA comes crashing into town, who do you think is going to be the American scapegoat back home? Ambassador Hadden Walker. They'll nail him as the guy who failed to forecast the collapse of ARVN. The guy who resisted negotiations with the Communists while there was still a chance to avoid total defeat and to establish a coalition government. The guy responsible for the U.S. debacle in Viet

Nam. *Not* the ambassadors who preceded him. *Not* the Presidents who got us into this. *Not* anyone else. *Your father! He* blew it, not them!" Tony stood up. "Only you can help your father out of this mess."

"Only me? How?"

"With this." He pointed to the recorder on the bed. "By going to your father and encouraging him to tell you how he really feels about ARVN, not what he's cabling Washington. Find out if he's painting an upbeat picture here in a desperate effort to squeeze out those emergency funds. Look, two months ago, four months ago, these funds might have helped. It's too late now. If they took the goddamned Pentagon and gave it to ARVN as a present, it wouldn't make any difference now. It's over, except for the finale. The only question now is *what kind* of a finale. A coalition government in which the Communists *share* power? Or an all-out NVA victory, American defeat?"

Suzanne was stunned. "You are actually asking me to —"

"Getting it word for word would reveal what your father really thinks," Tony said. "It would enable Washington to make a decision based on reality rather than on your father's deceptions."

"Tony, you've got to be mad," Suzanne shot back. "Nha Trang one day. Now this."

"It's gone beyond what I am, what your father is. Something *must* be done. This is not just another firefight. It's the end! Don't you see?"

Suzanne stared at the recorder on the bed. "You want me to . . . *spy* on my father?"

"Suzanne, it's for his sake. For yours. For all of us. In normal times, would I ask this? I love you."

"Yes," she said angrily. "But for a price. For a reel of tape."

"Think about it," Tony answered quietly. "Or rather, *don't* think about it. Once the recorder is in place, you don't have to touch it, don't have to remember it's there. It works by itself, takes on a life of its own." He approached her slowly, and, without saying another word, slipped the recorder into her handbag. He smiled reassuringly, and kissed her cheek.

Suzanne held the handbag at arm's length, as though it were live ammunition, a grenade with the fuse already pulled. A look of defiance swept over her face. "And suppose I do this thing and then it turns out that what he tells me is exactly what he has told you. Then what?"

Tony couldn't resist laughing. "I'd eat the fucking tape recorder."

"Well," she said grimly, "you just may get that chance!" She turned and walked out, slamming the door behind her.

Tony stood in front of the mirror opposite the bed, searching his face. Suddenly, he lifted his hand, and, with his bare fist, smashed the glass. The face shattered into a thousand slivers.

18

It was almost eleven o'clock, and Suzanne had collapsed onto the couch in the living room at the residence. She felt unable to move. Tired of the war, tired of Viet Nam, tired most of all of being trapped in the middle. Merciless, both of them. What do *they* care? Two men — obsessed by their private visions of what's right for the world. Using her, grinding her to bits in the process.

The houseboy kept an impassive face when she asked for a bourbon on the rocks so early in the day. "Yes, Miss," he said tonelessly.

Her eyes roamed the familiar room — its slatted blinds and heavy cretonne drapery, its big comfortable wing chairs in a washy pattern of blues and greens, its ornate Vietnamese ironwood cabinet. Suzanne had purchased the cabinet on her own during her first few weeks in Saigon. She remembered telling her father of her difficulty in deciding between two similar pieces of furniture — this one with its geometric design, and another with the more usual floral motif. "My compliments on your choice," he had said. "It shows discriminating taste." How easy the choices had been, then.

The houseboy returned with her drink. "Thanks," she said abruptly. "I'll have it later."

She raced up the stairs to her room, clutching the brown canvas handbag. Angrily, she shut the door behind her and dumped the contents of the bag on the bed. A lipstick. Two ball-point pens. A small Vietnamese–English dictionary. A comb. Some Vietnamese coins and paper currency. A street map of Saigon. The micro-recorder.

"Hello," she said very quietly. "Testing . . . testing. . . ."

She picked up the recorder, depressed the "rewind" button, and watched the tape roll back. Then she hit the "play" button.

"Hello," her voice said. "Testing, testing. . . ."

Testing what? Loyalty? Love? Patriotism?

She pushed the contents of the handbag aside and stretched out across the bed. A photograph, gilt-framed, in faded color, looked back at her from the dressser. The three of them — her mother, her father, herself — on a holiday in Capri. She must have been nine at the time. Her mother elegant, slightly shy; her father young, confident, magnificently handsome. She remembered how he would sit with her sometimes at night, dressed in what he called his "work clothes" — black tuxedo with satin lapels, fancy white shirt — and tell her bedtime stories about people he had met: Truman, Eisenhower, Khrushchev, de Gaulle, Nehru, Sukarno. She had always listened happily, fighting off the moment when he would tuck her in, flatten her nose with a kiss, and call to her mother: "Louise — ready or not — the world is waiting!" And her mother would appear, fresh and sparkling, in some pastel of violet or sea green, lean over the bed, kiss her, and whisper, "I'd rather be here with you." Suzanne would smile, going along with the ritual. Before she fell asleep, she would breathe in the fragrance of the perfume left behind by her mother.

Many times she had wished for those days back again, had wished for her mother, alive, had wished for *somebody* to talk to. But never more than now.

Reluctantly, she got up, washed her face, and brushed her hair. She put her things back into her handbag, flung it over her shoulder, and left the house, heading for the Embassy.

She found her father, when she entered the office, standing in front of the display shelves, admiring his latest acquisition.

"Morning, Suzanne," he began. "This" — he ran his palms over the Swatow vase — "is really a lovely piece. Funny thing, every time I find a piece I love, I am always amazed that I was ever able to get along without it." He could sense that she wasn't listening. "Anything wrong?"

"Not really," she replied, moving toward the sofa near the window. "But I was looking at that picture of the three of us — you, me, mother — that was taken on Capri ten thousand years ago. It occurred to me that we never get a chance to talk the way we once did."

"The years will do that." He walked across the room and sat down next to her, kissing her lightly on the cheek. The handbag lay between them.

"Viet Nam is a monster," he said with a wry smile. "It devours everything — including me." He took her hands. "I'd like to think I'm indigestible."

"Dad," she said, "I have a confession to make, unless you've already heard about it."

He looked at her intently. "I may not have heard, but in Viet Nam nothing would surprise me," he said. "What is it?"

"In Nha Trang yesterday. In the plane . . . with Tony. I was there."

"That sonofabitch," Walker shouted, incensed. "I just can't believe it. He never even told me." He leaned toward Suzanne. "He took *you* — to Nha Trang?"

"Look, I'm all right," she hastened to reassure him. "And I got a close-up look at the war that I never would have otherwise."

"And you also got a close-up look at that boyfriend of yours that you never would have otherwise," Walker added coldly. "Did you talk to him today?"

"Yes."

"And did he tell you?"

"Yes."

Suzanne tried to look into her father's eyes but he turned away. "I would never have gotten out alive," she finally said, "if it had not been for Tony."

"I suppose Mr. Catlett expects a Congressional Medal of Honor," Walker said contemptuously.

Suzanne ignored the comment. "But couldn't you possibly reconsider what you told him?"

"No." His voice was hard.

"Even if it meant that I would follow him out of the country?" It was a spur-of-the-moment response, taking Suzanne by surprise.

Walker was no less surprised. "Suzanne," he said, staring at her, "you would never do such a thing. *I* know you wouldn't. *You* know you wouldn't."

"You're very sure of me, aren't you?" she answered. She was stunned by her continuing defiance and, for a moment, she had the uneasy feeling that she was being manipulated, long-distance, by Tony.

"You may have noticed," he answered, "that it's getting harder and harder to be sure of anyone. Of anything."

The painful weariness in his voice softened her irritation. "Dad," she said, "I watch you every day, struggling to hold this place together, and I see the toll it takes. You're never easy anymore. Always on edge. Fighting all kind of wars. With your staff. With the Vietnamese. With Washington. How is all this going to come out? How are *you* going to come out?"

"Good questions. I used to think I knew the answers."

"Look, I'm not a Senate committee. I'm not asking for a policy statement. It's just us. Tell me what you're thinking. Maybe it will help."

Walker sighed. "Maybe you're right. I hadn't realized how long it's been since we talked. I've been abandoning you — to the hero of Nha Trang."

Suzanne glanced guiltily at the handbag. "That's unfair, Dad. You can't expect me to —"

"All right, all right. But hear me out. . . ."

"I'm listening. . . ."

"Look, Suzanne, it's not my job to play God — I know what people, even in this Embassy, say about me, that I'm a domino-theory man, outdated, unrealistic. But the domino theory I am concerned about is not the conventional one: that if South Viet Nam falls to the Communists, then the other Southeast Asian countries will fall one by one. I've got *another* domino theory, *more* terrifying. It's that America's *allies* around the world will fall away, convinced that our word is worthless. One ally after another. *That* domino theory is the one the Russians are hoping will turn out to be true."

Suzanne shook her head. "And you — all alone — are going to prop up the whole structure?"

"No harm" — he smiled — "in trying. After all, I'm not out to save the world. That would be showing off." The smile became a laugh. "Only Washington — and Saigon."

He poured two cups of coffee.

"Listen to me, Suzanne," Walker went on. "If Washington will commit those emergency funds, ARVN will fight on. And if ARVN fights on, maybe — *maybe* — Hanoi will see that the U.S. is here to stay. Maybe — *maybe"* — he approached the huge map of South Viet Nam on the wall and pointed to the capital and the sprawling Delta region to the south — "Saigon will be able to hold on to this area. This is where most of the people live, where the rice is; this is the nondeficit area of the country. And offshore, Suzanne" — he pointed to the South China Sea — "there is *oil!* Oil in the hundreds of millions of barrels. Some American companies are already salivating at the prospect of setting their rigs in place. Oil — once it starts flowing — will pick up the bill for the war, pay for what ARVN needs to fight, maybe even knock a little sense in Hanoi's head."

Suzanne thought of Tony's accusation: *this* man, now talking in such emotional gusts, *this* man, right in front of her, was creating his own make-believe world, Disneyland in South Viet Nam. *Her father!* "But isn't all that . . . a one-in-a-million

146

chance? Aren't you . . . pretending" — the very word filled her with a sense of betrayal — "that things are better than they are in order to —"

"To what?" His face closed in on hers.

"To . . . force . . . Washington into coming through with the emergency aid. . . ." She stared at his face: a sheet of steel. She remembered those smiling eyes, the amused lips, the music in his voice when he used to put her to bed.

"Suzanne, listen to me. Please let me give you my best estimate of the situation. All right?" He reached out and took her hands.

"With emergency aid, Saigon has a chance. *Not* a guaranteed chance; no man in his right mind would guarantee anything about this country. But a chance. That's why I am . . . polishing ARVN's image, reassuring Washington that ARVN is still in there scrambling, so Washington can't use the excuse of a 'hopeless situation' as a way out of its responsibility: getting that hardware here. Now" — he walked to the window and watched the Vietnamese crowds below scurrying in both directions along Thong Nhat — "without the aid . . ." He shrugged his shoulders. "I wouldn't go shouting that from the rooftops, 'Saigon is finished!' but I'm telling it to you — to you alone!" He looked at her in a way that reminded her of those nights long ago, those special bedtime stories. "Call it what you will. Call it . . . role-playing, if you like. But grant me this one thing: Do you agree that it is for a worthy cause?"

Suzanne did not answer; she sat rigidly, trying to smile. It was obvious that he was playing his role in the hope that it would ensure South Viet Nam's survival and America's integrity, that he did not feel as though he were doing anything immoral. Just the opposite. But meantime he was withholding the full story from Washington — while the war churned on. Viet Nam, the corruptor of us all, Suzanne thought. My father included. Tony was right.

"Dammit!" Walker went on. "I'm not living in a fool's paradise. This isn't my first assignment; in fact, it's probably my last because no matter how this comes out, the wolves will be after me. So I'm playing it in a way that I think is best for our country. The tragedy is that the real world doesn't offer you the luxury of truly ethical choices — as your friend Tony would have you believe."

There it was, Suzanne thought: Tony and Hadden — with Suzanne in the middle. Same old trap. Both of them full of their own morality. Tony accusing her father of shading the truth in his cables to State. Her father convinced the shading was vital to avoid the worst possible disaster.

"I'm really glad we've had this chance to talk," he said, reaching over and patting her cheek. "Normally it's a sentence or two on the run. Now you've got it all."

He kissed her, and he could sense her restlessness. "Anything wrong?" he asked.

She shook her head. "You must be busy," she said, standing up. "I'm going to run."

"Not too fast," he said with a laugh. "In Saigon these days, that can be contagious. Besides" — he looked at his watch — "I'm going out myself. Let me drop you."

She picked up her handbag, and he steered her through the anteroom to his private elevator. As the door opened on the ground floor, Suzanne spotted Tony making his way through the lobby. Their eyes met. Tony glanced swiftly at the handbag, at Walker, at the handbag again. Then he disappeared down the corridor.

Suzanne, somewhat shaken, was relieved that her father had not seen Tony. His eyes were on the crowds in front of the consular office: hundreds of Vietnamese trying to apply for visas to the U.S. These were the longest lines she had ever seen. She took her father's arm, sensing his tension.

They walked out of the lobby, past the tamarind tree in the parking lot, and stepped into the waiting limousine. "Head down Thong Nhat toward Le Loi," Walker told the driver.

Suzanne drew the glass partition separating the front and rear seats. "I've been wanting to talk to you privately," she said to her father. "I've been thinking of Thi and Thach."

"Of course," Walker answered. He was clearly preoccupied.

"My two kids at the orphanage," Suzanne went on. "If things are all that bleak, maybe I'd better arrange some stand-by plans to evacuate them."

" 'Evacuate'?" Walker said, trying to control his impatience. "It is precisely because things *are* that bleak that you cannot do anything."

"But that's crazy. . . . What possible reason . . . ?"

"The answer is right outside the window."

She looked out at the familiar street scene. "I don't see anything different," she finally said.

"Look again."

It was more of the same: Vietnamese — on foot, in cars, on bicycles, on Honda motorcycles — streaming in both directions.

"I *still* don't see anything," she repeated.

"Suzanne," he said, looking through the window, "do you know what these people would do if I — and the same goes for the Ambassador's daughter — as much as walked in the *direction* of a suitcase? They'd conclude that it's all over, the Americans are pulling out. There would be a stampede to every boat, every plane — but mostly to the American Embassy. They would see us as their last refuge. Saigon would make the panic in Nha Trang look like a fire drill. *No one* would get out. The South Vietnamese would turn on us. Our allies would become our enemies."

"But I just can't . . . abandon Thi and Thach."

"I am not recommending abandonment," Walker said firmly. "I am recommending postponement."

"Postponement could mean . . . I just can't wait, just sit around and let disaster overtake us."

"Your way," he said, his voice tense, "would guarantee disaster. My way at least forestalls it."

149

"You must," she persisted, "have some plans for evac—"

"I don't even want to *hear* that word," he snapped. He stared through the window and watched the Vietnamese crowds on Le Loi. "Just let me say that we are not *un*prepared for any contingency. Look, Suzanne, I'm not some kind of tyrant . . . when I say that I cannot permit you to make any such plans on your own. In fact, I need your help. I want you to act as though we all planned to stay here forever."

"You want *me* to 'role-play'?" She looked at him in disbelief. Tony, first, asking her to betray her father. Now her father asking her to betray herself. "When is this going to end?"

He turned toward her with a puzzled look.

"I've got to get out," she said, her voice rising. "Now."

"Now? Right now? What is it?"

"It's just that I'm beginning to feel . . . *used!*"

Walker jerked back his head, as though he had been stung, and Suzanne quickly tried to soften the impact of the word. "Used up, I mean. Tired. Exhausted." She rapped sharply on the glass partition and motioned for the driver to stop.

"You all right, Suzanne?"

"Yes, yes, yes."

The instant the car pulled to a complete stop, Suzanne bolted into the hot Saigon street. She felt as though she had broken out of a cage — free from the cycle of the morning's tensions, from the need to choose; she stood along the curb and waved goodbye to her father. Her raised arms crisscrossed back and forth, making Xs against the sky — until they stopped in midair. Suddenly, she dashed headlong into the middle of the wide boulevard. Cars, motorcycles, and trucks slammed on their brakes; she missed being hit by a few inches. She could make out her father's limousine ahead, stopped by a red light, and she began weaving frantically between the rows of automobiles. But when she was just three cars away, the light turned green, and the traffic shot forward. Suzanne stood motionless, in a gray-blue haze of exhaust. She had left her handbag on the rear seat of the limousine.

19

"Have you heard anything from your Embassy in Hanoi?"

Walker, sitting in the sunny office of the French Ambassador, tried to sound nonchalant. To Bodard, the question had all the casualness of a condemned man's appeal for a last-minute reprieve.

The French Ambassador nodded. "As a matter of fact, I have — just this morning. I was going to telephone you. . . ."

"Well," Walker said, with a forced smile, "I just happened to be in the neighborhood."

"Always a pleasure to see you," Bodard said, somewhat grimly.

The news from Hanoi had, predictably, brought no reprieve; it was instead a clear signal that the North Vietnamese were not going to pause in their drive for total victory. They had smashed much closer to the capital since Bodard had last talked with Walker; in fact, the military situation, from Saigon's view, had deteriorated disastrously. Hue and Da Nang in MR 1, Ban Me Thuot and Nha Trang in MR 2, half a dozen provinces in MR 3, and a whole gazetteer of villages and hamlets in MR 4 — all were now threatened or had been overrun by the NVA. The collapse of ARVN on all fronts — except in some scattered areas within fifty miles of the capital where the South Vietnamese were now struggling to hold on — had taken even Hanoi by surprise. And the cable from Hanoi only underscored how the North Vietnamese were now moving aggressively on the diplomatic front as well — specifically, trying to pit the French against the Americans.

"And what did Hanoi say?" Walker leaned forward, all pretensions of nonchalance now abandoned.

Bodard lit a Gauloise and watched the smoke spiral toward the high ceiling. Then he went to a filing cabinet in one corner of the room. He took a key from his jacket pocket, turned the lock of the top drawer, extracted a cable. "From our Embassy in Hanoi," he volunteered as he returned to the desk and slid into his upholstered chair. "Routed to me via the Quai d'Orsay. The gist of it is simple, deviously simple, you might say. Hanoi" — he began paraphrasing from the cable, looking up occasionally — "is saying that the war is now in its final stages and that, to avoid further bloodshed —"

"How compassionate," Walker interrupted, spitting out the syllables. He glanced at Bodard. "Sorry."

Bodard shrugged. "— the Americans must be made to realize that their cause is now hopeless," he resumed. "The cable goes on to remind France that, once the Americans are driven out, a vacuum will develop in the South, and" — he cleared his throat — "that France, with its long-standing economic and cultural links with Indochina, would be the natural inheritor of whatever foreign opportunities may arise in the country." Bodard crushed the Gauloise in an ashtray. "It's as though they were inviting us to dance on the American grave in Viet Nam." He lit another Gauloise. "I hate it."

"And Paris?" Walker inquired softly. He knew what the answer was even as he asked the question.

Bodard sighed. "I must tell you that, for Paris, the current crisis has a quality of *déjà vu*. So rather than antagonize Hanoi in a situation that would seem to have no future, the Quai may find it more sensible all around to capitalize on its ties with the

North Vietnamese to find a way out of this mess." He slipped the cable into his desk drawer. "No, my dear Hadden, it is not a question of national self-interest, of putting our relations with Hanoi over our alliances with you. Rather, it's a question of cold pragmatism — trying to shape the outcome to everybody's ultimate advantage."

The image of rats deserting a sinking ship inevitably came to Walker's mind. "Of course, I disagree," he finally said.

"Disagree?"

Walker nodded.

"Do you really believe that?"

"I do." Walker said, more defiantly than he had intended. "But it is not easy." He stared at Bodard. "And it is getting lonelier every day."

The room grew quiet, the only sound the ticking of the cloisonné clock on the mantel.

"At least you, Henri, haven't taken to wearing your nationality all over your clothes."

Bodard looked embarrassed. He understood Walker's allusion. The French community in Saigon had in the past few days been conspicuously displaying badges with the French *tricolore* on shirts, jackets, even bathing suits at the Cercle Sportif. The red-white-and-blue bands of the national flag had also begun to appear on French-owned automobiles and villas. French passports were suddenly sprouting from shirt pockets, official pronouncements that the bearers were not Americans.

"I am not happy about it, but what can I do?" Bodard explained. "People become frightened. They look for protection. A pin. A flag. A passport. *C'est la guerre.*"

He picked up a copy of *Le Monde* from his desk. "This just arrived today." He scanned the front page. "Names from the past, famous French generals who had served in Indochina. Christian de Castries, who was captured by the Viet Minh at Dien Bien Phu. Pierre Langlais, the parachute leader at Dien Bien Phu. Raoul Salan, commander-in-chief here in the early 'fifties." His pudgy fingers moved down the news columns. "Now they are all old men, in Paris, poring nostalgically over their maps, reliving the war. Here, listen to Salan. . . ."

"All those generals were *defeated* by Ho Chi Minh, weren't they?" Walker remarked coldly.

Bodard smiled. " *'Fini pour l'Indochine,'* Salan says," Bodard began reading. " 'The South Vietnamese have no army now. Nobody helps them. The North has the support of Russia and China. . . . It is the Free World which is losing face. . . . All of Indochina will become Communist. I have always spoken, always written, of this possibility. . . . This will have a short ending. The North Vietnamese have everything in their hands. They will take Saigon. They have won the war, and they have won it all.' "

Walker slammed his hand on the desk; Bodard was startled.

"Henri," Walker said bitterly, "there are no greater pessimists than defeated generals. They cannot tolerate the idea that someone else might succeed where they failed."

"*Mais* —"

"There is one critical omission in everything you have just read."

"I think I know what you are getting at," Bodard said, his eyes downcast.

"The United States, the greatest power on earth," Walker continued, speaking slowly and deliberately, "will never allow its strategic policy to be dictated by . . . defeatists." He knew that he should not divulge a confidential conversation with the President to the ambassador of a foreign country, not even to his friend Bodard, but he could not restrain his compulsion to say out loud what the President had said privately. "The President told me, in the Oval Office, when I accepted this assignment a year ago, that the United States would carry out its pledge, to this government, to these people. 'Hadden,' he said, 'you have my word of honor.' We shook hands. I left the White House . . . believing him." His words had a hollow sound.

Bodard, subdued, searched for a word of comfort. "My dear

Hadden," he said, "you are describing France in nineteen fifty-four — at the time of Dien Bien Phu. We too once talked in terms of 'honor' and victory, yet in the end . . ." He lifted his hands in resignation. "But" — he got up from his desk and moved toward Walker — "Viet Nam is just one move on the chessboard. You may have lost a pawn — here — but America is not checkmated everywhere. It is still . . . America. And there may yet be a way to avoid total humiliation in Viet Nam."

Walker looked up. "How?"

"By negotiating with 'the other side.' "

Walker's glance at Bodard betrayed bitter disappointment. So Bodard too had joined the ranks of those calling for negotiations with the Communists! One thing you had to say: the Vichy mentality of World War Two, of making a deal with the enemy, was still alive and well. History had, after all, provided no lessons.

"I take it, Henri," Walker finally answered, "that there's no mention of Marshal Pétain in *Le Monde*. He would have some interesting recommendations for the United States."

Bodard smiled the question away. He knew that Walker detested the idea of negotiations with the Communists, but he felt that the issue had to be met head-on, especially now. "Negotiations with 'the other side,' " Bodard repeated.

"Negotiations?" Walker asked sharply. "Is *Hanoi* telling you that?"

"Perhaps," Bodard said, returning to his desk. "I'm an old hand at reading between the lines of diplomatic cables, and my sense is that Hanoi would not slam the door on that possibility, at least *not yet*. Of course" — he paused to make sure that he had Walker's full attention — "it *could* be a trap, a hint at negotiations in order to suck in the Americans. But in any case, for Saigon, it could be a way of avoiding bloody chaos a hundred times worse than what's been taking place in MR One and MR Two."

"Henri," Walker replied patiently, as though he were embarrassed to spell out the obvious, "they will always be ready to negotiate. But now, if ever, is not the time. Not while *we* are still holding Saigon, what *they* want most of all. Not while there is still a possibility that Washington may come through with an emergency airlift of military supplies for ARVN."

"Do you really, Hadden, really believe that is possible — now?"

"*Not* to believe it would be to brand the President of the United States a man without a shred of geopolitical sense. . . ."

"Ah, my dear Hadden," Bodard sighed. "Gloom everywhere." His face suddenly brightened. "Wouldn't you like a little snack? A fresh *pâté de foie* has just arrived from Paris and I find it irresistible." Without even waiting for a reply, he picked up the intercom and gave a swift order in French. A white-gloved Vietnamese waiter served up, within moments, a crock of pâté, a tray of water biscuits, and a chilled bottle of sauterne.

"*Merci*," said Bodard. The waiter left. Bodard covered a cracker with pâté and offered it to Walker. "Have a taste, my friend. In moments of crisis I have found that an excellent *terrine* helps me to survive."

"But I do not have a French palate," Walker said. He regretted the remark instantly; he could see Bodard's face tighten.

"I'm sorry, Henri," Walker followed up quickly. "I guess it's just that I'm a minority of one. I still believe that *if* the South Vietnamese can hold on where they are now, and *if* the aid is forthcoming, Hanoi may decide that it is simply not worth fighting on. That would leave the South Vietnamese with the most valuable part of the country, Saigon and the rich Delta area — with oil offshore. They could make it then, and we could get out with at least a scrap of honor."

Bodard by now had consumed half the pâté. "Do forgive me for being outspoken, my dear Hadden," he said, speaking through a mouthful of crackers, "but I believe that the *only* strategy that makes sense now is to push for a coalition with the

Communists. We French have a reputation for realism, you Americans for idealism, and my realism dictates negotiations now — to avoid total defeat, tomorrow, the next day, or the day after that."

"No, Henri," Walker said. "No negotations now." He glanced at his watch and stood up.

"Will you do me the honor, Hadden, of raising a toast, just the two of us, to our friendship, yours and mine?" Bodard said. He quickly poured two glasses of wine.

Walker couldn't help laughing. "You are incorrigible, my dear Henri," he said. "Whatever the outcome, I shall always treasure your willingness to put up with an irascible, ill-mannered, know-it-all American Ambassador."

They clinked glasses and drank the wine.

" 'Fifty-four," Bodard said, smacking his lips. "A good year for French wine, a terrible year for war. I fervently hope that 'seventy-five is better on *both* counts."

Their moment of relative calm was interrupted by a message, delivered on a tray, advising Walker that Washington was urgently trying to reach him; the U.S. Embassy had tracked him down in Bodard's office. Walker shook hands with Bodard, departed swiftly, and stepped into his waiting limousine for the short drive around the corner to the U.S. Embassy.

The car pulled to a stop next to the tamarind tree in the Embassy parking lot. Walker spotted Suzanne's handbag on the seat, and slipping it under his arm, approached the Embassy building.

A sharp ray of sunlight glinted off the official plaque mounted on the wall next to the entrance: EMBASSY UNITED STATES OF AMERICA. The plaque, with its American bald eagle, suddenly reminded Walker of a nasty little joke he had heard when he first came to Saigon. "Question: If the eagle is the national bird of the United States, what is the national bird of South Viet Nam? Answer: the mosquito."

His eye fixed on the eagle, one claw extending an olive branch, the other brandishing thirteen arrows, symbolizing both U.S. dedication to peace and readiness to defend the nation against all enemies. The eagle — strong, brave, unconquerable. One of these days, perhaps, extinct.

20

Walker opened the door to his office. Within an instant he was staggering backwards, the breath knocked out of him by an assailant. For one wild moment, he imagined that he was the victim of a mugging, or that the NVA had taken over the Embassy while he was at Bodard's.

A split-second was all it took. Then he recognized Suzanne. She had hurled herself at him, ripping the handbag from under his arm.

"Thank God you've got it!"

"You left it in the car," he said, stunned. "Calm down. What's happened? You'd think you had a bunch of eyes-only cables in there."

She ignored him.

He watched as she plunged her hand into the canvas bag, trying to identify the contents by touch. The handbag now seemed to be alive, changing shape as her fingers pushed into all the corners. Walker put his arm around her shoulder. Her body was rigid. "What is it, Suzanne?" he asked. "Did you lose something?"

Suddenly, her hand stopped groping, and Walker could feel her body loosen with relief.

"You find what you are looking for?" he asked gently.

"Yes, it's here. Was this bag always in the car?" Her voice was trembling.

"Yes, all the time," he said, his fingers gently massaging her neck. "On the back seat. Nobody touched it."

"You're sure?"

"Sure." But Walker sensed a remaining trace of anxiety in her.

She pushed herself up from the chair. "I'm very sorry about all this," she murmured.

"What can it be that's got you in such a state?"

"Oh, it's . . ." She stopped. She suddenly realized that it would be best to defuse his curiosity, to leave him with the feeling she was all right now. "It's a little personal memento."

The explanation was weak, given her outburst, and she knew it and she knew that he knew it, but it was the best she could do. She mumbled something about the heat, about not feeling herself lately.

Helen knocked on the door and stuck her head in to tell Walker that Washington was on the scrambler telephone line. Suzanne gratefully seized the chance to skip out, waving a quick nervous goodbye to her father and indicating that she would see him later. He watched her as she half-walked, half-ran down the hall, and wondered if her distraught behavior had anything to do with Tony.

It was the Secretary of State, and Walker, the instant he put the receiver to his ear, realized this was going to be a difficult conversation. The Secretary was at his unctuous best, trying to package the bad news in a ribbon of compliments.

"The President told me just a few minutes ago to convey to you how much he admires you, how grateful, how lucky the country is to have a man of your strength of character on the spot, representing America at a critical hour," the Secretary began.

Walker's diplomatic unscrambler was already at work. That means that the emergency aid program is dead. *What else?*

"Hadden," the voice from the State Department continued,

"we've known each other too long, been through too many crises together, for me to play games with you." Walker could visualize the Secretary scanning the notes from his conversation with the President. "Are you sitting down?"

What else? "I hear you fine," Walker finally said.

"Hadden, we've broken our asses with those idiots on Capitol Hill. I've tried every trick in the book, promised them a billion-dollar dam for each of their states, explained the repercussions of a disaster in Viet Nam, how it could affect the perception of U.S. power throughout the world. They are deaf, deaf, DEAF!"

A lot of words, Walker thought, a lot of big fat words. The fatter the words, the worse the news. "I've got the context, Mr. Secretary. The specifics, please."

"I'm going to give it to you straight, Hadden. First: no more aid. Not another penny. The people on the Hill see the Viet Nam stories on television every night, ARVN on the run, the NVA moving closer and closer to Saigon, and they've decided it's all hopeless now. I'm sorry, Hadden. I know how badly you were counting on the aid. Now, second —"

Second? What was "second"? "Why don't you give me all the good news at once?" Walker said, making no effort to conceal his sarcasm.

"Look, Hadden," the Secretary answered defensively, "I've always been on your side on Viet Nam, and you know it."

"Go ahead, please."

"Second: B-fifty-two air strikes — absolutely out of the question. There would be a coast-to-coast uprising here at home if those planes ever took off again in the direction of Hanoi. We are out of the war."

"So South Viet Nam is simply . . . abandoned?"

"Believe me, I appreciate your agony. When I came into this office, I had the same strategy you had: to try to give Saigon enough support, and time, so that the South Vietnamese would have a chance of their own to survive and we would have a chance to extricate ourselves with at least a shred of honor. But it's always been a race — a race to come up with that aid before we were swamped by the opposition. Well, we've been . . . swamped."

"Mr. Secretary," Walker, furious, cut in, "do you remember that conversation the three of us had in the Oval Office when I was sworn in as Ambassador to South Viet Nam?"

"Yes." The impatience in the Secretary's voice came through loud and clear.

"The President gave me his word of honor that —"

"And the President meant every word of it. But, Hadden, he's boxed in. He's tried. And he's lost the fight."

"The President told me that even if it meant his own political downfall, he would get the goddamned aid before he would let South Viet Nam go down."

"Yes, I remember that conversation very well."

"And you told me the same thing."

"Yes, I remember that, too." It was the voice of a man who would prefer not to be confronted by his own past pledges. "Look, you know very well that if I had my way, you'd have the money. But both of us are stuck with a democracy and we have no choice."

"Mr. Secretary, I —"

"Wait a minute, Hadden, you haven't heard everything yet."

Third?

"There's also a third point. Now listen carefully — and try to keep the apoplexy to a minimum."

Walker held the receiver a little farther from his ear.

"I've been ordered by the President," the voice said very slowly and precisely, "to instruct you to make contact with 'the other side' to determine whether Hanoi is willing to enter negotiations looking toward the formation of a government of national reconciliation between Saigon and the Communists."

Walker resisted a strong temptation to tear the phone from the wall and hurl it through the window.

"Hadden, did you hear me?"

Walker remained silent, his knuckles white as he clenched the receiver.

"For Chrissakes, Hadden, will you let me know you're still there."

"I'm here," Walker finally said.

"Look, Hadden," the Secretary's voice picked up. "I know this is a heartbreaking assignment, especially for you. But the alternative is an America torn by riots and violence. You haven't been here. You don't know what's happening. This country is not going to get reinvolved in the war, and that leaves us with a choice of which is the lesser horror — a coalition with the Communists in Saigon or anarchy in the streets of America."

So this is it, this is what it comes to. Fifty thousand Americans dead, three hundred thousand Americans wounded, a hundred and fifty billion dollars in military aid, the U.S. ripped by years of violence on the campuses, a President driven out of office. Now this — from Washington: Sorry, Viet Nam, but I have another engagement. Let's have lunch some day. Don't call me. I'll call you.

"Why did we ever bother sending in all those troops here ten years ago?" Walker asked angrily. "Why didn't we just send in gravediggers at the very outset and they could have buried South Viet Nam in 'sixty-five, nice and simple. Been much cheaper, too. In all ways."

"Look, Hadden, cut the sarcasm. I don't feel any better about this than you do, and you're not the only one who's fighting a war. I've been fighting it on a hundred fronts myself. With the doves right here in the goddamned State Department. With Capitol Hill. With the press. With college professors. With Viet Nam veterans. Everybody wants out, out, OUT."

Walker picked up the latest copy of the armed forces newspaper, *Stars and Stripes*, just flown in from U.S. military headquarters in Tokyo. A front-page photograph showed the President sprinting away from a group of college reporters at a stadium in the Midwest. The President had a big phony smile on his face, and the reporters were trying to shove microphones at him. The caption read: "Commander-in-Chief Runs From Questions on Viet Nam."

"The President, too? I'm looking at a picture showing him . . ."

"Oh, *that* picture. Unfortunate, but one of those things. I hate to tell you this, but it was published in newspapers all over the world.

"Does he *understand* that he, through you, is instructing me to negotiate the first military defeat of the United States in history?"

"Oh, come on, Hadden, let's not be so melodramatic." The Secretary's patience was wearing very thin.

"There are times," Walker said in a half mumble, "when I think we ought to drop him on North Viet Nam. He'd really mess it up for them — and maybe *we* would win."

"What was that you said?"

"Never mind."

"I heard enough. Do you want me to relay your sentiments to *him?*"

What difference will it really make? The thought suddenly struck Walker that he would have to inform the Vietnamese President about this reversal of U.S. policy — from no negotiations to negotiations. No reason to rush, though. Best to stall as long as possible, to try to keep the whole thing from collapsing.

"You do remember, Mr. Secretary, my cable to you on what the President of South Viet Nam threatened to do, if no aid were forthcoming?"

"Yes."

"Well?"

"Well, what?" The Secretary's voice was exasperated. "The sonofabitch is bluffing. What's he going to do? Resign? Do you really believe that? Where's he going to go? The only place he would be welcome is you-know-where."

"Where?"

"Hanoi. They'd give him a lovely reception."

The Secretary's attempt at humor was wasted on Walker. "But what about Moscow's and Peking's influence on Hanoi?" he shot back. "The Russians and Chinese want détente — not with each other, but with us. Can't we make them pay for that? Can't we lean on them to lean on Hanoi?"

"We've tried that too, Hadden." A laugh crackled over the line. "You won't believe what the Russians told us. They said that the United States, given its own experience with South Viet Nam, surely has learned that client states have an irritating habit of wanting to go their own way. The Chinese say the same thing, even more so, given the tensions that have existed for hundreds of years between themselves and the Vietnamese. Hadden, you don't really think that when our Communist friends have us by the balls, they're going to let go, do you?"

Walker kept staring at the photograph of the running President. "Once the word gets out the U.S. is interested in negotiations with the Communists, we're going to be faced by a pandemonium that's never been seen before, anywhere."

"I know that, Hadden, and you're going to have a monumental job on your hands," the Secretary replied. "You've got to begin a wholesale evacuation of all Americans in such a way that it is kept a secret."

"A *secret?*"

"Yes, as secretly as possible."

"Here? In Saigon? We're going to be sitting ducks. When we first arrived here, we had one friend, the South, and one enemy, the North. Now, ten years later, we're going to leave with no friends and two enemies."

"Hadden, let me say once again that the country is extraordinarily fortunate to have you as the man on the spot. If anyone can carry out these assignments, it's you. No one has your ex-

1 6 5

perience, your courage, your sixth sense in dealing with crises."

"Thanks for the endorsement."

"Look, I know what it feels like. Let me just run through it all again. One, no more aid. Two, no B-fifty-twos. Three, initiate negotiations with 'the other side' with a view toward forming a coalition. And fourth . . ."

Fourth?

". . . watch your own ass."

Walker couldn't stifle a bitter laugh. "What you're really asking me to do," he said, "is the following: one, become the undertaker for South Viet Nam; two, become the traffic cop for the evacuation; and three, become the scapegoat for the U.S. defeat in South Viet Nam."

"You won't be the only one. They're already gunning for *me*. Anything else?"

"Yes," said Walker. "I have a fourth point for you, too."

"Shoot."

"You'd better watch out for America's ass when this is all over."

"Good advice," the Secretary answered. "I wish I could find it funny. And good luck, Hadden. Your instructions for the negotiations will reach you via back channels. I'd be on the lookout for any premature leaks. And again, and I mean it, Hadden, I'm glad you're our man there."

Almost inaudibly, Walker murmured, "Up yours."

"You're welcome," answered the Secretary briskly.

They hung up, simultaneously.

21

Walker hunched over his desk, the copy of *Stars and Stripes* spread out before him, and studied the photograph of the President at full gallop. Another photograph suddenly focused in his mind. six U.S. Marines defying Japanese bullets to raise the U.S. flag on a tiny atoll in the Pacific, Iwo Jima. That single snapshot had stirred the emotions of the country during World War Two, had become a symbol, celluloid ultimately cast in bronze, immortalized in a heroic statue near Arlington National Cemetery. But *this* photograph? Was it the symbol of the *new* America? The tragedy was that no one seemed to care; the people he had showed it to found it amusing, predictable.

Walker's first thought had been that somebody should have confiscated the film on the spot and burned it as subversive. The second thought was that the photograph should be required study for all psychiatrists; a classic case, in black and white, of a man meant for lesser things who was now camouflaging his inadequacy by running away.

Walker tossed the *Stars and Stripes* into the wastebasket, then dialed his CIA station chief and asked to see him. During the few minutes it took John Sommers to trot down the three flights of stairs, Walker began to envision the vague outlines of a counterstrategy to the Secretary's instructions. The Secretary has his own approach, he thought. Fine. But that does not mean that I cannot have *my* own.

Sommers looked more disheveled than usual, as though he had slept in one of his whirling intelligence computers. He was also gloomier than usual. When Walker asked for the latest update on the military situation, Sommers had only one word. "Bad," he said.

The starkness of Sommers's assessment took Walker by surprise. He wondered out loud whether there wasn't anything, not even a scrap, that was "good."

"None," Sommers said.

"You're monosyllabic today, John."

"Yes."

Walker gave Sommers one of his famous hard looks. "Why?" he asked.

"Because," replied Sommers, "epitaphs are usually brief."

Walker decided to let that one go. Sommers, his shirt collar open, his tie askew, showed signs of extreme fatigue. It was obvious that, after the Ban Me Thuot surprise, he didn't want to get caught red-handed in a second failure. That was the goddamned trouble with the CIA, Walker thought. The spooks were convinced that any challenge to their conclusions was an insult to their intelligence — in all meanings of the word. Walker was used to the fact that Sommers's assessments were bleaker than his own.

"*All* the indicators are negative, Mr. Ambassador," Sommers continued, his voice raspy with exhaustion. "The North Vietnamese have just about succeeded in isolating Saigon. Russkie and Chicom supplies are pouring into the South at record levels. The NVA now has more firepower than it has had at any time during the war and, worse yet, that firepower is now being positioned all around the city. Our latest reading now puts some advance units of the NVA only thirty miles from Doc Lap Palace."

"And what about ARVN?"

"ARVN? ARVN is running."

1 6 8

Walker couldn't resist a smile. They're in good company, he thought, with a glance at the wastebasket.

"Well," Walker resumed, "let me put the hundred-and-fifty-billion-dollar question to you. Do you see any way out of this . . . less than promising situation?"

"Aid of any kind is what Saigon desperately needs right now and, even so, it wouldn't do much good," Sommers replied matter-of-factly. "Maybe just delay the grand finale, not much else."

Walker considered briefing Sommers on the conversation with the Secretary. But he wanted Sommers's independent appraisal of the military situation. Besides, Sommers would hear soon enough — through his own channels, from Langley — about the cutoff of the military pipeline to ARVN and the decision to negotiate with Hanoi.

"In other words, Mr. Ambassador," Sommers went on dryly, "aid, no matter what kind, would be a long shot — at best."

"That's exactly what we need," Walker said, zeroing in on Sommers's offhand remark and thinking about his own evolving counterstrategy. "A long shot." He lit a cigar. "The B-fifty-two shot?"

Sommers grunted. "Those days are gone, Mr. Ambassador. Finito. Not after Watergate. Not after Cambodia. Not now."

"True," Walker echoed. "But suppose we signal Hanoi that the B-fifty-twos *may* be on their way back into the war. That might give those bastards up there something to think about."

Sommers was puzzled. Was Walker playing games?

"Well," Sommers remarked, "let's not forget that the B-fifty-twos, even when they were being used, didn't exactly stop Hanoi."

But Walker wasn't listening; his counterstrategy was now ready to go.

"In fact, Mr. Ambassador," Sommers went on, "how do you threaten Hanoi with nonexistent B-fifty-twos?"

"John," Walker said, drawing deeply on his cigar, "leave that little chore to me."

The moment Sommers had left the office, Walker dialed Helen and asked her to get in touch with the correspondent of *The Washington Post* and say that the Ambassador would like to see him. "That may come as something of a surprise to poor Bill Starnes," Walker cautioned, not unmindful that he had turned down every correspondent's requests for an interview over the past year. "Tell him it's no April Fool's Day joke, Helen. Tell him the Ambassador is serious."

"When are you free to see him?"

"Immediately."

Walker leaned back in his chair. He felt perfectly justified in what he was about to do. Madness to do it Washington's way, nice and friendly. It was late in the game, but why not try to strengthen the U.S. hand? Why sit down at the negotiating table knowing that "the other side" held all the aces?

Which is where Starnes came in. The trump card, Walker thought, in his own counterstrategy. The manipulation would have to be very delicate, with no trace of Walker's fingerprints. He would have to pick his words carefully. Give the correspondent the feeling that he was on the verge of an exclusive, leave him sniffing a Pulitzer. The journalistic appetite would do the rest. It was one of the accepted tools of the diplomatic trade, using the press to send a signal to friends or enemies, whomever and wherever. What is more, a story on the front page of the *Post* would have more of an impact on Washington and Hanoi than the publication of top-secret cables. The goddamned doves in the State Department had been leaking Saigon cables left and right in the hope of making Walker's pleas for ARVN support sound like the screamings of a rabid hawk. Top-secret cables were — the very thought brought a smile to Walker's face — a dime a dozen in Washington. Even the *Post* cost more. Fifteen cents a copy.

Helen buzzed him on the intercom: Starnes would be here in thirty minutes.

"Was he surprised?" Walker asked.

"Well, he told me that he dropped his cup of coffee."

"Did you tell him I was serious?"

"I did, but he still thought I was playing a joke on him."

"And?"

"And I convinced him that I got the request right from, if you'll excuse the expression, the horse's mouth."

"Well done," Walker laughed. "I'll get you a medal for that."

Again, he leaned back in his chair. He could already see the banner headline and the story in the *Post*, and he could anticipate the dividends, from both Hanoi and Washington.

One, the story would be instantly relayed to Moscow by the Soviet Embassy in Washington, and Moscow, in turn, would instantly relay it to Hanoi. The Administration, under pressure from the doves, would be forced to deny the story, but Hanoi, wary of official U.S. denials, would still *not* be able to ignore it.

Two, the story might prompt Hanoi to reconsider any strategy to pounce on Saigon in a final humiliation of the United States in South Viet Nam.

Three, the story might maneuver Hanoi into a much softer negotiating stance.

Four, the story might embolden certain hard-line Congressmen and Pentagon generals, all of whom had complained that the U.S. military had been forced to fight the war with one hand tied behind its back, to demand that the U.S. take dramatic action: drop America's "calling card" on Hanoi, you might say.

And five, Walker thought, there was the little matter of the history books. When it was all over, however it ended, he wanted to be sure that the scholarly postmortems would single out Washington, not Ambassador Hadden Walker, as the misguided betrayer of Viet Nam.

The buzzer rang. "He's here, Mr. Ambassador," said Helen.

"Send him in."

Starnes, a lanky, red-haired Midwesterner in Saigon press corps uniform — short-sleeved khaki safari suit with at least a dozen pockets — entered the office cautiously, as though it were a mine field. It was the first time he had ever set foot inside Walker's private domain, and his eyes darted around, taking it all in: the flags, the shelves of porcelain, and the Ambassador puffing on a cigar.

"This isn't 'Indian country.' " Walker laughed, using the DAO description of enemy-held territory. "Come on in."

Starnes smiled. "I've got to admit, Mr. Ambassador, that I was more than a little surprised when your secretary telephoned."

"Understandable," Walker replied noncommittally. "Very understandable. I appreciate your getting over here — on the double." He pointed to a chair directly in front of his desk.

Starnes walked cautiously across the room; he was suspicious, but curious, reminding himself to listen very carefully now, sort out the real from the fake later. After a year in Viet Nam, he felt fairly competent at poking through the constant upbeat gibberish being put out by U.S. officials. He had heard a million stories from old-time correspondents about "The Five O'Clock Follies" — the U.S. military briefings in the old days of MACV — when the colonels and majors would hand out mimeographed optimism disguised as war communiqués. He remembered that when he came to Viet Nam, people asked what he had brought with him, and Starnes had a stock reply: "Two suitcases — one filled with notebooks, the other filled with skepticism." Starnes, though uneasy, had no doubt that if this session with the Ambassador turned out to be a kind of "Midday Follies," he would recognize it.

"Bill," Walker began softly, "I thought I'd ask you over to compare notes on how the war is going. What do *you* think?"

Starnes smiled, but said nothing. Bastard, he thought; I've been after him for a year for an interview and now that I'm finally in his office, at *his* invitation, he asks *me* to talk first. In less than a minute of exposure, Starnes could see that Walker was living up to his reputation in the Saigon press corps as a master manipulator.

"First, though, before we get down to brass tacks," Walker continued, "maybe we ought to establish the ground rules. I'd be grateful, Bill" — Walker tried smiling — "if nothing I say here was attributed to me, and the reason," he went on quickly, preempting Starnes, "is that I'd like to be able to speak to you as candidly as possible. If your story should have such phrases as 'Walker said' and 'Walker suggested' and so on, well, you can appreciate how that would inhibit me and, besides, give me all kinds of problems with Washington."

Starnes shook his head. "But that gives *me* terrible problems, Mr. Ambassador."

"I realize that, Bill, but you can take my word for it that everything I tell you will be accurate," Walker countered. "If you use it — no attribution."

Starnes didn't like it. No attribution? Fuck him. "I'm not sure I can work that way, Mr. Ambassador," he said, stiffly.

Walker looked chagrined. "Gee," he said, putting on his best Southern aw-shucks candor, "I was hoping it would be okay. Matter of fact, I had thought of asking *The New York Times* over but it was out of loyalty to the Washington press crowd that I finally decided on you. Now, Bill" — he got up from his chair and sat on the edge of his desk — "if you feel that my request cramps your style unbearably . . . well, let's just forget it and we'll have a cup of coffee."

The old threat-of-competition gambit, Starnes thought. Play the *Post* off against the *Times*. Tricky sonofabitch. But there was an alternative: he would listen, take notes, and if Walker was simply peddling a line of shit, he wouldn't write the story.

"Okay, Mr. Ambassador, no attribution."

Walker hid his relief behind a cloud of cigar smoke. He sat down in his swivel armchair, and Starnes opened his notebook.

"The Administration is now in the midst of an intensive decision-making process concerning steps to be taken in connection with the current situation," Walker began, loading his phrases with exploitable possibilities. "The review is underway in the National Security Council, in the White House, the State Department, the Pentagon, and the CIA."

"What kind of steps?" Starnes probed.

"A variety of steps," Walker said, with deliberate vagueness. "Even the guys back there appreciate that the situation here is very delicate, very dicey, and even they are not keen on seeing the U.S. go down to its first clear-cut military defeat in history."

Starnes looked up from his notebook. "You're not just talking about more military aid for ARVN, are you?"

Beautiful, Walker thought as he smiled at Starnes. Now don't rush it and, for God's sake, let him lead. Just keep throwing the bait.

Walker half-nodded. "I don't think you can rule that out, until Saigon is down for the ten-count," he replied. He rather liked that answer: it wasn't a total lie (Saigon was still on its feet) and it wasn't the total truth (the Secretary had said that aid was dead). He remembered a line that had been attributed to a top NSC official during JFK's presidency: ". . . a communiqué should say nothing — in such a way as to fool the press without deceiving them."

"You mean," Starnes persisted, "that you believe that aid is still a possibility?"

"I don't think that possibilities can ever be dismissed — as such," Walker said. "But you know, even above and beyond aid, the real challenge is to cut the North Vietnamese down in their tracks, quickly."

Starnes leaned across the desk. "Air power?" he asked. "You mean U.S. air power?"

Ah, Walker thought. Excellent; I didn't say it. He did.

"You remember Hanoi's Easter offensive in 'seventy-two?" Walker asked. "Between Nixon's summits in Peking and Moscow? Well, if it weren't for U.S. air power stopping them dead up around Hue, the NVA might have rolled right on down into Saigon."

Starnes was now scribbling furiously in his notebook. "Mr.

Ambassador, are you suggesting that the Aministration's review includes the possibility of U.S. air power — specifically, sending the B-fifty-twos back into the war?"

Outstanding, Walker thought. *The record will show that it was Starnes, not I, who raised the subject of B-52s.* He looked at Starnes, said nothing.

"I take it," Starnes said carefully, "that your silence means the B-fifty-twos are a live option." He stopped short. "I can't believe it. Not this late in the war."

"I can't believe it either," Walker said, blowing a giant smoke ring into the air. "I've always felt that the B-fifty-twos were like using elephants to swat mosquitoes. This has been, as you yourself have written more than once, a political war while Washington" — he sought to convey that he too shared Starnes's published view that Washington was populated by nincompoops when it came to Viet Nam — "has always tried to win this conflict with technology. But . . ."

"But what?"

"But when *you* mentioned the B-fifty-twos, I couldn't help pointing out that it was U.S. air power — and not ARVN — that stopped the NVA in the Easter offensive."

"Can't you be a bit more specific, Mr. Ambassador? Is there such a possibility now? Is that what Washington is thinking about?"

"Bill, as an old Saigon hand, you can appreciate that I can go only so far. I cannot be more specific."

Starnes tried to broaden his spectrum of questions in the hope that Walker might be more forthcoming. "So you think Washington is searching around for some sort of rescue operation for Viet Nam?"

"The words are yours, Bill, not mine," Walker replied. "My own feeling is that, even with all the problems that the South Vietnamese have given us over the years, there was always a better way to fight this war. The Pentagon was always looking through the prism of World War Two, seeing the conflict here in terms of conventional warfare instead of guerrilla warfare, in terms of taking over the conflict in the massive American way rather than training the South Vietnamese to fight on their own. I've always been skeptical about that."

Starnes's pencil was racing across the pages of his notebook.

"This is for your ears only, Bill," Walker added. "And remember — you didn't get it from me."

Walker was pleased to see his comments being taken down on the spot. He was afraid that, having avoided the press corps in Saigon up until now, he might have grown a little rusty at the care, feeding, and manipulation of journalists. Obviously, he had not forgotten his old skills, nor had he forgotten that the right word to the right reporter at the right time could make a critical difference in an ambassador's reputation. He remembered his own experience in Prague in 1968, how, after the Russian tanks had invaded the city, he had privately invited a senior American journalist to his office and read him excerpts from his own top-secret cables warning Washington that the Russians would never allow Dubček to stay in power — cables that Washington had ignored, pushing ahead with plans for a summit meeting with Brezhnev until suddenly the Soviets were all over Prague. As Washington stood wiping egg off its face, the published story portraying Walker as a prophet without honor did not exactly endear him to the President and Secretary of State at the time. To an angry cable from State, Walker shot back an equally angry cable saying he resented being accused of leaking secret information to the press, and goddammit, Washington had better cut out that backstabbing.

"I want to get back to that B-fifty two option, Mr. Ambassador," Starnes said. "Is it real?"

"Let me just say, Bill, that Washington is in the midst of decision, and I don't want to be in a position of saying yes to some of your questions and no to others. But what I *would* like to say is this, Bill." He looked directly at Starnes. "Anyone with any familiarity with the history of U.S. involvement in this war can draw his own conclusions." He paused meaningfully and leaned forward, offering Starnes his full attention. "What do you think of the situation, Bill?"

"I think it's a terminal case," Starnes said, putting his pencil in one pocket of his safari jacket. "I've been writing Saigon's obituary for the last few days. It's now only a question of *when* the patient draws his last breath."

Walker nodded, his face expressionless.

There is something eerie, something theatrical about this bastard, Starnes thought. Sitting there so relaxed, so unflappable, the Southern aristocrat blowing smoke rings at his porcelain while just outside, the country is disintegrating, the war creeping up to the windowsill. What a performance!

"Well," said Walker, "that's always been one of my problems with the press and one of the reasons why I've stayed away from your colleagues." He tried to keep the sarcasm out of his voice. "I didn't want to get in the way of your thinking." He studied his fingernails. "But I must say there is such a thing as a premature burial."

But Starnes wanted to get back to the only subject on his mind. "I hope you won't find this impertinent, Mr. Ambassador, but why should I take the B-fifty-two possibility seriously?"

"Well, Bill," Walker answered very carefully, "there's no reason you should. But I have always admired enterprising reporters who know how to put two and two together. I know that you fellows assume that, if it's a U.S. official who's providing basic statistics, two and two add up to five. Or three. Or six. But sometimes . . . two and two *do* add up to four."

Starnes tucked his notebook into one of the jacket pockets. "Well, I guess that's it, Mr. Ambassador," he said, standing up. "Thanks for seeing me."

"The pleasure is mine, Bill. Now that I've finally met you, I truly regret not having had the chance to talk with you in the year I've been here. We might have done some great work together."

"Well," said Starnes, "maybe we've made up for it today."

Walker shook hands with Starnes and wished him good luck. Starnes took a last look around the office, studied Walker's professionally dead-pan face, and left.

Walker glanced at his watch. About 5 P.M. That made it 4 A.M., Washington time, thirteen hours earlier. Too late, assuming Starnes decided to write a story, for it to make that day's final edition of the *Post*. Well, the next day would have to do. If the piece appeared, Walker knew that he would hear about it, without delay, from an interested reader on the seventh floor at State.

He picked up the phone and dialed Phan Thanh Giang. Giang was surprised to hear from him. Walker heard a trembling in the old man's voice.

"Giang," Walker said, choosing his words carefully, "I've been thinking about our last conversation and what you talked about. I still don't believe that the temperature is as hot as you do . . . but it could get hotter. So maybe you had better prepare your *grandchildren*" — the perfect word, Walker thought, for Giang's Vietnamese antiques — "for a little excursion." He stared at the receiver in his hand. "Do you understand what I mean?"

"Oh, I do, I do," Giang replied, his voice hoarse with emotion. "God bless you."

"And Giang, let's keep it to ourselves."

"Oh, yes, yes."

"We wouldn't want to attract a crowd, would we, Giang?"

22

For the first time in her two decades with the Quai d'Orsay, Jeanne de Clery had been entrusted to carry out a sensitive diplomatic assignment — ironically, not for the French. It gave her an exhilarating feeling: executing the mission would take only a sentence of her time, but she did not have to be told — and *he* certainly had not told her — that those ten or fifteen words, once uttered, would have an extraordinary impact on the outcome of the long war. Now, as she strolled through the party crowd in the grand salon of the Continental Palace Hotel, she could not resist reveling in the knowledge that no one in the room — not the assorted diplomats from some twenty countries, not the military representatives of the four-nation ICCS "peace-keeping" team, not the journalists, not even the South Vietnamese government officials — knew what she knew.

"How beautiful you look." Ambassador Bodard bit into a rice cookie as he raised his glass to her.

"Thank you," replied Madame de Clery. It had been an amusing game, choosing what to wear tonight — her black Yves St. Laurent or a new crimson *ao dai* made by Mr. Minh on Tu Do Street, and she had decided that the form-hugging *ao dai* was more seductively appropriate for a dragon lady on an undercover mission. Moreover, this was one of those nights when she felt more Vietnamese than French, and she wondered whether it had anything to do with her feeling that Viet Nam, once again, was on the verge of a great upheaval.

"Yes, Jeanne, you look more beautiful than ever," Bodard said with a wink. "Are you in love?"

"Knowledge is beauty, Monsieur l'Ambassadeur," she murmured, flirting with him over the rim of her champagne glass.

"Ah." His eyes widened in anticipation of a bulletin.

"It's an old Vietnamese proverb," she said with a laugh.

Bodard, bowing slightly, turned and billowed off in the direction of the buffet table laden with all sorts of tasty Vietnamese "small chow."

As discreetly as possible, Madame de Clery began to reconnoiter the faces in the crowd — but she could not find the face she wanted. She could recognize the Hungarian military representative on the International Commission of Control and Supervision — the tall man in the musical-comedy uniform, talking to the Ambassador from Japan. She could recognize the Indonesian military representative; he was standing alone, searching for company. She could recognize the Iranian military representative, with gold braid on his shoulder, looking almost like the Shah he worked for. But the Polish military representative was nowhere in sight.

She found herself exchanging hellos with dozens of guests who had turned out for a free drink, a chance to swap the latest rumors. The party host was a Japanese construction company that, notwithstanding the deteriorating military situation — perhaps because of it — could smell a fortune waiting to be amassed. Viet Nam, once the shooting stopped, would need to be rebuilt, and the Japanese were clearly hoping that, by spreading a little of their wealth now, they could make a lot more later.

Her own delicate mission aside, Madame de Clery thought, this party might be worth remembering as the last gasp before what the demoralized Saigon intellectuals were now calling "The Grand Finale." Extraordinary that these people here should be carrying on this way; a newcomer to town would never have guessed that North Vietnamese combat units were already poised within thirty miles of the capital. Vietnamese waiters, in worn but starched and spotless white uniforms, threaded softly through the crowd, balancing trays of glasses filled with scotch, vodka, champagne, wine, and orange soda. The very walls adorned with intricate Vietnamese lacquerware paintings portrayed a peaceful landscape: rice terraces, wispy maidens, shimmering gold fish. The paintings, like just about everything else in Saigon, were for sale.

But tonight Madame de Clery had no interest in the scenery. She hurried across the salon into the hotel lobby. This gave her an excellent vantage point; she could spot any new arrivals and she could also amuse herself by taking in the nightly show on the Continental's open-air veranda. The wicker chairs were all occupied, as usual, by foreign businessmen and journalists and Vietnamese girls, drinking local beer and black-market liquor. Hawkers in discarded army clothing wandered through the crowd, offering pornographic postcards and a variety of drugs. Teenage whores lounged around the edge of the veranda, smiling and occasionally calling out, in their highly pitched children's voices: "Want to make boom-boom?" It was a typical night at the Continental; the war creeping up to the outskirts of the city seemed to make no difference. A faded *grande dame*, the Continental was still offering its special divertissement to the present company, just as it had to French Foreign Legionnaires before World War Two, to the French colonial army after World War Two, and to American GIs who arrived in the years after Dien Bien Phu. The Continental seemed not so much to have been built as to have grown here; old Indochina hands were known to claim that when the first Europeans — the Portuguese — landed in 1535, the Continental was already doing a thriving business.

Now, out of the corner of her eye, Madame de Clery spotted a black Citroën flying the red-and-white flag of Poland. As the car pulled up the curb, she retreated into the grand salon, innocently mingling with the other guests. She had decided to allow the Polish military representative a drink or two before closing in and carrying out her assignment, word for word, just as she had rehearsed it an hour earlier for Ambassador Walker.

His telephone call, as she was dressing for the party, had taken her by surprise. He needed to see her urgently, Walker said. This time of the day? she wondered. But his businesslike voice ruled out any possibility of romance. She agreed, warning him that she had only a few moments because she was already late for a reception at the Continental.

Five minutes later, he was at her house; he entered the usual way, through the back door. He looked anxious and tired; even his unfailingly crisp linen suit had wilted. He told her that he needed her help, but only on the condition that she ask no questions and that not a word of their talk be repeated to anyone else. They both knew that the second request — superfluous, he hastened to assure her — referred especially to the French Embassy. She had never before seen him so tense. She hesitated only for a moment before agreeing.

"Do you know the senior Polish military representative on the ICCS?" he asked.

"The *Polish* representative?" She nodded.

"Could you pick him out in a crowd?"

"But yes. I've exchanged a few words with him at one reception or another. He is not very amusing, I think, but then again I have never been comfortable in the company of Communists." She laughed. "It probably has to do with my background."

Her effort at humor did not produce even a hint of a smile on Walker's taut face.

"Would you do this for me, Jeanne?" he asked, his voice very low, almost a whisper. "He will be at the reception. Please tell him the following: 'The American Ambassador would like to see you at my house at ten o'clock tonight.' "

Walker, meeting secretly with the representative of *Poland?*

182

So it had finally come to that, she thought. The collapse of everything that Hadden had stood for. She held back the surge of compassion she felt for him.

"Will you do it?" he asked anxiously. "I don't want to do this through my own people — too much risk of a leak. And if I were to be seen talking to the Polish military representative, *at this time*, it would touch off alarm bells all over town."

She nodded, reaching for his hand. He pulled away.

"Let me repeat the sentence once again. 'The American Ambassador would like to see you at my house at ten o'clock tonight.' "

" 'The American Ambassador would like to see you at my house at ten o'clock tonight,' " she repeated. She searched his face. "May I ask you a question, Hadden?"

"We made a deal, Jeanne," he said softly. "No questions asked. Right?"

She nodded. He smiled and reached for her hand. "But there should be some reward in this for you," he said. "All I'm prepared to tell you now is that you will become part of the history of this war. Please try to understand."

This war, she thought. Always *this* war. Nothing but *this* war. My father from Paris and my mother from Hanoi met in *this* war. I was born in *this* war. I was married in *this* war. I lost a husband in *this* war. My Vietnamese blood will always identify me with *this* war. Is there no other life but *this* war?

"And when he comes here," Walker continued, "and he will — the Communists always do when they smell blood — I would be indebted if you could arrange to be out of the house. All it should take is a few minutes."

He kissed her swiftly and left.

The Polish military representative, an American cigarette in one hand, a tumbler of vodka in the other, his nameplate — "COL. STANKIEWICZ, POLAND" — pinned to his right breast pocket, was engaged in an animated conversation with his Hungarian colleague. From a distance, Madame de Clery watched the Colonel as he beckoned the circulating waiter, picked up a fresh vodka, and drifted through the crowd to exchange a few words with the Ambassador from Thailand. Moving on, the Colonel approached a South Vietnamese officer in military uniform; the South Vietnamese turned his back, deliberately. The Colonel shrugged and joined a circle of diplomats.

Madame de Clery inched closer. She tuned in on a discussion of the soaring black-market rate for the piastre — from a few hundred to the dollar to a few thousand to the dollar within the last twenty-four hours. "A sign of the times," someone added with a laugh. "The value of the piastre is the best military intelligence you can get in Saigon."

At precisely this moment, Madame de Clery saw her chance to bump accidentally into the Colonel.

He smiled, with an exaggerated half bow. "Pardon, Madame," he said.

She assured him that she had been at fault, offered him her most charming smile, and led him toward the potted palms in the corner of the salon. She flattered him with questions about his family back home in Warsaw and the frustrations of the lonely military man abroad. The whole maneuver was so easy, she was almost ashamed. Suddenly, they were detached from the crowd, beyond hearing distance of any of the guests.

"I have a message for you," she said.

"Excellent," he replied, his eyes misting with self-congratulation. "It isn't often that I am given a message from someone as beautiful as you are."

Madame de Clery could not resist a flicker of amusement. *"Merci mille fois,"* she responded, looking directly into his eyes. Then, in the same light tone, she continued: "The American Ambassador would like to see you at my house at ten o'clock tonight."

His face reddened and he coughed, almost choking.

Madame de Clery stood still, observing the impact of her message.

"Would you be so kind as to say that again, please," he asked.

"I said, 'The American Ambassador would like to see you at my house at ten o'clock tonight,' " she repeated.

"That is what I thought you said. I just wanted to be sure." He stared mournfully at Madame de Clery, sheathed in her silken *aoi dai*, her ivory face smooth and unrevealing except for a tiny bead of sweat on her upper lip. He took a large swallow of vodka. "I will be there," he said.

She quickly gave him her address and rejoined the party. Weaving through the crowd, she stopped before a handsome young diplomat, a complete stranger, and poured out a stream of inconsequential chitchat. He said he was the Italian consular officer. He had arrived in Saigon only four months before, he volunteered, adding that he had seen enough to last a lifetime. Madame de Clery smiled, but she wasn't listening. She was looking past his sharply tailored suit at the Polish military representative who, nodding to the right and left, was making his way out through the front door.

Relieved, she leaned over and kissed the young Italian, once on each cheek. "A little something to add to your memories of Saigon," she said with a piquant smile. As she left, she waved goodbye to Ambassador Bodard, but his eyes were riveted on a tray of fresh crayfish, and he did not see her.

At precisely five minutes before ten, Walker arrived at Madame de Clery's back door. She had assured him by telephone that the message had been delivered, that her servants had been dismissed, and that she herself would leave the house and not return until eleven-thirty.

"But this will take only a few minutes," he had told her. His voice sounded lonely, as though he were marooned.

"I'll make it eleven then," she had replied softly.

Once inside the house, he went directly to the rattan bar in the living room. Jeanne must have left only a few minutes before. She had filled a short glass with ice for him and left a bottle of brandy next to it. He poured himself a drink.

The thought of the upcoming meeting nauseated Walker. The very presence of the Poles and the Hungarians had been a constant reminder of the maddening unreality of the war. They, along with the Canadians and the Indonesians, had been part of the original team set up at the time of the so-called Paris Peace Agreement of 1973 to monitor the "cease-fire." But predictably, every time Saigon accused Hanoi of violating the agreement, the Poles and the Hungarians counteraccused Saigon of engaging in propaganda to cover its own land-grabbing operations. The Canadians and the Indonesians defended Saigon whenever North Viet Nam lodged a protest against South Viet Nam. Since a unanimous vote among the four ICCS members was required before any investigation could be carried out, nobody ever seriously investigated anything. The whole thing got to be a bloody joke. The Canadians, after six months, went home in disgust, to be replaced by the Indonesians. Meantime, the charade continued, allowing the North to infiltrate a steady supply of men and supplies below the seventeenth parallel. Now, the NVA was in perfect position to launch a death blow at Saigon.

And here he was — he, the American Ambassador — waiting to make contact with the Polish Colonel.

He glanced at his watch. It was not yet ten o'clock. He wandered restlessly around the room and came to a stop before the familiar photograph on the wall: a smiling Vietnamese woman in a flowered *ao dai* and a serious, mustachioed young man. Jeanne's parents.

Within a few minutes, he heard a car brake to a stop. When the doorbell sounded, Walker went to the bar and slowly poured himself another brandy. Then, with great reluctance, he moved to open the front door.

A short, stout man stood before him. In civilian clothes. Well, that was considerate, Walker thought.

"How do you do, Colonel?" he said crisply.

"It's a great pleasure to meet you, at last," the Colonel replied.

Walker did not offer the Colonel a drink. He preferred to raise toasts with those Communists on the ICCS who had slipped into the American Embassy asking for asylum. He pointed to a chair — Stankiewicz sat down immediately — and Walker seated himself directly opposite.

The Colonel gave Walker a smile full of large tobacco-stained teeth.

"The United States," Walker began stiffly, "wishes to relay a message to the regime in North Viet Nam. . . ."

The Colonel kept smiling.

"The message is this," Walker said in a monotone. "The United States is prepared to enter negotiations with a view toward forming a government of national reconciliation in Saigon."

Sitting at the edge of his seat, his pudgy hand outstretched, the Colonel had opened his mouth to reply when Walker cut him off. "I have nothing more to say."

But the Colonel was not to be silenced. He could not contain his triumphant excitement. The Americans were at last facing the inevitable, officially. The U.S. Ambassador sat opposite him, begging for political negotiations with Hanoi. "You are talking, of course, about a 'coalition' government," the Colonel said.

The word revolted Walker. "Call it what you will," he answered. Then, coldly, he added, "One other thing. Perhaps you can make your necessary contacts as quickly as possible and telephone me tomorrow, so that we can arrange a follow-up meeting to work out the necessary preliminary details before any formal talks take place — if that in fact should happen."

The Colonel, clearly jubilant at the prospect of vaulting from the boredom of the ICCS to the very forefront of secret diplomacy, said he had some questions.

But Walker made it clear that he was not prepared to hear any questions. "I think," he said sharply, "that you have all the information that is required. I shall be waiting for your phone call. Talk only to me; I alone am authorized to deal with this matter. And I trust it is not necessary to stress the importance of secrecy — if these negotiations are to succeed."

The word "succeed" stuck in his throat. How could he have used it? *Succeed* — at what? At turning over South Viet Nam to the Communists? At giving the United States its first military defeat? At tempting the Communist world to embark on new Viet Nams? At disillusioning America's allies? *That* was success?

Walker got up from his chair and walked toward the door. The Colonel followed him.

"Good evening, Colonel," Walker said.

"Good evening, Mr. Ambassador," the Colonel replied cheerfully.

The whole process had taken less than five minutes.

At precisely eleven o'clock, Madame de Clery returned to the house.

"Jeanne . . . ," Walker began.

"No," she said. "Not a word." She led him by the hand to the bedroom.

"But I want you to know —"

"Later," she said.

As they made love, the events of the past few hours unreeled through his mind. The Polish Colonel's yellow-toothed grin surfaced again and again, an ineradicable symbol of his own humiliation that he knew would be forever scratched in his soul.

"You are not your usual passionate self tonight, Monsieur l'Ambassadeur."

"Yes" — his voice was almost inaudible — "and I'm not your usual 'Monsieur l'Ambassadeur' tonight. Just an errand boy at the end of a telephone line. Carrying out instructions. What diplomats call 'an instrument of policy.' No blood. No heart. No mind."

She put her warm fingers on his lips. "Enough," she said. "I may not be able to ask questions but that does not mean that I do not know the answers."

He put his arms around her and held her.

"While you were having your meeting," she began, "I walked through the streets of Saigon, and I found myself looking at faces, Vietnamese faces, wondering what will happen to these people when it's all over." She rested her head on his chest. "Particularly to people like me."

"You?"

"Oh, I don't mean 'me' in the sense that I am endangered, not at all," she said. "I'm one of the lucky ones; I have a French passport. No, I mean 'me' in the sense of those people like me who fled from the North in nineteen fifty-four after Dien Bien Phu. Those people *then* had a place to flee to — the South. Almost a million of them, by boat, train, foot. And for all kinds of reasons — religious, political, because they could not stand the repressions of the regime in Hanoi. The Communists had their own explanation. They said the Catholics fled south because the priests told them that God had gone south and if they did not follow God they would lose their souls and maybe even their lives."

Walker remembered seeing film of the ragged 1954 exodus of refugees from the North to the South.

"But when the Communists take over here," Jeanne went on, "where will they flee to now? Nowhere. Unless they simply get into their sampans and float out to sea."

Where would they flee to now, Walker thought, these Vietnamese whom Jeanne had been looking at only an hour ago in the streets of Saigon? Even "God" was trapped.

"Jeanne, you said '*when*' the Communists take over here. '*If*' is a more accurate way to put it."

"If?"

"*If* they take over," Walker emphasized. "I'm not telling you anything you haven't guessed. Only three people in all of Saigon know about it — I, you, and the Polish Colonel. The Poles will tell Hanoi that the U.S. is ready to enter into negotiations, and Hanoi will negotiate. I have no doubt of that, none at all. And maybe, just maybe, the Saigon half of a coalition government will be able to prevent a total Communist takeover."

"You're wrong, Hadden," Jeanne said.

"Wrong?" He knew what she was getting at but he just could not bear the feeling of being forced into retreat again.

"The Vietnamese half of me," Jeanne said, "tells me that Hanoi will *not* negotiate. They did that in Geneva in nineteen fifty-four — and they later felt betrayed. The Geneva agreement called for an election in 'fifty-six, to reunify the North and the South. But when the time came, everyone realized that Ho Chi Minh would win. So the South said no elections. And the Americans supported the South. Hadden" — it was almost a command — "look at me."

He pulled his head out of the pillow.

"Why in the world," she asked, "when they are moving closer and closer to Saigon every day, would the North want to negotiate with the Americans now?"

"They will!" Walker countered. "I have always believed they will. They're going to need us one day — for money, maybe even for support against their ancient enemy, the Chinese. They'll negotiate — as a down payment on future 'friendship.' "

"You have a way with words, Hadden, but I know the Vietnamese. You're wrong."

"Not many people say that — and keep their jobs," Walker responded with a weak smile.

"Not many people, I hope, have a 'job' like mine."

He leaned over, pushed away the cascading black hair, and kissed the small strawberry mark between her breasts. "Your one, your only . . . imperfection," he whispered.

"And you, Hadden," she said teasingly, "are a perfectionist. . . ."

Walker smiled. "I used to be, but I am becoming more tolerant. Did I tell you I bought a vase — a beautiful Swatow, but imperfect?"

"No, you didn't. Where did you find it? At the Nguyen Dynasty?"

Walker nodded. "Part of the collection you mentioned at Bodard's. Professor Hoan knows I buy only perfect pieces. But he encouraged me to buy this one. He'll take it back, he says, if I have regrets. But he knows I'll never give it up . . . any more than I will give you up." He kissed the strawberry mark again.

"In a perfect world, you would not have to . . ."

"In a perfect world, I would not even have to leave this warm bed."

She kissed him, and he pulled her close, and they held each other very tightly.

"Time to go," he finally said, with reluctance.

When he returned to the residence, he found Suzanne in the living room sipping a Coke. She looked up at him. The very sight of her, in her pink bathrobe, curled up in the big wing chair, comforted him. He leaned over and kissed her.

"Hope you had a good time," she said cheerfully.

"Suzanne," he said, "it has been an extraordinary day."

23

Tiny though it was, the micro-recorder weighed heavily in Suzanne's handbag. She had been up since six in the morning but had waited an hour or so before leaving the residence and heading for Tony's place on Gia Long, ten blocks away. She had avoided taking any of his telephone calls since they had glimpsed each other in the Embassy lobby the day before. She felt like a shuttlecock — batted back and forth between him and her father — disfigured, deformed, *deselfed*. But she knew the worst was yet to come. Tony would claw and dig and tear at her. It would be difficult, but she would get it over with and spare herself the further humiliation of being too cowardly to face him.

Still, she knew she was putting off the encounter when she decided, on turning the corner into Thong Nhat, to stop at the Embassy snack bar for a cup of coffee. From a block away, she could see a swarm of Vietnamese jammed up against the ten-foot walls surrounding the Embassy compound. So yesterday's crowds in the lobby were now beginning to back up into the streets, she thought. The crowds, as she walked by, were strained, anxious — but still quiet, still orderly. What would happen when — *if* — the NVA moved even closer to the city? It suddenly made her problems seem trivial. She was an American with a sure ticket to escape. But what about *these* people? Her appetite for coffee suddenly vanished. She hurried past the

Embassy directly into the big square that the Vietnamese years earlier had renamed John F. Kennedy Square, to symbolize what they then saw as America's undying commitment to South Viet Nam. She passed the towering cathedral that the French had built almost a century before, and turned left down Tu Do. When she reached Tony's apartment building on Gia Long, she looked up at his balcony. He stood there, waiting for her.

He was at the door when she arrived. "I couldn't get through on the phone," he began, kissing her lightly on the forehead. "I was worried about you."

Suzanne smiled mechanically, staring at the shattered mirror on the floor. "What happened?"

"Oh, that?" Tony laughed. "I hit it with a dart."

They studied each other, neither yet ready to cut through the unspoken tension, each waiting for the other to make the first move.

"Well?" Tony finally asked.

Wordlessly, she reached into her handbag, took out the micro-recorder, tossed it on the bed.

Tony, his lips curving into a smile, glanced swiftly at the recorder. "Suzanne," he said, "I know how difficult it must have been. The crisscrossing emotions. Your feelings about your father." He leaned toward her. "But, believe me, it was the right thing to do." He reached over and picked up the recorder.

A feeling of exultation swept through him. He suddenly saw himself as an excavator, ax in hand, standing on the tortured terrain of Walker's mind, about to crack through the surface. In just a moment, he would dig up the secret Walker!

His index finger pressed the "on" button. He held the recorder to his ear, his face eager, his eyes on Suzanne.

Suzanne, her face a dead blank, watched Tony's smile fade into a puzzled expression. The only sound in the room was the muted hum of the recorder's transistorized motor. He thrust the recorder in front of his eyes — then shot a questioning glance at her.

"The cassette!" His voice, tender a moment ago, was now inquisitorial. "Where is the fucking cassette?"

Suzanne looked at him, her face now a mix of compassion and disgust. After a moment, in a voice filled with tension, she answered. "I destroyed it."

His eyes blazed at her.

"I had told myself I was doing it in the interest of truth — for my father — to convince you of his integrity. But that was an excuse, a way out. I was doing it because I was weak. I couldn't say no to you. I couldn't choose between you and him. So I compromised, and told myself that was *honorable*. But it wasn't. We both know that. It was contemptible. Despicable. Vile."

Tony turned away from her. Brusquely, she grabbed his face and turned it back toward her.

"Look at me!" she shouted.

He obeyed, stunned by the change in her.

"I went to his office. I got him to talk. To tell me exactly how he felt, what he thought the outcome would be . . . and all the time the tape was spinning in my handbag, taking it all down, every syllable of it." Her voice was strong, the earlier anxiety gone. "And then I took the recorder back to my room with me. I held it in my hands. And then I knew what all this was. *Betrayal!* I was all set to betray my father. I took out the cassette. I smashed it — with the heel of my shoe. Then I took a scissors and I cut the tape into a thousand pieces and flushed it all down the toilet." Her eyes never left Tony's, as though she knew instinctively that she had to communicate with more than just words.

Tony tried unlocking his eyes from hers. He had come so close, but he had lost. Dimly he could hear her saying that she understood why he had wanted her to do what he'd asked her to do but now it was his turn to understand why she had not been able to go through with it.

"SHIT!" He hurled the recorder against the wall. It chipped a hole in the concrete and crashed to the floor. "You know what the destruction of the tape means? Do you? Do you?" His clenched fist slashed through the air, his angry face now closing in on her. "It means that the killing will go on!" His head shook from side to side. "Me — with that fucking M-sixteen, at Nha Trang. You — with the fucking heel of your shoe. Both of us — gutless!"

"No, Tony, not gutless. Human! Do you remember what you felt, after Nha Trang? Filled with shame. Horrified. You couldn't believe it was you. Well, what about me? You wanted me to catch him . . . red-handed. To get him to confess that he was the criminal who was prolonging a war he knew was lost. His *daughter!* Your accomplice! Using his love and his confidence."

Tony turned away and stared emptily at the chip in the wall.

"Listen to me," she implored. "I know the anguish you are going through. Believe me. But, Tony, I think you're losing control. You're being carried away with some kind of obsession that he —"

"Forget the tape recorder," Tony snapped. "What did he tell you?" His face was now five inches from hers, a face that looked familiar yet was one she had never before seen: full of hate, an enemy's face.

"He told me that he thought that Washington would come through with the aid."

"How? Pushed by his lies?"

She ignored the question. It was a risk, and she knew it, but she was now beginning to feel stronger, even strong enough to face the risk of a showdown. "I want to be as honest as I can. The you I know and care about is not somebody who would even think of such a scheme. I don't know what it is — the intrigue of Saigon, your 'spook' instincts, the corruption of the war — but you weren't like this when we first met. You —"

"*Nothing* was like this when we first met," he shouted. "Did you see what I saw in the streets this morning? I was out at six A.M., walking along Tu Do, Nguyen Hue, Le Loi, and I could feel the nervousness in this town. Nervousness today, terror tomorrow. Did *you* see any of that? Did you?"

She nodded. "I saw. People jammed up this early in the morning, desperate for U.S. visas. I'm not blind. But what makes you think that . . . *you* will lead them out? You've been carrying on these last few days like some kind of wild man who can control what's happening. Tony, you're *not* the Messiah!"

"No, but —"

"Oh, come on, Tony," she cut in. "You really don't think you have some kind of secret formula, do you?"

"Call it what you like," he shot back. "All I know is — your father fucking well doesn't have it!"

Suzanne was still. After this outburst, she hoped that his anger would ease.

"Well," he said, his voice becoming less shrill, "you agree, don't you, that the next problem is getting out — not us, but them, those Vietnamese you saw on line at the Embassy? There are people all over this town who threw in their lot with the Americans, worked for them, took America at its word that it was here to stay. That's finished now. Now it all comes down to one word." Again, his face was just a few inches from hers. "Survival."

She remained still, waiting.

"Would you like some coffee?" he finally asked.

She had taken the risk of confronting him, and he was now pouring two cups of coffee.

"Oh, Tony . . . believe me. I know how this is tearing you up. But I think . . . this place, this war . . . it reaches into us and finds a hidden corner of rottenness. Everybody's got a corner like that. Most people live their whole lives without having to face it." She came toward him. "Forgiveness, Tony . . . it's not such a bad word."

"Suzanne" was all he said. He took her in his arms, buried his head in her neck. "I wish I could believe that."

"Shhhhh," she whispered, kissing him.

"You know your father has given me ten days to clear out?" he said. "If I go, what are you going to do? Go? Stay?"

196

There it was, again, even now, Suzanne thought, the old choice pursuing her.

"But you're lucky," Tony went on. "You'll never have to make that decision. We'll *all* be out of here in ten days."

Was that possible? Suzanne thought. The calendar suddenly seemed shrunken, and the image of Thi and Thach at the orphanage flashed once again in her mind. "I've been thinking about those two kids . . . ," she confessed. ". . . about them and all the other kids at the orphanage. What do *I* do?"

"Suzanne," he began, their roles suddenly changing, he now trying to console her, "one way or another, we'll get them out." His hands caressed her face. "*I* will get them out, if necessary. I promise you."

"Thank you . . . for saying that. But getting them out may be the easy part. What happens to them later? Can we treat these kids simply as cargo? Dump them on an America fed up with Vietnamese? That thinks of them as 'gooks,' 'slopes,' 'dinks'?"

" 'The only good dink is a dead dink,' " Tony said, almost to himself.

"What was that?"

"Choice quote from the battlefield, from my collection of 'Sayings of the Foot-Soldier.' You know, in all the years the Americans have been coming here, they still haven't learned to say 'thank you' in Vietnamese."

Suzanne looked through the window. The normal morning traffic crush. She wondered how many more days it would last.

"We, the pure," Tony said. "We, the truthful. We, the honest. They, the corrupt. They, the cowards. They, the pickpockets. I once heard Bob Hope, some years ago, tell a joke to the GIs here. 'I'm strolling along Tu Do,' he says, 'and a Vietnamese kid comes up to me and says, "Wanna buy a watch?" "I already have a watch," I say. Then the kid says, "Wanna bet?" ' The joke got a great laugh, but I was watching a replay of the show on Armed Forces TV that night with some Vietnamese friends of mine." He looked through the window, watching a group of young girls walking hand in hand, their long white tunics billowing in the breeze. They looked as though they were flowing across the asphalt. *"They* didn't think it was so funny."

There was a knock on the door. Tony glanced at his watch. Eight-ten. This time of the morning? He opened the door. A slim girl stood before him. She was wearing a green *ao dai*. Her long black hair plummeted to her waist. He caught his breath.

"It's me — Anh," she said. Her voice was a whisper. "Do you remember me?"

She looked as beautiful as ever, but her eyes had lost their sparkle. A face, a voice, from the past, his own past in Viet Nam, during his first tour in Saigon.

"Anh," he said, trying to suppress his embarrassment. "Of course I remember you."

A glimmer of a smile appeared on her face. Suddenly, through the open door, she saw Suzanne, and she backed away. "I'm sorry," she said, almost inaudibly. "I didn't know you had —"

"No, please . . . it's all right." He turned to Suzanne and excused himself; then he stepped out into the hallway, closing the door behind him.

Tony had first met Anh in 1970, a month after his arrival in Saigon. He had stopped in at Thanh Le, the local handicrafts emporium on Tu Do, and a lovely salesgirl had smiled at him and asked whether she could show him through the shop. She was extraordinarily beautiful, in a green *ao dai*. *Was she wearing the same dress now?* He had spent more time looking at *her* than at the assorted ceramics, lacquerware, teakwood statues, and elephant tusks. He had negotiated for a piece of lacquerware, as a way of prolonging their conversation. Finally, almost jokingly, he had asked her whether she would have dinner with him. "Oh, no," she had said, but she gave him the feeling that it would not hurt to try again. So he returned to Thanh Le every day for a week, buying one piece of unappealing bric-a-brac after another. Finally, she said yes. That was the way it began. He had spent the next three years with her. She spoke fluent French, the result of years in a *lycee*; her English had been acquired at Vietnamese–American Association night classes. She was gay and exciting, chatty and filled with fairytales and legends about Viet Nam. It was Anh who had introduced him to "the unheard voices" of the Vietnamese. It was Anh, on an occasional outing to the coastal resort of Vung Tau or to Antoine's seafood restaurant overlooking the beach at Nha Trang, who had escorted him out of the air-conditioned, A-1 meat sauce world of the Americans into the terra incognita of the Vietnamese. It was Anh who had described Viet Nam as a two-lane highway, one for the Vietnamese and one for the Americans, with no intersections; they needed each other, America and Viet Nam, she told him, but they didn't want to know each other; they slept in the same bed, but they had never been properly introduced. Anh, who had let him know how the Vietnamese felt about the war and how the conflict had turned the Vietnamese society on its head. Once, she had said, the scholars — the *si* — were at the very top, and the ordinary soldiers — the *binh* — at the very bottom. But the arrival of the Americans and their dollars had changed all that; *"nhat di, nhi tuong,"* she had said, explaining that now it was the prostitutes who were first, with the generals second. The *si* — her father among them — had become irrelevant people. She'd introduced him to her father, an elderly Vietnamese with an ascetic face and a wisp of a beard. She had talked about the customs of Vietnamese society, including the ritual of *coi mat*. Love was a Western luxury, she had said teasingly; most of the Vietnamese had their marriages arranged, and when the day came for the boy and girl to meet, it would be the astrologer who would decide which day was most auspicious. Tony had laughed, and she had asked what was so funny, did he think that American technology had more value than Vietnamese astrology? And then they both laughed, and she went on to say that the boy's family would call on the girl's family, bearing gifts of rice alcohol, flowers, and betel nuts, and the prospective bride and bridegroom would *coi mat* — "show the face." If the faces did not like each other, the meeting would be purely social, but if the faces did, a wedding would follow. But even that did not mean, she'd said with a laugh, that the couple would live happily ever after. In the rural areas, it was customary — after the first few nights — for the bride to return to her family and wait until the husband came calling, carrying a roast pig. If the pig was whole, the bride would go back with her husband. But if one of the pig's ears was cut off, it meant that the husband had discovered that the bride was not a virgin. He gave her back to her family. Tony's reaction was that the war had long since cut an ear off Viet Nam, and she had laughed, and they had gone back to his place and made love over and over again. Tony had thought that she was the only girl in the world for him, but then he had flown off to the United States for three months of home leave in early '74. When he returned to Saigon, he had found Suzanne. She had displaced Anh.

They looked at each other self-consciously. "Anh, how are you?" Tony finally asked. "How have you been?"

"I did not want to come here. I did not want to bother you. But my brother said I must." She half-looked into his eyes. "You remember Duc?"

Tony pictured a handsome teenager with an alert face, always tagging along to the softball games at the old MACV compound near Tan Son Nhut. "Of course," he said. "Of course I remember Duc. Is he in the army now?" It was a silly question, Tony thought, but it was a way of breaking the awkward tension between them.

Anh turned, called down the hallway. A moment later, a young man appeared, on crutches, one trouser leg on his ARVN uniform pinned to his waist.

"I'm sorry," Tony mumbled. "I didn't know." He reached out and shook Duc's hand. "How are you, Duc?"

Duc smiled with embarrassment and looked down at the floor. "I am all right," he said in halting English. "We are all right."

"Is there anything I can do?" Tony asked, his eyes going from Anh's face to Duc's face. He tried not to look down at Duc's pinned trouser leg.

"Yes," said Duc, readjusting his body on the crutches. "Marry my sister."

Tony was stunned. Anh looked away, her eyes pointed down the empty hallway.

"If you marry Anh, she can get an entry visa to the United States," Duc pleaded. "When the North Vietnamese come, they will say that we were friends of the Americans — because of Anh and you. They will find out. They will find out everything — about everybody. Marry Anh, please. To save her."

Tony found himself speechless.

"If she goes, she can take us with her," Duc went on. "Our mother is no longer alive. Just our father, me, and her. And then in America, you can go away. The marriage is not real. It's just on paper."

Anh was overwhelmed with embarrassment. "I didn't want to come here. I did not want to trouble you," she said in a whisper. "But Duc saw you one day in the street and followed you and found out where you lived. I didn't want to trouble you. Duc made me."

Duc cut in softly. "We know that what we are asking is much difficulty for you," he said, reaching into his torn military jacket and taking out a thin packet of U.S. bills. "Take it," he said. "It's all the money our family has. Four hundred and forty dollars."

Tony could barely fight back tears. He pushed the money away.

"Do you still remember our telephone number?" Duc asked. "Five six four seven nine. Please. We have no one else we can ask."

"Anh, Duc," he said hoarsely. "I will help you. *How*, I am not sure, but I will. If the North Vietnamese come, I will help you." His voice was cracking.

"I am sure you will." Anh's face lit with a tiny smile. She turned, and the two of them went down the hallway, Anh walking very slowly so as not to outpace Duc on his crutches. Tony's eyes never left them.

Suzanne opened the door of the apartment. Without saying a word, she took him by the hand and led him back into the room. He sat down, sobbing convulsively. Suzanne waited. Suddenly, the whole story poured out — how he had first met Anh and how he had spent all his time with her and how, when he had returned to Saigon after his home leave, he hadn't even telephoned her.

"I'm just like all the others," he cried. "Use these people, discard them." He blotted the tears awkwardly with his handkerchief. "Here I am, convinced I'm a special case, better than the other Americans, better than your father . . ."

"What did Anh want?" Suzanne asked softly.

"Anh didn't ask for anything," Tony answered in a low voice. "It was Duc, her brother. He asked me to marry Anh, as a way of getting her and her family out of the country. Oh, God, Suzanne — her whole family — reduced to begging."

"If it can help," Suzanne said very softly, "then marry her."

"Marry her?" he echoed, limply.

"There are no rules anymore, only instincts," she went on. "We'll get out. We're Americans. We've got our whole lives ahead of us. She may have only days."

He hurled himself out of the chair and threw his arms around Suzanne. They held on tightly, as if to save each other from disaster.

24

Suzanne had known about Anh — in a shadowy way, but never by name. Tony had once mentioned a Vietnamese girl, someone who had been a friend of his, long ago. She had tucked away that bit of his past in the back of her mind.

Now, Anh was painfully real, a part of Tony's responsibility. Suzanne, a few moments ago, had done what she could to help — but then she had decided to leave him alone, with a promise that they would meet later in the day. The desperation of Anh and Duc, their helpless dependence on the goodwill of Americans — that whole scene had pushed her thoughts in the direction of Thi and Thach, *her* Vietnamese.

She found herself walking in the direction of the "Home for the Children of Parents Killed by the Viet Cong." It was a long walk, she knew, maybe two miles, but she felt it was just what she needed: time to be alone, out of the range of Tony's embraces and her father's presence, time to concentrate on the challenge she felt stalking her, even as she headed down Gia Long toward Tu Do. Tony had already been tested. Now it was her turn.

ARVN was everywhere. Saigon's streets had turned into streams of khaki; the South Vietnamese military, routed throughout the country, on the run, had flooded the capital. Suzanne could see soldiers wandering about aimlessly; one of them, maybe seventeen, with angry eyes, aimed his M-16 at an old Vietnamese woman selling *pho*, laughed, then lowered his rifle and kicked over her soup stall. Up ahead, a dozen or so soldiers, very drunk and bellowing hysterically, were racing down Tu Do, arm in arm, scattering everyone before them. These young boys, revved up for war over the years, now suddenly unplugged and gone berserk, demoralized, leaderless, roaming the streets, aiming their frustrations at the very people they were supposed to defend. In their tattered uniforms, they contrasted surrealistically with the beautiful Vietnamese girls in their elegant *ao dais*. ARVN soldiers: invaders of their own capital.

Up to now, it all had been theories and war games; she had been caught in her father's scenario versus Tony's. Now, reality crashed through. Ban Me Thuot. Nha Trang. The frantic crowds at the Embassy. Anh. And the soldiers.

Suzanne's vision began to blur. Her hands felt sweaty, her legs weak. She had never felt this before but she knew what it was: plain fear. She stood still for a moment. The faintness passed. But the heat of the morning had already begun to incinerate Saigon, overwhelming her. She felt that she had better sit down in some cool place.

The Givral, a favorite meeting place for the city's resident cynics, was just down the street, at the intersection of Tu Do and Le Loi, across from the Continental Palace Hotel. Suzanne moved quickly through the Vietnamese crowds and pushed open the bistro's heavy glass door. Even though it was not yet 9 A.M., the place was jammed with its usual clientele — unemployed sophisticates, café intellectuals, a few journalists, a scattering of anonymous espresso-drinkers, all sitting around Formica-topped tables, analyzing the first of the day's output of plots, conspiracies, and gossip. The Givral was not *haute cuisine* but it was *haut rumeur*, and *tout Saigon* crossed its portals at one time or another during the day to tune in on "Radio Givral."

All the tables were taken. Suzanne was about to leave when

she felt another wave of faintness. She looked around and spotted a table for two occupied by a Vietnamese woman in her forties, sleekly groomed, in a blue *ao dai*. Swiftly, Suzanne brushed past the maître d' and sat down in the vacant chair. She smiled at the woman, murmuring an apology. The woman responded with a tense, preoccupied nod. A waiter approached, Suzanne ordered a *citron soda*, and it was set before her a moment or two later.

As she picked up the tall cool glass and put the straw to her lips, Suzanne tried to avoid the disquieting gaze of the woman. The staring eyes had suddenly turned menacing. Suzanne was about to excuse herself, to look for another table, when the woman began to shout, her manicured hands pounding the table, her high-heeled shoes stomping on the floor. It was as though Suzanne's very presence had detonated her.

"You are an American, yes?" she shrieked in English. The Givral's clientele went silent, in itself a rare occurrence. All heads turned toward the two of them.

Suzanne tried smiling but the smile was short-circuited by the woman's high-voltage fury. Am I *ashamed* to say yes? Suzanne looked helplessly at the woman and at the other customers. Their eyes were fixed on her; no one spoke. Suzanne finally nodded.

"You Americans — you have had enough of us! You will . . . . abandon us!" The woman was screaming now. "And what will happen?" She leaned across the table, her face rigid with hostility.

Suzanne stiffened. The waiter who had brought her the *citron soda* came over and pleaded with the woman in Vietnamese, trying to calm her.

"What will happen to us?" the woman kept shouting, pushing the waiter away. "I don't know who you are but you are an American. That is enough. *You* will all go home — and leave *us* to the *Communists*." Again, she leaned toward Suzanne. "And do you know what will happen to us?" She spat out the words. "They will kill us."

Suzanne was stunned by the woman's outburst. She tried to stand but her legs would not hold her. Her hands trembled. She felt as though she had just been stripped and was sitting there fully exposed — naked, white, her very nationality a crime.

This time, the manager of the Givral approached the table. Speaking gently, he half-lifted the woman from her chair, took her by the arm, and led her to the entrance of the Givral. *"They will kill us!"* were her last words as the heavy glass door closed behind her.

Suzanne stared around the room. No one offered her so much as a smile of comfort. For the Givral's habitués, it was just another little episode in the constant drama of Saigon. They went back to their espresso. Suzanne finally managed to push herself out of the chair; she walked toward the door.

"Oh, that lady is crazy," muttered a middle-aged Vietnamese man, sitting at a table with three friends. "She comes here every day now looking for Americans. She made a mistake yesterday. She shouted at an Australian." His friends nodded their heads in confirmation. "It's like that with all the Vietnamese these days." His friends nodded again. "But don't worry, mademoiselle. She's harmless."

"Harmless," one of the other men at the table repeated. "Why? Because she's Vietnamese."

The Givral erupted in laughter.

Suzanne pushed open the glass door. She stood on the sidewalk, numbed, shocked by the assault.

It was much hotter now, the crowds were beginning to thicken, and so was the traffic. In fact, traffic was at a complete standstill. Suzanne looked down Le Loi and saw the cause of the massive jam-up: a big black hearse, with funeral wreaths hanging from the windows, blocked all movement at the other end of the street. The vehicles trapped by the hearse were honking their high-pitched horns, and Saigon's policemen in white uniforms — "the white mice," as they were known — were blasting their whistles. Even by Saigon standards, it was a major traffic jam. Window-shoppers along Le Loi stood staring at the snarled traffic, storekeepers spilled into the street, children on their way to school stopped to watch the show. A Saigon spectacle, Suzanne thought: the crowds, the cars, all immobilized by the black limousine of death. She stared at the hearse. Perhaps the shimmering heat was playing tricks with her eyes; she could see no driver in the front seat.

Within an instant, before she could look again, she heard a massive, ear-splitting explosion. The hearse — vanished. Nothing but thick black smoke. Automobiles, bicycles, pedicabs — demolished, scattered in all directions. Bodies — strewn over Le Loi. A woman in a white blouse and black pantaloons. A man in a blue shirt. Two little girls and a boy in their school clothes, their books crazily intact, piled neatly beside them. Pools of blood staining the asphalt. Shattered glass cascading to the ground. A few ARVN soldiers contributed to the pandemonium by firing their M-16s into the sky. Everyone in the Givral had raced out onto the sidewalk. Suzanne could see the woman in the blue *ao dai*, nearby, cross herself.

"VC," said a French journalist whom Suzanne recognized from the Givral. "Fill a coffin with explosives, load it on the hearse, and drive it into the center of town. Boom!" The smoke was now beginning to billow above the five-story apartment buildings. "Their whole strategy is to frighten the people here, spread the panic. Same thing as during the Tet offensive in 'sixty-eight." He shook his head. "Only this time it will be worse."

Within a few minutes, ambulances, their sirens wailing, arrived at the scene, and a bulldozer was being rolled in to clear away the twisted bits and pieces of the hearse and the nearby vehicles. Suzanne stood with the crowd, watching. By late afternoon, the street would return to normal. Traffic would flow again, window-shopping would begin again, and the only reminder of the blast would be a deep hole in the middle of Le Loi.

Suzanne began walking slowly toward the orphanage. She

looked at her watch. Only a few minutes past ten. What would the rest of the day bring?

"Sooz-zinn." Thi, trailed by Thach, broke out of the circle of Vietnamese children playing on the lawn and leaped up to throw her arms around Suzanne. Thach was around Suzanne's neck a leap later. She hugged and kissed them. They were wearing the same outfits as the other kids — hand-me-down black rayon trousers, white shirts, and plastic sandals — but Suzanne could not resist the feeling that "my two kids" seemed to have more spark, vitality, just plain excitement. She walked them back to their friends and pulled up a wicker chair to watch them play *nhay lo co*. Thi, a big grin on her face, her long black hair flying wildly, hopped on one foot from square to square but couldn't make it to the end and collapsed on the ground in a burst of laughter. All the other kids applauded. Thach then tried his luck, made it all the way, and the kids hoisted him onto their shoulders. Thach was the winner; he smiled shyly, covering his mouth with both his hands to hide his missing front tooth.

But even as she joined in the applause, Suzanne found herself besieged by questions. Are you really serious about these kids, about being responsible for them? Or are you simply playing "mother," Junior League lady who puts in an hour or two a week at the foundling home — so long as these visits do not conflict with tennis or a lunch date? Do you really love these kids, I mean, love them enough to undertake the obligations that go with love? Or are they just a whim, a Saigon diversion?

For almost a year now, ever since her arrival in Saigon, she had spent time with them and gotten to know their strengths, weaknesses, moods. Once, when Thi came down with a recurrence of malaria, Suzanne had stayed six days in a row at the orphanage; during that period, Thi and Thach had become "my two kids." But Suzanne also knew that "my two kids" were "my two kids" only within the unreality of a wartime capital, where a "lifelong" friendship between an American and a Vietnamese ended abruptly the day the American was rotated back home.

She reached out, one hand for Thi, the other for Thach, and led them inside the house for lunch.

Lunch turned out to be a special treat; the Vietnamese women volunteers had brought a variety of tasty dishes. Suzanne and the two children sat together at a rickety wooden table. Suzanne had allowed them to believe it was they who had taught her to use chopsticks, and now they looked on proudly as she picked the miniature egg-roll the Vietnamese called *cha gio*, and dipped it neatly into the saucer of *nuoc mam*, the indispensable, powerfully pungent fish sauce. Thi had mischievously held Suzanne's nose the first few times she had tried *nuoc mam*. Now Thach, as always eager to please her, raced off and came back with a glass of iced tea. For an instant, Suzanne worried about whether the water used to make the ice had been boiled, but the thought shamed her, and she dropped three extra cubes into her glass and drank the tea quickly.

She walked Thi and Thach back to their friends — there were about a hundred kids in all, and the chatter was deafening — then she returned to the house for a private talk with Madame Nguyen Thi Can, who ran the orphanage.

"How are the kids getting along?" Suzanne asked.

Madam Can did not need any translations. "Given the way things are going," she replied, loosening the collar of her *ao dai*, "they're getting along remarkably well. They are young but, even at five, six, or seven, they are already war veterans. Somehow they find a way to adjust."

"What about *later*?"

"*Later?*" she asked. "It all depends on *where* later is. If it's in America, it's one thing. If it's here, who at this point really knows?" She realized that Suzanne was struggling with a decision. "You still have time, Miss Walker," she said.

"Yes," Suzanne replied quietly. "But not much."

She walked outside with Madame Can, and they stood

watching a hopscotch game. The kids were having a great time, jumping, laughing, a smooth stream of Vietnamese chatter linking them together. There was a happy intimacy about the group, safe, for the moment, in their world. Who has the right, Suzanne asked herself, to plunge them into an alien culture? *This* is their home, not America. Here, they have their own friends, customs, language; here, they are not strangers, not targets of America's resentments about Viet Nam, not curiosities.

She looked into their faces, shining, alert, eager, and remembered a recent incident. An American civilian contract-worker for whom Saigon had been a gold mine was throwing a spectacular farewell party for himself at the Continental. Open house for Americans in town. Tony had asked Suzanne to join him there for a drink, and Suzanne had been surprised to see, in the midst of the crowd of Americans, two Vietnamese children, about Thi and Thach's age, standing alone.

"Who are they?" Suzanne had asked.

"Sheeeet, Mizz Walker," the host had replied, taking another gulp of gin. "Who knows? Picked them up in the street an hour ago. Maybe I'll take 'em home with me." He giggled, winked at Suzanne. "Couple of little 'gooks' to show the neighbors I been to the war. Souvenirs, like. Yeah—a couple of souvenirs! Right, Mizz Walker?"

The thought struck her, as she watched Thi and Thach, that the truly moral answer to the question of whether or not to evacuate them was not an automatic patriotic "yes"; a "no" might have even more validity. The decision had to go beyond any readiness on her part to assume the full-time job of raising them, educating them, nourishing them into adulthood, beyond her own distaste for abandoning them to the Communist victors; the decision had to be based on something as simple and elusive as what would be best for Thi and Thach. How could she know? All she had to work with was her own intuition, and she realized that whatever she decided would not be foolproof.

Suzanne felt Thi and Thach tugging at her. She kissed each

of them and asked Madame Can to explain that she would be back very soon. She passed through the gates of the orphanage and started toward the residence. The traffic was worse than usual — held up by streams of refugees from areas newly overrun by the NVA. They filled the streets, carrying sacks of belongings, pulling loaded wooden carts, dragging small children behind them. The dull thud of artillery fire from the suburbs of the capital was growing steadily louder.

25

"It's a Colonel Stankiewicz," Helen said over the intercom. "He's sure you'll want to talk to him immediately."

"Let him wait, Helen," Walker said. "Count to twenty before you put him on."

Walker stared at the ceiling, trying not to think of what he would like to tell the Colonel to do, right now. Finally, he picked up the phone. "Colonel?" He kept his voice a flat monotone.

"Mr. Ambassador?" The Colonel's voice, by contrast, was eager.

"Yes, this is Ambassador Walker." Walker allowed his voice an edge of impatience. He had no interest in how he came through; this was a job, a despicable job to which he'd been assigned by the marathon runner in the White House. "Do you have a reply for me?"

"Yes."

"What is it?" he asked curtly.

"I have been authorized," the Colonel said, "to say that the Democratic Republic of Viet Nam, given its desire for peace and in keeping with its unswerving commitment to the 'Agreement on Ending the War and Restoring Peace in Viet Nam,' reached in Paris in January, nineteen seventy-three, has given serious consideration to the proposal put forth by the Government of the United States of America and accepts . . ."

I never had any doubt that the Democratic Republic of Viet Nam would accept. So much for the geniuses who insisted that the North Vietnamese, once they were within striking distance of Saigon, would refuse to negotiate.

". . . the American proposal for a 'National Council of Reconciliation and Concord,' as set forth in the 'Agreement on Ending the War and Restoring Peace in Viet Nam,' as signed in Paris."

The sonofabitch is programmed. They stick the words deep into his throat and he regurgitates them syllable for syllable.

"In other words, a coalition," the Colonel emphasized.

"I never said 'coalition,' " Walker cut in.

"A coalition," the Colonel repeated. "A coalition."

"In other words, yes, you agree to a meeting," Walker said impatiently.

"Yes! To discuss a 'coalition'!" The Colonel's voice was triumphant.

Walker knifed in in an effort to cut out the sense of victory. "The immediate question," he said, "is to set up a meeting to work out the necessary preliminary details before any formal talks take place."

"Yes," the Colonel replied. "I have been authorized to say that the Democratic Republic of Viet Nam is ready to dispatch its senior representative on the four-party Joint Military Commission, now based at Tan Son Nhut airport in accordance with the Paris Agreement, to meet the representative of the United States at any mutually agreed site."

Walker had already thought about a suitable site for the first sensitive contact to take place. It was a "safe house" operated by the CIA right in the middle of Saigon. So far as the "spooks" knew, the secrecy linking the "safe house" to the CIA had never been penetrated.

"The U.S. proposes that the meeting take place at a private

and well-protected residence at twenty-two Hong Thap Tu," Walker said.

A barely controlled chuckle sounded in Walker's ear. "That is agreeable," the Colonel said. "That house is well known to the Democratic Republic of Viet Nam."

Walker winced. Goddamn Sommers and his "safe house." "Time?" Walker asked.

"Four o'clock this afternoon."

Walker glanced at his watch. It was now 2 P.M. "All right," he said. "Our side will be represented by one of my —"

"That is *not* agreeable."

Too bad. Starting the negotiations on a lower level would slow things down, maybe produce a useful deadlock.

"Would you repeat that?" Walker asked.

"That is *not* agreeable," the Colonel said. "I have been specifically authorized to state that the representative of the Democratic Republic of Viet Nam is prepared to meet only with the Ambassador from the United States."

"Only with the Ambassador?"

"Only with the Ambassador."

Dilemma. If I agree to meet with them, to begin the negotiations at the highest level, that might be rushing things, conceding eagerness. But if I don't agree and then am obligated by Washington to reverse my position, that would be perceived as a retreat.

"Let me restate my position," Walker said diplomatically, clearing his throat. "The United States will of course be represented by the Ambassador."

"Then you have agreed to all the points that I have set forth on behalf of the DRV?"

"No," Walker said sharply. "We have *both* agreed to the various details in connection with establishing the first contact."

"Mr. Ambassador, it would therefore seem that all has been agreed —"

"I don't think we have anything more to say to each other,"

214

Walker interrupted. Without saying goodbye, he put down the phone. Then he picked up a pencil and began to write:

SECRET SPECAT EXCLUSIVE
FROM AMEMBASSY SAIGON
TO SECSTATE WASHINGTON
POLISH CONTACT JUST TELEPHONED TO SAY DRV HAS AGREED TO MEETING TO DISCUSS NEGOTIATIONS AS PER YOUR INSTRUCTIONS. SESSION SET FOR FOUR PYEM SAIGON TIME. FYI PERSONAL EYE HAVE NO HEART FOR THIS ASSIGNMENT WHICH EYE REGARD ABSOLUTELY CONTRARY TO U.S. INTERESTS.

WALKER

He reread the cable. It would, he knew, be rushed to the Secretary the instant it clicked into the Ops room at State, then it would be locked up in the archives for the required quarter of a century. Twenty-five years? Walker smiled. A discreet leak, at the proper moment, was always possible, wasn't it? To prove that he had consistently warned against negotiating with the DRV.

He walked down the hallway to the communications room and handed the cable to the code clerk for immediate transmission via back channels. He glanced at his watch. It was now 2:30.

First, the DAO. Then, the CIA. Last, the DRV — and the contact with the DRV was less than ninety minutes from now.

That did not leave Walker with much time to get a final sitrep, a situation report, prior to his critical sessions with "the other side," but even so he decided that it would be most productive to arrange for separate briefings by General Collins and by John Sommers; otherwise, the DAO general and the station chief would simply echo each other, nod in each other's direction, find safety in numbers even though the number was only two. Failure to forecast the NVA attack on Ban Me Thuot had shaken them badly. Since then, Collins and Sommers had taken to predicting nothing but disaster regardless of the indicators. It was their insurance policy; no one ever wrote a bureaucrat a letter of commendation for predicting success but all he had to do was fail to predict a fiasco and he'd find himself drawn and quartered.

Collins's and Sommers's preoccupation with self-protection was an extravagance that Walker could not afford, not just now. What he needed most urgently was an accurate and independent readout of just how close the NVA had penetrated to Saigon and the degree of ARVN's resistance — if any. Plus an assessment of Hanoi's immediate strategy. These details would be critical at any time, never more so than now; they would determine the strengths and weaknesses — in reverse order, Walker thought wryly — of his own negotiating hand. True, in the final analysis, if your side was losing the war on the battlefield, you didn't win it at the conference table — but that did not mean that you simply hoisted the white flag. The trick was to keep your adversaries on edge about the military options still at your disposal. Not that you could extract victory from defeat. But maybe you could extract what he had taken to calling "positive negatives." Non-humiliation. Non-surrender. Non-dishonor.

The DAO first; the CIA, twenty minutes later. He would get their separate assessments before briefing either of them on the latest news: the upcoming DRV contact.

Collins, his two stars glittering on his military uniform, entered the Ambassador's office. His lean face was etched with its usual worry. "The only reason ARVN is still in position around Saigon," he began as he pulled his chair away from Walker's desk, "is that the NVA simply hasn't given the final push. All the indicators are on the NVA's side." He began ticking them off on his fingers. "Manpower. Ordnance. Morale. Hell, the NVA can already feel Saigon in the palm of its hand."

"See any way for Saigon to hang on?" Walker asked. A Saigon that was still hanging on could be a negotiating counter-point in his bargaining with the DRV. But Walker knew what Collins's answer would be.

"Hang on? No. Hang? Yes." The General seemed eager to wrap up his assessment.

Why do I have the feeling that Collins can't wait to send his uniform and his face to the dry cleaner so that they'll be nice and fresh for the next war? Walker pinned the General to the chair with questions for another few minutes, but Collins responded with variations of his first reply: no openings anywhere, no ideas on how to thwart the NVA. Walker gave a slight nod of thanks to Collins for his sitrep and asked him to wait outside.

Two minutes later, Sommers had replaced the General in the chair opposite the Ambassador's desk.

"Just saw Collins as I was coming in," the CIA station chief began, clenching his hands. "Want him here?"

Walker shook his head. "I'd like to have your views now," he said. "And then we can all get together." The look on Sommers's face suggested that he was not too happy being played off against Collins. Walker ignored it. "Shoot," he said. "What's the latest you have?"

The station chief's voice was gloomy. "That 'firecracker' that the VC set off on Le Loi today gives you some idea of where the North Vietnamese now see themselves," Sommers began. "Smack in the middle of town. Yeah, I know, there are still thousands of ARVN troops positioned around Saigon but that's a statistic, not a fighting army." He rubbed his eyes. "Let me put it this way. The NVA could take this town with a telephone call." His fingertips drummed against each other.

"Any way of . . . cutting the phone line?"

"None."

Sommers and Collins, Walker thought. Interchangeable mind sets. "Any idea of their negotiating strategy at this time?" he asked.

"All-out victory," Sommers replied. "They'd be crazy to settle for anything less."

"Do you see any way, John," Walker asked, restraining his impatience with Sommers's negative outlook, "assuming that the NVA does decide to attack the city, that Hanoi can be induced to accept a continuing U.S. presence?"

"Why should they?"

Walker stared at Sommers. "Well, I have always maintained that they may need us once the shooting stops," Walker argued. "For economic reconstruction. As a play-off against China. I thought you might have some ideas on that."

Sommers shook his head. "I don't see it that way," he reiterated.

Walker wondered whether Sommers or Collins would have had the imagination to try to bomb Hanoi with nonexistent B-52s. *Had Starnes ever written that story?*

The intercom buzzed on Walker's desk; he picked up the receiver. "Helen," he said sharply, "I told you, no interruptions."

"I know, Mr. Ambassador, but it's the Secretary of State. He said he must speak to you right away. He's on the line."

Walker glanced at his watch. "Okay," he said, "put him on." He turned to Sommers. "Sorry, John. I have an urgent call from Washington. Would you mind waiting in the other room until I'm through? Should only take a few minutes." Enough time, Walker thought, for another battle in the secret war between the U.S. Embassy and the State Department. Sommers left the office, and Walker picked up the scrambler telephone.

"Hello," said Walker, holding the telephone receiver a good three inches from his ear.

"Goddammit, Hadden!" The Secretary was obviously in no mood for polite preliminaries. "This story in *The Washington Post* this morning. I just can't believe that you would —"

Starnes, you've got my vote for the Pulitzer. "What story?" Walker asked, feigning innocence.

"Come on, Hadden, it's too late for games," the Secretary snapped. "You know goddamned well what I'm talking about. A story datelined 'Saigon' and written by William Starnes. He says . . . let me read you the headline. The *banner* headline."

Walker could hear newspaper crackling at the other end of the line. "Here it is," the Secretary said. " 'ADMINISTRA-TION CONSIDERING USE OF B-FIFTY-TWOS TO HALT NVA OFFENSIVE.' I —"

"Just a minute, Mr. Secretary," Walker cut in, taking the aggrieved offensive. "Does it *quote* me? Or is Starnes concocting it on his own?"

"No, it doesn't quote you," the Secretary thundered, "but a State Department courier just rushed a copy of the *Post* to my house. The ink is all over my pajamas, and your fingerprints are all over the front page."

You can handle that problem with a little soap, Mr. Secretary. The problems you've given me are a lot dirtier.

"I had to wake up the President to tell him about this," the Secretary went on. "He's even more furious than I am. Listen, Hadden, I don't know whether the word has ever reached you but we are at the *end* of the war, not the beginning. We are on our way *out*, not back in."

Walker counted to five before replying. "I don't need any reminders about that," he finally said. "But I still think you could have come up with that extra money for ARVN. Just to give them a fighting chance. If I were in any way involved in the Starnes story . . ."

Walker could hear a snort over the line.

". . . it would be no more immoral than the U.S. decision to cut off ARVN's fighting arm."

"Hadden, goddammit," the Secretary cut in, "you don't know what the hell is going on back here. Congress, the media, the public — they're interested in only one thing: getting the Americans out before the NVA turns up on your doorstep. In other words, you've got to speed things up. The Pentagon tells me planes are leaving from Saigon half, two-thirds empty." The line was silent for a moment. "Nobody's saying it out loud, but everybody's thinking it. . . ."

"Thinking what?"

"That you've been dragging your feet on evacuating Americans. Deliberately."

"Would you translate that for me?" Walker said with barely concealed irritation.

"Goddammit, Hadden, you don't need any translation. People are saying that you are using Americans in Saigon as pawns, keeping them there deliberately even though the NVA is closing in on you so that we, at this end, will have no choice. We will be forced to send in the B-fifty-twos to protect the Americans that you are holding."

"You're all going crazy back there," Walker yelled, his voice just short of conviction.

"Maybe so, but I'm telling you that people here believe it, and more people are believing it every hour. It's in all the newspapers, Hadden. 'Walker — Evacuation Bottleneck.'"

"I'm not surprised," Walker said. "Just a little character-assassination by my colleagues at State, I take it. A little obfuscation of the *real* issue so that they'll come out smelling like roses and I'll be on the shit pile of history."

"That doesn't sound like you, Hadden."

"Mr. Secretary," Walker shot back. "I'm sitting on the edge of a volcano. If Saigon thinks that the U.S. has ordered a full-scale evacuation, this place will panic, and no one, I repeat no one, will get out even if you send in every goddamn plane in the U.S. Air Force to Tan Son Nhut. If I send out what you regard as too few people, then Washington accuses me of foot-dragging. It's a no-win situation."

"Hadden, I'm telling you again, you don't know what the hell is going on back here."

"And you don't know what the hell is going on *here*."

Both sides opted for a twenty-second cease-fire.

"Well, just get the Americans moving out, for Chrissakes," the Secretary finally erupted. "As fast as possible."

"I thought that you of all people would understand that I must proceed with what is known as 'all deliberate speed.'"

"Look, Hadden, I do understand," the Secretary said in a softer tone. "Is there anything we can do at this end to help you?"

"Such as?"

"I mean, what else do you need to make the evacuation work smoothly? I'm thinking about that itemized list of assets that have been made available to you. You know the list I mean?"

"I do."

"Well, it shows that you've got all the evacuation assets in place or moving into place at top speed right now. We've set up a whole task force for you. TF-Seventy-six. You've got half the U.S. Navy standing by within twenty miles of the South Vietnamese coast. You've got carriers loaded with helicopters waiting to take out Americans. You've got Air Force transports standing by at Clark in the Philippines. All waiting — for you to give the go-ahead signal." A pause. "That decision is being left to *you*."

"But the environment here is explosive. You flash the go-signal now and Ban Me Thuot will look like a Sunday outing."

"Maybe so, Hadden, but what I want to know from you is what you need to make the evacuation work. More ships? More helicopters? More planes? More of whatever? We all want it to be a success."

"The problem isn't the assets," Walker shouted. "The problem is to use them in such a way that the evacuation effort does not produce chaos and trap everyone, including the Americans. Can't you people in Washington understand my predicament?"

"Of course we do, Hadden. Everyone back here is rooting for you. But you've got to move faster." The Secretary grunted. "All we need for the grand finale is the sight of hundreds of Americans — taken prisoner by the NVA. That would be the *coup de grâce* for us."

Walker nodded.

"I didn't hear you," the Secretary said.

"What else?" Walker said impatiently. He glanced at his watch. Still an hour to go before the meeting with the DRV.

"Your last back-channel cable says you're going to be meeting with them soon."

"Yes."

"Well, Hadden, you and I have been through a lot of this war together, and I must say that I had never thought it would all come to this."

"Our strategy, if that's the word, made it inevitable."

"Let's not go through that again, Hadden. I just want to wish you good luck."

"Good luck is not enough. Wish me miracles."

"You never give up, do you?" A small laugh traveled halfway around the world. "Good thing, too," the Secretary observed, "given your immediate destination."

As soon as the Secretary hung up, Walker called Collins and Sommers back in. "That was the Secretary," he told them. "He wants to know why we can't do anything right out here." He slammed the desk. "I tell you this — and you can quote me when it's all over: The only policy in Washington right now is CYA! CYA!"

Collins and Somers were staring at him.

"*They* tell me the U.S. Navy is offshore, waiting. *They* tell me that the helicopters are offshore, waiting. *They* tell me that transport planes are at Clark, waiting. 'All waiting for you, Mr. Ambassador, to give the signal; we've provided you with everything necessary to make the evacuation a success!' " Walker was now shouting. "CYA. *Cover your ass.* Well, they're covering *their* asses, all right." He pointed to the telephone. "CYA son-ofabitch."

Walker leaped out of his chair and began pacing the room. "They've set it up in such a way that it is already *my* ass," he said bitterly. He looked at Collins, then Sommers; they both remained silent. "But what they don't realize is that by setting me up in advance . . . the designated scapegoat . . . they've given me freedom of action to do what I think is best — best for the Americans here, best for the United States, best for the Vietnamese."

He looked at his watch. If the Secretary had seen *The Washington Post*, so had the Soviet Embassy in Washington; for fifteen cents, the Russians got more intelligence in a single day than all the KGB operations in Washington got in a year. That would mean that the headline had already been flashed from Washington to Moscow, then from Moscow to Hanoi, then from Hanoi to the representative of the DRV who would be meeting with Walker in less than an hour. Would the headline, the threat of B-52s, in any way alter Hanoi's negotiating position? Well, he would know soon enough.

"All right gentlemen," he said, "that does it. I want you to know that I'll be sitting face to face with the DRV within an hour."

Collins and Sommers looked at each other, surprised.

"All I want to say now is that a contact has been made," Walker explained, "the objective being to see whether some kind of Saigon–Hanoi regime can be set up here. Maybe, just maybe, we can forestall an absolute Hanoi takeover." He glanced at Sommers. "I'll tell you something you'll find hard to believe, John, but when I suggested that we meet at twenty-two Hong Thap Tu, they said they knew all about twenty-two Hong Thap Tu."

"They could, you know, be bluffing . . . ," Sommers said defensively.

"Never mind, John. That house hasn't much of a future now."

Walker reached into his desk and took out a thick loose-leaf folder. A label on the jacket read: "Operation Frequent Wind." It was the top-secret plan for the emergency evacuation of the United States from South Viet Nam. He riffled through the pages.

"All set to go . . . when the signal is given. Correct?" he asked.

Collins and Sommers nodded.

"Quick review," Walker went on. "Our first three options differ only in detail but they are all based on using fixed-wing airplanes operating out of Tan Son Nhut. Fixed-wing planes mean evacuating more people. But if Tan Son Nhut comes under NVA attack and is closed down, then it's Option Four — an evacuation by helicopters only. The main evacuation points in that case will be at the LZs at the DAO but we'll also be using the chopper pad on the roof of the Embassy and the chopper pad we will be creating in the Embassy parking lot. Both of these LZs, you understand, will be small-scale — only for Americans here and the few Vietnamese staffers at the Embassy. Right?"

Sommers suddenly spoke. "To use the Embassy parking lot, we're going to have to" — he suddenly lapsed into CIA language — "terminate the tamarind tree with extreme prejudice."

"No," Walker said firmly. "Not until I give the order. Cut that tree down too early and you might as well stand on top of Doc Lap and sound the fire alarm! You'll touch off a riot." He stared at Sommers. "The tree stands."

"But it's got to come down," Sommers persisted. "Wait till later — and it may be too late. Even our own people here in the Embassy are getting restless, itchy."

"No," Walker repeated icily. "The tree stands. Until the last moment. Until I say it comes down."

Sommers shrugged. He looked at Collins but Collins said nothing.

" 'Frequent Wind' goes into effect automatically on only one condition," Walker cautioned. "Only if the NVA should start to attack Saigon. Not before. There still may be some cards we can play to head off total humiliation."

"Listen, Mr. Ambassador," Sommers said, "I wouldn't count too much on your meeting with the DRV. The NVA has practically got it all anyway."

Walker gave Sommers a cutting look. "They have agreed to meet with me to negotiate, haven't they?"

Sommers, his jaw clenched, looked at the ceiling.

"That's it, gentlemen," Walker said.

"Good luck," said Sommers lamely.

"Same," said Collins.

As they opened the door and left, Helen brushed by them. "I can't hold him off much longer, Mr. Ambassador. He says he's got to see you — right away!"

"Calm down. *Who's* got to see me?"

"The police chief — General Xuan."

"You told him I'll be tied up all afternoon . . . ?"

"If you took a look at him, you'd know he's not in any mood to make an appointment. What do I do?"

Walker knew Xuan was brutal, dangerous, unpredictable — and that his cooperation would be indispensable in any all-out U.S. evacuation.

"Okay," Walker said with disgust. "Send him in."

Xuan was in Walker's office within seconds.

Walker was stunned by the sight of him; Xuan had obviously tried to disguise his identity. His immaculate white uniform as chief of the city's "white mice" had been replaced by a baggy gray suit, his merciless eyes hidden behind huge dark sunglasses, his aura of power gone. It was difficult to believe that this man, single-handedly, had terrified all of Saigon for years. Want to buy an exit visa? See Xuan and fill his hands with dollars. Need a permit to open a bar on Tu Do and stock it with whores? Just give Xuan a kickback. Want to peddle drugs without any harassment by the police? Make sure Xuan gets his rake-off. Bribery, embezzlement, and extortion were his way of life, and the first words out of his mouth made it clear that his outer transformation had not changed his way of doing business.

"I need an airplane right away," Xuan began, his voice threatening. "To get my family out of Saigon. No time for discussions now. I just want you to make the plane available." Walker, staring at Xuan, had no doubt that his bulging pockets were filled with hundred-dollar bills; Saigon's top law-enforcement officer had packed up his essentials and wanted out. The panic that Walker feared stood right here in front of him. But Walker knew that he had better play it cool, reminding himself that he would need Xuan and his police force to keep the mobs under control once an evacuation got underway.

"General," Walker replied with exaggerated patience, "I have an urgent appointment now. Can we talk about this a little later in the day?" He left his chair and began walking toward the door.

"No," Xuan shouted. "Not later. Now." He blocked the door. "And you have no choice. You will give me the plane."

Walker stopped short. "What do you mean, I have no choice?" he asked angrily.

"You are making your plans to get out, and I am making my plans. I need a plane," he demanded. *"Now."*

"General, you force me to be blunt. *No!"*

"Yes! Because I am holding your daughter . . . hostage."

Walker felt a sudden tightening in his chest. He reached for his chair and sat down heavily.

"Don't worry," Xuan added swiftly. "She's all right, unhurt. Just being . . . held."

"You sonofabitch!" Walker shouted.

"No, *you* sonofabitch!" Xuan outshouted Walker. "We've already been listening to you for too long. I'm going to save myself. And you'll give me that plane — if you want your daughter."

Walker stared at Xuan with contempt. "How can you think of trying to save your own skin — *now* — when South Viet Nam is fighting to stay alive? Do you know what *I* am trying to do — to prevent a bloodbath?"

Xuan laughed. "We know everything. You think we are stupid — but it is *you* who are stupid. Stupid for thinking that because you have white faces you can run the world. When they come here — the 'gooks' from the North — they will wipe the floor with you!"

Walker leaped from his chair, made a move toward the door.

Xuan stepped forward to block the exit, then with a swift thrust of his right arm, knocked Walker to the floor. Xuan, legs apart, hands on hips, stood over him.

"And don't tell me," Xuan shouted, "that there are no planes available, either. I know that you've made a plane available to fly out — broken old dishes."

The telephone conversation with Phan Thanh Giang flashed through Walker's mind.

"You have no choice, Mr. Ambassador," Xuan stared down at him.

Walker, trying to collect his thoughts, to prepare for his next move, braced himself against a chair and pulled himself, as slowly as possible, to his feet. He faced Xuan and spoke as calmly as he could manage. "General, if you go, and the word gets out that even the Vietnamese generals are fleeing, how can you expect ARVN to fight on?"

Xuan laughed contemptuously. "Don't appeal to my honor. I have none left. Neither do you."

It was hopeless. "Where is my daughter?" Walker asked, his voice suddenly a whisper. The very question filled him with shame; it was as though he were witnessing the collapse of his own integrity by even hinting that Suzanne's personal safety could be used as blackmail against him.

"Oh, she's in a safe place," Xuan said, his voice now less threatening, convinced that he was on the verge of success. "She understands."

"I would appreciate it, General," Walker said with iron control, "if you did not hurt her."

"My people won't hurt her," Xuan muttered. "But if you call for your Marine guards to move against me, I would not be able to communicate with my people and then I could not be in a position to guarantee her safety." He grinned.

Walker could think of no immediate strategy, except to stall for time. He glanced at his watch. Forty minutes to go. "Look, General," he said, "I *must* keep this appointment. I'll call as soon as I get back here."

Xuan nodded. "I will wait for you — here."

They exchanged looks of mutual hostility. Walker stormed out of the office, Xuan right behind him. Xuan sat down in the anteroom. Walker took his private elevator to the lobby.

He emerged into a mass of pushing and shoving Vietnamese, now frantic to fight their way into the consular office. Shouldering his way through the crowd, he stepped out into the sunlight.

The weather was unconscionably beautiful, the sky clear, a slight breeze ruffling the leaves of the tamarind tree. Walker was, for a moment, soothed by the sight of its sturdy, invulnerable trunk. But his eye caught a slash, a whiteness in the brown bark. No mistaking it. Axes had dug V-shaped wedges into the tamarind. Against his orders. They'd done it behind his back. He stared at the tree. The slashes were on the side he couldn't see from his office window.

Bastards. Chopping away. Ready to run. Preparing for the end.

His voice, when he gave instructions to the driver, was so weak that he had to repeat the address three times. Finally, they headed toward 22 Hong Thap Tu.

26

The first time Tony simply misdialed the number. The second time he forgot the number midway in the dialing. The third time he dialed the first two numbers — and then stopped. The fourth time, tensing up like a sniper looking through the crosshairs of a gunsight, he took careful aim at the ring of digits and then picked the numbers off one after the other: Five. Six. Four. Seven. Nine.

"*Chao ong.*"

Damn, it was her father. As soon as he heard the Vietnamese "hello," Tony remembered the silken voice, sounds that clung together for only an instant before evaporating.

"Hello," said Tony. He waited. "Hello?" No answer. "Anybody there?" Still no answer, but he could hear two voices whispering urgently in the background.

"Hel-lo. . . ." The silken voice was gone. This one, he knew at once, belonged to Duc.

"Hello," answered Tony, trying not to convey impatience. He had hoped for Anh to pick up the phone the moment it rang so that he would not have to go through the whole family before he got to her; the voices of her father and her brother revived his guilt for having so casually abandoned Anh on his return to Saigon in 1974, guilt long buried under his feeling for Suzanne and rekindled by Anh and Duc's appearance at his door earlier in the day, guilt now compounded by their anguished appeal for help.

"Tony?" said Duc eagerly.

"Yes, Duc," he said. "It's Tony. Is Anh home?"

More whispering at the other end.

"Tony," Duc finally responded, "Anh went out of the house for a moment, but . . ."

Goddamn.

". . . she told me that if you called" — his voice now had nervous laughter tinging the edges — "to say that she would be back in ten minutes."

Tony glanced at his watch. Two-thirty P.M. Six hours since he had seen Anh and Duc.

"Ten minutes?"

"Yes."

"Tell Anh I'm on my way over to see her."

"Oh, that is good," said Duc. Tony could hear the rush of relief in Duc's voice. "She will be very happy to see you. I will tell her."

Tony was not looking forward to this visit. To go at all meant a personal pledge to help Anh's family out of Saigon: I, Anthony Catlett, Central Intelligence Agency, U.S. Passport 4687623, am your magic carpet out of here — if it comes to that. His humiliating behavior at Nha Trang suddenly surfaced and he tried to sweep it away, his mind suddenly a windmill blowing gusts of memories: a visit to the Hollywoodish Cao Dai Temple at Tay Ninh, a Sunday at the beach in the coastal city of Vung Tau, a moonlight sampan ride along Hue's Perfume River. Was it with Anh or Suzanne that he had gone to Tay Ninh? It suddenly struck him that in dialing Anh he was really dialing himself and he was not getting through. The line, somehow, was out of order.

"I'll be there," said Tony. He was about to put down the telephone but he could still hear Duc's voice, frantic now. "Yes, Duc . . . ?"

"Do you still remember where we live?" Duc asked breathlessly, the relief of a moment ago replaced by embarrassment.

"Still on Le Van Duyet?"

"Yes" — a smile in Duc's voice now. "Number forty-five. The little brown house with the Vietnamese flag in the window."

"Oh yes, I remember, Duc," Tony replied reassuringly. "I'll find it." He hung up.

He picked up a handful of darts and launched them at the bull's-eye on the wall. All misses. Well, at least he was in sync with reality, he thought. He was on his way out the door when he realized that he was still wearing his office clothes — suit and tie. He quickly changed into what the tailors on Tu Do called "a TV suit" — a short-sleeved safari outfit — and rushed down the stairs. The Vietnamese woman who cleaned his apartment was on her way up and she tried to stop him, calling "Mister Catlett," and though he could see the fright in her eyes he kept taking the stairs two at a time. Only when he was outside, racing down Gia Long toward Le Van Duyet, did it strike him that the woman usually cleaned up during the morning and here it was early afternoon. He suddenly realized what it was that she wanted to talk to him about. He could feel it in the street, in the crowds, in the anxiety on the faces of Vietnamese. Escape.

The house was exactly as he remembered: small, one-story, bordered by a narrow strip of grass on each side. The front door still had a crack near the bottom. He tapped once but he recalled that he had, when he was no stranger to 45 Le Van Duyet, established a code to announce his arrival. Four quick taps in a row. He quickly tapped three more times, and there was Anh, in the green *ao dai*, glowing, shyly pleased to see him.

But there was still the barricade of an empty year separating them. They sat down on wicker chairs, facing each other.

2 3 1

"About this morning . . . ," Anh said with embarrassment. "It was Duc who —"

"Oh no, Anh," Tony said. "It's all right. I understand. I should have been in touch with you much earlier. It is I who should be embarrassed."

She smiled. "I understand, too," she said softly.

But the exchange of words had no meaning, just depersonalized sounds, and Tony knew as he looked at her and she looked at him that their emotions were already locked in an intimate dialogue.

"Something to drink?" she asked nervously, and she ran to the kitchen and came back with two glasses of orange crush.

Tony was aware that neither Duc nor her father was in the house. "I just spoke to your —" Tony began, but Anh quickly interrupted. "Oh, they had something to do . . . and decided to do it now." Anh blushed. "About this morning again . . . ," she said, and this time Tony interrupted, "Oh, it's all right," and she said, "No, I mean, you had *company*," and it was Tony's turn to blush, and he said, "Anh . . . ," and she overwhelmed him with a smile that left him wordless.

"How have you been, Anh?" he finally was able to say, reaching for the drink. But even as she began talking, he remembered how her voice always seemed to have a caress in it, a warmth that eddied up to him, and he only half-listened, his mind reaching back to the excitement of their first meeting at the Thanh Le curio shop in 1970. The year since he had last seen her had only ripened her beauty. The old Asian hands had always told him that of all women they preferred the Vietnamese. The Japanese were cool and bowlegged, the Koreans stoic and big-boned, the Chinese businesslike. Only the Vietnamese were both delicately beautiful and unabashedly passionate.

Tony tried again to concentrate on Anh's words. But just a glance at her, at the *ao dai* tugging at her bosom, and he discovered that the feelings he thought were dead had only been lying in ambush, waiting to strike. He suddenly leaped from the chair and reached out to Anh. She stood up, they put their arms around each other, tenderly, and moved toward the open bedroom door.

Anh's love spilled over, as though she had been hoarding it for the last year, inundating him with waves of full-bodied warmth. Her lips began moving over his body, tickling him, nuzzling him. They looked at each other, the untouched year wiped away with a glance, and they reached out again and Tony wrapped his arms tightly around her. Around Suzanne.

Suzanne! He went limp and Anh could sense it and she asked him what was the matter even as she kissed his ears and his arms and his nipples and he said nothing but she said oh yes I can feel it and he said no really and she said yes really and Tony knew she was right but he said nothing and instead he dug his face into Anh's warm neck and let his fingers play along her tiny breasts and damp thighs and he wondered how was it possible for him to be in bed with Anh so suddenly so uncontrollably so explosively when he could have sworn that his own passions were locked into Suzanne and he told himself in what he knew was an obvious effort to break free from the *double* sense of guilt he now felt, Anh *and* Suzanne, that life in Saigon was not anchored in any kind of honesty but rather that Saigon was a hotbed of artificiality frightened people everywhere believing that what they did here was spur-of-the-moment nothing permanent nothing to be recorded in the ledgers but rather that everything here was erasable discardable unreal and that it was the ultimate bit of naiveté of innocence a joke to think that truth and decency were at all possible in a city that was so rotten corrupt for sale. A doomed city, a war civilization on the verge of extinction, people hiding their true identities in their hearts and engaging in a hundred different forgettable lives, especially now with the NVA knocking at the door. A fuck before dying.

Everything false? Even his feelings about Suzanne?

"I understand, Tony," Anh whispered. She tried to comfort him told him not to agonize about their being together it was just a souvenir of their friendship and he shook his head and shouted no no no and he stared at her and demanded to know whether her father and Duc had left the house so that she could be alone with him her body for an exit visa and she turned away and he kept shouting answer me and he could see tears forming in those incredibly beautiful almond-shaped eyes and he leaned over and kissed her and they wrapped themselves together.

Gently, afterwards, he tucked her into his arms and promised her that he would take her and Duc and her father out of Saigon.

"I will call you when the time comes to leave," he said, and Anh looked at him and nodded. "But if for some crazy reason I can't reach you, if the telephone lines are cut or I'm not near a telephone or whatever, what I want, Anh, is for you to come to the Embassy, you and Duc and your father. There will be a mob there, so what you must do if you are stuck outside is to tie your green *ao dai*" — he pointed to the dress heaped on the bedroom floor — "to a bamboo pole and wave it. I will see it from inside the Embassy and I will come out to get you."

Anh was crying and laughing. "The green *ao dai?*"

He nodded.

She smiled and she pulled him close and kissed him.

Fifteen minutes later, he was racing through the streets in the direction of the Embassy. The mood of the crowd was increasingly anxious, even ominous. He suddenly stopped, spun around, certain that Suzanne was pursuing him. But the only person behind him was a grinning old Vietnamese peasant woman, a black turban on her head, her face gnarled, her teeth stained black with betel juice. He reached into his pocket and came up with a handful of piastres — eager to pay for the sheer relief of finding that it wasn't Suzanne. He resumed his sprint toward the Embassy but, just as he approached the main gate, he had to pull back to avoid being hit by a small departing car. He caught a glimpse of the passenger in the rear seat. The Ambassador? Tony couldn't help laughing. Shit, even Walker's limousine had broken down.

27

The Ambassador had deliberately chosen an unmarked car for the rendezvous. According to his calculations, it would take six minutes to reach 22 Hong Thap Tu and another two minutes to reconnoiter the outside and inside. That would leave him seven minutes before the representative of DRV was due to arrive, at exactly 4:00 P.M. Walker recognized that under the circumstances a seven-minute wait could be an eternity, but, precisely because of the circumstances, he wanted the time to solo amid his own emotions.

What would it feel like, waiting for the enemy to cross the threshold? Being the *first American* ever instructed to negotiate a U.S. defeat? Not only was he curious about what his state of mind would be during those split seconds just prior to the face-to-face meeting, he also wanted time to ready himself for his role as the U.S. representative, as well as for his *private* role as the third man at the negotiations. The invisible onlooker. The outraged American. Hadden Walker, U.S. citizen, in contrast to Ambassador Hadden Walker, diplomatic machine, dials controlled by Washington. Two totally different men, he felt, sharing an antagonistic coexistence, with the Citizen determined to keep the Ambassador at arm's length, as though it were an embarrassment to be seen with him. Yes, when it was all over, however it ended, he would promptly shed his official identity and write his own account of the collapse of South Viet Nam. "AN AMERICAN BETRAYAL" BY HADDEN WALKER, AMERICA'S LAST AMBASSADOR TO SAIGON. He could see the books stacked across the country, the dust jacket showing a triumphant Ho and a cringing America. A book setting it all out. Just as war was too dangerous to entrust to the generals, so too was history too critical to entrust to the historians. Or to the politicians. Or, worst of all, to the CYA idiots at the State Department. Someone on the inside had to tell the truth.

But his fifteen-minute timetable was quickly thrown off by the traffic. Thong Nhat, the main boulevard, was clogged, a pile-up of cars and tanks, bicycles and Hondas, *ao dais* and khaki, men, women, children, whipped by fear, beginning to descend on the Embassy as their last refuge. Saigon: a sewer backing up. Wouldn't it be a lovely touch, the last straw, Saigon's ultimate revenge, Walker thought wryly, if it turned out that he missed his appointment with the DRV because he was trapped in a traffic jam? The driver lost three full minutes just carving his way through the tangle of vehicles and people and then he broke free and made a right turn on Hai Ba Trung and headed for Hong Thap Tu, just up the street. The car passed the Nguyen Dynasty shop along the way, and Walker for a fleeting instant wondered when he would ever haggle again with Professor Hoan over a sixteenth-century Chinese vase.

Hai Ba Trung! There it was, spelled out — a symbol of Viet Nam's suspicions of the Chinese. He must exploit that in his negotiations with the DRV, play on the latent Vietnamese hostility toward their neighbors. The war may have thrown the Vietnamese and the Chinese together, Walker thought, but history had more often cast them as enemies. The evidence was on street-corner signposts all over Saigon: Hai Ba Trung, Tran Hung Dao, Le Loi, among others, all major thoroughfares in the capital city, all named for Vietnamese heroes and heroines who over the centuries had fought the invaders sent south by the Forbidden City in Peking.

Pages of Viet Nam's bloodied past began turning over in his

mind; he had, on being named Ambassador, plunged into the history books in search of clues to the enigmatic makeup of the Vietnamese. It was the least he could do, he remembered thinking, to offset America's crippling ignorance of its ally south of the seventeenth parallel and its enemy north of it. He recalled a story making the rounds in the early 'sixties about two American generals meeting in the Pentagon and one saying, "What are you doing?" and the other replying, "Studying Vietnamese," and the first general saying, "How interesting; where are you going?"

All right, *he* knew better. Knew that during the thousand years that China's emperors lorded it over Viet Nam, the Vietnamese had revolted *ten times*. But the Chinese, after finally being forced into retreat, in A.D. 939, kept trying to come back, the last effort to reconquer Viet Nam made as recently as two centuries ago. In his talk with the DRV, he would scratch at the scabs of the old wounds. Tell them that the Mao Dynasty wasn't much different from its predecessors. Point out that the aid from "Big Brother" was prompted not by love for Hanoi but by hate for the "American Imperialists." The Chinese, my dear friend, are ready to fight to the last Vietnamese. God, he would stick that sentence in like a knife and twist it. Yes, he would hold out a little bait, dangle the possibility that the U.S., postwar, *might* shore up Hanoi's own determination not to be turned into a Chinese satellite — this, not free, oh no, but in return for several things: *no* NVA assault on Saigon, *no* NVA humiliation of the United States, *no* NVA resistance to a continuing U.S. presence in Saigon after the establishment of a Saigon–Hanoi government of national union.

But even as he was rehearsing his lines, he wondered too whether Starnes's B-52s would in any way affect the strategy Hanoi would follow when the DRV representative sat down on the other side of the table. One thing for sure, Walker promised to himself: he would not be outwitted by Hanoi, as the American negotiators had been during the Paris "peace" negotiations in 1973.

When the car finally pulled to a stop in front of 22 Hong Thap Tu, Walker told the driver to drive back to the Embassy and to return to 22 at 4:30 and wait; he wanted no one loitering outside. When the car had left, Walker approached the villa. The house was one story, wood and stucco, with a red-tile roof, just like the other houses on the street. A stranger passing by would not have given it a second glance, which was why it had been chosen.

He quickly reconnoitered the grassy backyard; nothing unusual. He mounted the three stairs and, as a precaution, rang the bell. No one answered. He reached into his pocket for the key and let himself in. The furnishings in the living room were middle-class Vietnamese: a wicker couch covered with green bark cloth, four chairs, and a rattan table with a glass top. All very ordinary looking, but he knew that some unusual footnotes to the war had taken place in this room. Bribes passed to Saigon generals to provide the CIA with details of upcoming ARVN battle plans. Payoffs to Vietnamese politicians to support U.S. policies. Private "debriefings" of senior VC and NVA prisoners. Walker remembered the way the Agency in its gung-ho enthusiasm had even tried to recruit one of the Vietnamese houseboys at Doc Lap Palace to accumulate discarded presidential papers, bring them to 22, and hide them in a tank in the bathroom; the spooks had given the boy a hundred-dollar bill. He came back with a sheaf of notebook pages that turned out to be the cook's market lists for the previous month. On top of that, he stuffed them in the toilet instead of the tank, putting the plumbing out of commission. Hundreds of thousands, maybe millions, of dollars had changed hands here; in the grand scheme of things in Viet Nam, mere petty cash. How, Walker wondered, recalling the gleeful jibe of the Polish Colonel, had "the other side" penetrated the secrecy of 22? Not that it made much difference now, but he guessed that one of the ARVN generals on the CIA payroll had sold the Hong Thap Tu address to the VC. The general playing both sides for suckers. Viet Nam.

Walker sat down in the living room. He looked at his watch.

Three minutes to four. He went to the window and glanced down the street. No car in sight.

He tried to sit, to relax, but could not. He found himself pacing back and forth to the window. America and Viet Nam, he thought. Flung together by fear — America's fear of communism, South Viet Nam's fear of obliteration. Never allies — just uneasy, temporary partners in fear. A complicated and tortuous relationship, booby traps of suspicion blowing up in their faces, hopes amputated, the two sides blasted apart, developing a contempt for each other and a secret, perverse admiration for the enemy. The Americans finally took their napalm and Cokes and went home. A decade, Walker thought, buried in coffins.

Two minutes to four. He began to feel the old diplomatic juices at work, the familiar excitement of approaching combat. The challenge was to salvage something out of nothing.

Exactly one minute to four. He returned to the window. He looked down the street, both ways. No car in sight. Now that was cutting it a bit too fine. He sat down again, his eyes fixed on his watch. Ten seconds to go. Nine. Eight. Seven. Six. Five. Four. Three. Two. One. Four o'clock sharp!

The boom deafened him. *BOOM! BOOM! BOOM!* He held his hands to his ears. He grabbed the armrests of his chair to avoid being hurled to the floor. INCOMING! He staggered to the window. He could see dirty red columns of smoke climbing to the sky. People were running from their houses. The blasts of artillery echoed throughout the city.

"SONSOFBITCHES!" he shouted. The four-o'clock appointment. H-hour for the NVA's all-out assault on Saigon. They wanted it all. No compromise. No way to stop them now. Saigon blowing away. Finished. Ho Chi Minh City.

He burst out of the house, racing down Hong Thap Tu toward Hai Ba Trung in the direction of the Embassy. The streets were wild with terrified people, pandemonium everywhere, the war now exploding in the capital itself. His breath came in sharp gasps. Suzanne! In a second of blinding guilty terror he remembered Suzanne. He had to get to her. He had not thought once of Suzanne since he had left that bastard Xuan. Where was she?

Walker found himself in the middle of a crowd of screaming Vietnamese, swept up in the human debris of Saigon.

28

You didn't need feet to reach the Embassy, not now. All you had to do was relax, as though you were floating on water, and the waves of Vietnamese pouring through the streets scooped you up. Walker found himself swept along, jostled, tossed, pummeled, until the torrent of bodies splashed to a stop against the concrete wall surrounding the U.S. compound, ten feet high, two feet wide, topped with barbed wire. Struggling forward, Walker looked up and found himself staring into the muzzle of an M-16 pointed at the mob by a U.S. Marine on top of the wall.

Walker tried to break free. He twisted his shoulders from side to side, but all he got for his effort was a sharp jab in the ribs. Pain shot through his body. He was terrified that he would collapse, be trampled underfoot. Again, he tried to pry himself loose; this time he lunged to within shouting distance of the Marine on the wall.

"OPEN THE GATE!" Walker's voice could barely be heard over the tumult of the crowd. "LET ME IN!"

"Sorry, buddy," the Marine shouted down from the wall. "No one gets in right now. Those are orders."

Orders? Had the whole world gone mad in the last few minutes?

The Vietnamese around Walker tried to shove him to the

rear, but he fought them off, his elbows chopping at every hand that touched him. He drilled his eyes on the Marine. "Open the gate, goddamn you, and let me in." But his words were a thin echo by the time they reached the Marine.

"Fuck off, buddy," the Marine shouted, waving his M-16. "Orders are orders. Who do you think you are?"

"I AM THE AMBASSADOR!"

"If you're the Ambassador," the Marine barked, a hard angry look on his face, "then I'm the Queen of England." His rifle made an arc across the crowd. "Try again in an hour. Maybe they'll be letting more people in."

"I AM THE AMBASSADOR!"

Their eyes met; there was something about Walker's bearing that got through to the Marine. He turned and looked down on the other side of the wall. "There's a guy in the crowd who says he's an American," the Marine shouted. "He keeps yelling he's 'the Ambassador.' What do you want me to do?"

A head began to inch over the top of the Embassy side of the wall: the disheveled hair, heavy-lidded tired eyes, round face of John Sommers.

"GODDAMMIT!" shouted the CIA station chief, stunned at seeing Walker trapped in the crowd below. "Let's get him over the wall. FAST!"

The Marine's face crumbled.

Sommers carefully worked his arms through the barbed wire and reached down to Walker. Their hands clasped. Sommers then began to pull him out of the mass of people jammed against the wall. Halfway up, Walker felt a sudden pain in his back; he had been hit by a sharp rock. The Marine fired a warning shot over the heads of the crowd. "Listen, you gooks, one more move," the Marine shouted, "and you'll get a bullet between your slanty eyes, you motherfuckers." By now, several other Americans inside the compound had climbed to the top of the wall and joined Sommers in helping Walker up and over.

"Christ," Sommers muttered, staring at the mob of Americans and Vietnamese on the Embassy grounds, "the whole place has gone crazy."

The Marine jumped down from the wall, his voice quaking. "Mr. Ambassador, I didn't know —" he began, but Sommers cut in, explaining to Walker that the Marine was a new arrival, part of a detachment that had just been helicoptered in from the U.S. fleet to beef up security at the Embassy.

"What's your name?" Walker asked.

"PFC Hawkins," the Marine mumbled. He looked eighteen years old at most; it was obvious that this was the closest he had ever been to a war zone. "I didn't know. . . ."

"It's all right, Hawkins," Walker said. "You were doing your job."

"Thank you, sir." The Marine vaulted onto the wall and glared menacingly at the crowd below. "Motherfuckers!" he screamed. "Gooks! Slopes! Dinks!"

A cloud of smoke suddenly choked Walker. He began waving his arms, gasping for air. "What the hell is that?" he asked, pointing to an oil drum throwing up a circle of fire.

"A few million bucks going up in smoke," Sommers explained matter-of-factly, pointing to a Marine who was tossing packets of new hundred-dollar bills into the flames. "Don't want to leave these for the next tenant."

They picked their way through the crowds and headed toward the Embassy building.

"What happened at twenty-two?" the CIA station chief asked.

Walker looked away, pained.

"Anything?"

"Nothing."

"Nothing?"

"The DRV didn't show."

Sommers's eyes widened, but he opted for silence; this, he knew, wasn't gloating time, not the moment to say he had known it all along: that negotiations never had a chance when the NVA was within walking distance of Doc Lap.

Walker could now see several thousand Vietnamese gathered around the swimming pool in the recreation area of the compound, their lifetime possessions crammed into over-the-shoulder travel bags, their faces reflecting relief to be inside the compound and uncertainty about what was next.

" 'Option Four' is already in effect," Sommers said. "First wave of choppers has taken off from TF-Seventy-six. Heading for the DAO pads at Tan Son Nhut. About six thousand Vietnamese are there. The main runways of Tan Son Nhut were hit. Long-range NVA artillery. Fixed-wing evacuation is out. Only helicopters now."

Just as they cut across the Embassy parking lot, as Walker was stepping on the T of VISITORS painted on the ground, he caught his breath. The tamarind tree's giant trunk, cut through by a crew of Marines working with a power saw, remained erect for one last majestic moment. Then, with agonizing slowness, the tree began to topple, crashing onto a row of parked vehicles.

Walker's eyes were riveted on the fallen tree. "Who did it? Who gave the orders to cut down the tree?"

"Couldn't control the Marines any longer," Sommers said defensively. "The CO told me the tree had to go *now* so that we could clear a pad for the choppers to land here on the lot."

The tamarind — KIA. The tree had lived through it all, the French, the Japanese, the French again, finally the Americans. An innocent victim, the tamarind. Deserves a real funeral, but there's nothing to do about it now. No one plays taps for a dead tree.

Walker, face taut, eyes darting, hurried through the crowd and into the Embassy building. Staff members were frantically axing everything in sight: desks, typewriters, water-coolers, pictures on the wall. A free-for-all smash-up.

"The tree isn't the worst of it," Sommers said, trying to overtake Walker. "There's something else you must know."

But Walker didn't hear him. He raced up the three flights of stairs and burst into the anteroom. General Xuan was still in the chair in which Walker had left him less than an hour ago.

"All over now." Xuan grinned. "Finished."

Walker looked at him with contempt. "Get your people together," Walker said. "Bring them here. But Xuan, let me warn you; you'd better be sure my daughter is all right — or . . ."

Xuan laughed, a brief staccato of a laugh.

"You understand?" Walker said, his eyes blazing. "Bring her here now."

"Yes, Mr. Ambassador," he said mockingly as he dashed for the elevator.

Walker entered his office, Sommers one step behind him. "Self-explanatory," Sommers said as he handed over a single sheet of typewritten paper. "It's all written down there."

"Is it really that urgent?" Walker asked, dropping into the chair behind his desk. "Must I read it now?"

Sommers nodded. "I think you'd better."

Walker's eyes raced over the paper. His head shook in disbelief.

Sommers looked away. "That's the *transcript* of the broadcast," he explained. "Monitored just as you left here at three forty-five. Now this" — he handed Walker a tape cassette — "is an actual *recording* of the broadcast." He hurried toward the door, as though at that moment he wanted to get as far away from Walker as possible. "If you need me, I'll be in my office. Shredding documents."

Walker hit the intercom button. "Helen, the minute Suzanne arrives —"

"She just walked in," Helen interrupted. "She's here."

"*Here?*" Walker was startled. "How could she have gotten here so quickly?"

Suzanne, in a white blouse and blue jeans, her face flushed, burst into the office. Before she could say a word, Walker cut in. "Are you all right?"

"Yes," she said. "I'm all right. But out there . . ." She could see that he was puzzled. "What . . . ?"

"Did they hurt you?"

"Did *who* hurt me? What are you talking about?"

---

2 4 5

"Did *they* hurt you?" He stood up. "That bastard Xuan. He told me he kidnapped you. . . ."

Suzanne shook her head. "Must be some kind of a joke. I've been at the orphanage. I got here just in time. And I was lucky. The Marine guard on duty at the rear gate knows me. He let me in. Otherwise, I might still be out there, with all the others. . . ." Her words trailed off as she sensed her father's growing anger.

"What is it?" she asked.

"Read this." He handed the paper to her.

Suzanne sat down, read the paper. She looked up, dazed.

He took a small tape recorder from his desk and inserted the cassette. He hit the "on" button, and a voice began speaking in English with a Vietnamese accent.

"This is Radio Hanoi speaking. The imperialist American Ambassador Hadden Walker is criminally guilty of keeping Vietnamese fighting Vietnamese — even though he secretly is convinced that the war is over and that the glorious People's Army of Viet Nam has emerged triumphant. We have reported this many times. Now we will present evidence — recorded in the Ambassador's own office during a conversation with his daughter. You will now hear the voice of the Ambassador. '. . . let me give you my best estimate of the situation. I wouldn't go shouting that from the rooftops — *Saigon is finished* — but I'm telling it to you, to you alone.' That was the voice of the United States Ambassador, the criminal who made the American puppets in Saigon fight on in the diabolical U.S. plan designed to keep Vietnamese killing one another — even though he knew that the situation was hopeless. . . ."

Walker clicked off the recorder.

Suzanne leaped to her feet. "How did they get this? Where did it . . . ?" For a moment, she was confused. Had she *not* destroyed the tape? Had she *dreamed* about destroying the tape?

Just then, the Embassy building was shaken by the staggering reverberations of a fresh rocket attack on the city. Walker and

Suzanne looked at each other, saw the furniture in the office tremble, then watched as the Swatow vase began to sway on the precariously narrow porcelain shelf. Walker rushed over to try to steady it. The vase crashed to the floor.

Suzanne gasped, but Walker ignored her. He dropped to his knees and ran his fingers through the bits and pieces of the treasured vase from the Nguyen Dynasty shop. Porcelain clinked against porcelain. He picked up one of the loops. Puzzled, he held it in his palm, then tossed it up and down, as though judging its weight. With an abrupt movement, he cracked it open.

"Sonofabitch!" he shouted.

"What is it?"

"You asked me where they got it — the tape of our conversation. *Here's* where they got it. From my . . . almost-perfect Swatow vase. From my dear, dear friend Professor Hoan."

Suddenly, Walker's face went rigid. *Jeanne!* The thought startled him. It was Jeanne, wasn't it, who had first mentioned the new porcelain pieces at the Nguyen Dynasty. *JEANNE?*

"Professor Hoan?" Suzanne knelt beside Walker. "Of the Nguyen Dynasty?"

Walker nodded, his lips clenched.

"And this small bit of metal buried in the loop . . . ?"

"A 'bug'!" Holding the disc between his fingertips he began to scream: "Do you hear me, Hoan? May your victory be your curse!" Then he stood up, went to the window, pushed it open, and stared down at the frantic Vietnamese fighting to climb over the wall into the U.S. compound. "Listen to the 'joy' your victory has brought to the Vietnamese people," he yelled into the bug. "Listen, Hoan, listen!" He drew his arm back and hurled the disc at the crowd.

Then he spun around and leaped three steps toward his shelves of porcelain, almost tripping over the pole that held the U.S. flag next to his desk.

Suzanne watched him in horror, unable to believe what she

saw. Her cool, dispassionate father, *her father*, unrecognizable now — his fists clenched, his eyes blank, the shock of a moment ago replaced by fury.

He kicked aside the remains of the shattered Swatow and scooped a blue-and-white Ming plate off the shelf. *Chia Ching, 1522–1566, bought it thirty years ago in a small antique shop off Djalan Sudirman in Jakarta.* "The White House!" he screamed, hurling the plate against the wall.

Suzanne catapulted out of her chair and tried to stop him but he pushed her away.

He reached for a pale-green celadon bowl. *Sung, 960–1279, picked it up at Peng's on Suriwongse Road in Bangkok in 1967.* "The State Department!" he shouted and smashed the bowl on the floor. His hand snaked out and seized a monochrome platter, creamy, with a foliated edge. *Yuan, 1279–1368, found it on a back shelf at Terry's in Manila ten years ago.* "Congress!" he screamed and flung the platter against the wall.

Again, Suzanne tried to restrain him; again, he thrust her away. Helen half-opened the door and stuck her head in, her eyes wide with surprise. But Walker glared at her and she quickly retreated.

He now placed his open hand at the far end of the top shelf and in one slashing motion swept off the remaining bowls, vases, and plates he had meticulously collected. His hand swept across the middle shelf, then the bottom shelf, until all the shelves were naked. He stared at the wreckage on the floor, at the treasures that only a few minutes before had been part of his life — now reduced to jagged bits and pieces. He booted the pile, chips flying in all directions.

Suzanne stood motionless, afraid to break through the barrier of his rage. Then, in a swift movement, she rushed toward him and he opened his arms and they embraced, clinging to each other as though they were on a life raft, adrift, no land in sight.

After a few moments, he lifted her chin and she smiled weakly. She could feel his body relax. He told her not to worry, he would be all right now.

Sommers burst into the office and stopped short, his eyes surveying the porcelain chunks and slivers. "What the hell happened?"

"It would take too long to explain," Walker said quietly, as though he were talking to himself.

Sommers looked bewildered, but Walker did not give him a chance to ask any questions. "What's the latest?" Walker asked.

Sommers's voice sounded like a heavy tank rolling across a field of boulders. "We're fighting the clock," he said. "I tell you, the sooner the choppers start landing here, the better I'll feel."

" '. . . the choppers start landing . . . ,' " Suzanne echoed, racing toward the door. "I haven't much time." She slipped out.

Sommers glanced at his watch. "They tell me it's about a forty-minute flight in from the carriers. That means they should be starting to touch down at the DAO pretty soon. Meantime, the NVA has thrown a ring of steel around the city. They've got S-A-seven surface-to-air, hand-held missiles, even radar-directed antiaircraft guns. They're making no effort to crash through — so far." He grunted bitterly. "Why even bother. They could waltz their way into Saigon."

Walker nodded, half-listening. *Whose failure was it? America's? South Viet Nam's? Mine? Mine? Oh no. Yours, his, theirs, not mine.* His built-in self-defense mechanism began whirling, the thousand fine-print lawyers on the permanent payroll in his mind feverishly carrying out an audit on the disaster, looking for loopholes, preparing their briefs. *Excellent work, gentlemen, excellent. Plenty of time to lay it all out later. Too much to do now. Expedite the evacuation. Avert panic. Yes, later. Plenty of time for accusations, charges, indictments. Later. Now was for now, gentlemen.*

"And in town," Sommers rasped on, "the Vietnamese are de-Americanizing themselves. The bar girls are shedding their miniskirts and getting back into their black-pajama pants and blouses. ARVN soldiers are throwing away their M-sixteens, right in the streets. Not only that, they're also tearing off their uniforms, running around Saigon in their underwear. All around town, people are ripping down English-language signs, especially those banners proclaiming U.S.–Vietnamese solidarity!"

Walker grimaced. "What an epitaph for America! 'WE NAKED VIETNAMESE SALUTE OUR INDOMITABLE ALLY THE UNITED STATES!' 'WE WHORES OF SAIGON WILL NEVER FORGET YOU!' " He leaned across the desk. "John, we've got one remaining obligation that we are *not* going to run from."

Sommers studied Walker's cold eyes.

"The Vietnamese inside the compound," Walker shouted. "I don't care who they are, but they're *inside* the U.S. compound and we're going to get every last one of them out with us or . . . we're not going out ourselves." He slammed the desk.

Sommers shifted uneasily in his chair.

Walker's voice sounded as though he were reading from a memorial plaque. "They won't get *me* out of here — until every last Vietnamese has gone."

The intercom buzzed. Helen said the White House was on the line and that the President wanted to speak with the Ambassador.

"Put him on — our Commander-in-Chief." He held his hand over the receiver and asked Sommers to check on the evacuation numbers: how many Americans and Vietnamese at the DAO, how many at the Embassy.

"I remind you," said Sommers as he headed for the door, "that the main evac center is the DAO, not the Embassy. The chopper pads here are primarily for Americans — plus the handful of Vietnamese on the Embassy staff who are still around."

Walker shook his head. "You look outside my window," he shouted, "and then I want you to tell me if you can live with that." He waved at Sommers. "Talk to you later."

2 5 0

Sommers closed the door and left Walker alone with the President at the other end of the line.

"Hello, Mr. President."

"Hello, Hadden."

Walker recognized the tone of instant camaraderie.

"The eyes of the nation are on you," the President said. "I want you to know how grateful I am that you are our man there and I know that you will carry out the evacuation in a way that will make all of us back here very proud."

Proud? Lose the war and win the evacuation?

"And Hadden," the President went on, "I also want you to know that we have gone the distance in every possible way, Navy, Air Force, Marines, carriers, helicopters, attack planes if you should need them — but God, I hope you don't — to make sure you have every possible piece of equipment to get our people out."

It's my ass that's on the line, right? CYA, at the very summit.

"Mr. President," Walker said, "all the equipment in the world isn't going to be of much help if the North Vietnamese should make a command decision to break up the evacuation."

"And the situation now?" A shakiness crept into the President's voice.

"Well, the NVA at least as of now are being gentlemanly — lovely people in Hanoi, you know. They've stopped their tanks on the edge of town. They're giving us a head start — on retreat."

The President ignored Walker's sarcasm. "Hadden, I want you to know that I personally have instructed the Pentagon to provide all the chopper sorties you'll need to carry out your job. Mostly for the DAO, I understand. A few for the Embassy."

Walker pushed out of his chair, the phone to his ear, and looked through the window at the thousands of Vietnamese huddled inside the compound. *A few for the Embassy?*

"Mr. President, we're going to need a lot more sorties than we ever dreamed of for the Embassy alone. The grounds below my window *inside* the Embassy compound are jammed with men, women, children . . . and" — his eye reconnoitered the thousands of frantic Vietnamese on the other side of the compound wall — "we're having one hell of a time trying to keep those on the outside from breaking in."

"Look, Hadden, we can't evacuate *all* of Viet Nam."

"Not all, I agree," Walker shot back. "But we simply can't abandon those who are already on our side of the wall, already on the Embassy grounds. There's precious little honor left to us. Let's not throw away the last scrap. We are simply going to need nonstop chopper sorties, and you'll have to authorize them."

"Look, Hadden, I don't want to be put into a position of approving an open-ended evacuation."

"I understand that, Mr. President" — it was becoming increasingly difficult to keep the fury out of his voice — "but this is our final move in Viet Nam and it should be without limits."

"But the Pentagon tells me they're ready to give you all the support you'll need."

"But let's make sure that that support has *rotors* attached to it. Look, Mr. President, I'm going to be blunt. I will not board a chopper out of here until the last Vietnamese on the Embassy grounds has been flown out."

The line cracked with static.

"Hadden, let's just see" — it was the President's peacemaking voice — "what happens."

"Fine. But I just want to make it clear that, apart from the Marine security force, I'm going to be the last one, American or Vietnamese, to leave this place."

"I hear you loud and clear, Hadden, but let's not get bogged down on that issue now."

"All right, just so you understand my position."

I'm going to be haunted by Viet Nam the rest of my life, haunted, hounded, stalked, and I don't want the added curse of having abandoned Vietnamese as though they were sacks of rice.

"Hadden, I'm going to be in and out of the Sitroom of the White House during these next few hours. If there's anything you need, anything I can do, please call me. I'll be near the phone."

"Thank you, Mr. President, but I still can't resist saying that it did not have to come to this, never, if only we —"

"No time for that now, Hadden. The challenge now is getting our people out. We don't want to go through a new POW crisis with Hanoi. Once was enough. And I want to tell you again, Hadden, that America will forever be indebted to you for the courage you're displaying at this critical moment in our history. I don't want to keep you on the line, Hadden. Call me if there's anything I can do. Good luck."

The line went dead.

The *chug chug chug* of whirling rotors could now be heard. Walker went to the window; the late-afternoon horizon was dotted with Jolly Green Giants, big, fat-bellied helicopters flying in the direction of the DAO. He looked down at the crowds of Vietnamese on both sides of the wall, their faces aimed at the sky. The last exit.

The intercom buzzed. Helen told him that the Marine guards were calling in on their walkie-talkies and reporting that General Xuan, accompanied by at least forty Vietnamese, was at the rear gate, demanding to be admitted to the compound. "He says you said it would be okay. The Marines want to know what they should do."

Tell the Marines to shoot them all, was the first thought that went through Walker's mind. "Tell the Marines to let the son-ofabitch in," he said. "Otherwise, Xuan's thugs could turn on us — with guns. Bad as it is now, it could be worse." He slammed down the phone. From the window, he could see the Marines swing open the rear gate and point their M-16s at the surrounding crowd while the General and his entourage were let in, all carrying shoulder bags so heavy that the whole group seemed to be walking at a tilt. Gold bars, Walker thought, their final loot of the war.

Sommers burst into the office. "Just to tell you," he said, "that the first choppers have touched down at the DAO and have begun loading Americans and Vietnamese. The pilots report they took some sniper fire on the way in."

"Probably ARVN," Walker said wearily.

"The choppers for the Embassy should be arriving shortly."

A streak of a face cut through Walker's mind. "What have we done about our friend at Doc Lap?" he asked. The South Vietnamese leader had been lurking in Walker's subconscious ever since the first rockets hit Saigon. "Has he called?"

Sommers shook his head. "He didn't call *us*. *We* called him. He's agreed to our plan."

Agreed?

"Our people have already picked him up at the palace and are escorting him to the DAO. We're laying on a helicopter — a private one — for him and his family." Sommers kicked a piece of porcelain. "Not just for protocol, either. I don't think he'd want any Vietnamese around him. Not now."

The President of South Viet Nam, being smuggled out of the country as though he were contraband cargo! And yet, this man, in exile somewhere, may have the last bitter laugh — the long-distance voyeur watching country after country fall away from faith in America's word. Who ever again will want to risk being a U.S. ally — ending up in an American chopper in the middle of the night?

"Messy business," said Sommers quietly.

"What else?" asked Walker.

"Self-destruct underway. Communications equipment being destroyed. Shredding machines working overtime. Sensitive documents being chewed up. Smashing everything we can. In fact, I've got some smashing of my own to do," Sommers said as he hurried out of the office.

So do I. Walker went to the wall safe, twirled the dials, and opened the small heavy door. He reached for a pile of top-secret cables, back-channel eyes-only messages to and from the President and the Secretary of State, and began scanning them. Promises from Washington that were never kept. Deceptions. Lies. The abandoned words now leaped from the pages, and he tried to blot out the memories they triggered. He was about to rip them to bits, when he stopped. He sorted through the cables very carefully, his own and those from the White House and the State Department. His warnings, their commitment. His alerts, their reassurances. His appeals, their pledges. It was all down here, a raw diary of his year in Saigon. He slid these select cables into a leather portfolio; the others he dropped into the metal wastebasket next to his desk. He struck a match and lit the discarded papers and watched the flames begin to curl around the edges, turning the teleprinted words gold and then brown and then black, a tissue of ash.

Walker was drawn back to the window as the first of the Embassy-bound choppers slanted into view. The Vietnamese inside the compound burst into frenzied applause, those outside again scrambled to scale the wall but were knocked back by the Marines on top. A Jolly Green Giant, its huge rotors barely clearing the foliage of the felled tamarind tree, touched down on the parking lot. The crowds surged forward in a wild effort to crash through the cordon of Marines; the Marines pointed their M-16s at them. The Vietnamese kept coming. The Marines fired above their heads. The Vietnamese stopped in their tracks. The Marines then forced the Vietnamese into queues, funneling them through the open hatch of the chopper. But after a momentary pause, the crowds surged forward again. The Marines tried to shove them back. The queues dissolved into an angry mob.

Walker, enraged, raced down the three flights of stairs to the lobby and pushed his way through the crowd. Suddenly he collided with Tony.

"You!" Walker shouted. "I want *you* to make sure that Suzanne is not lost in all this madness."

"Where is she?"

"She should be back here at any moment and you — *you* — better not let her out of your sight."

Before Tony could say a word, Walker pushed on, shouldering his way through the lobby, into the parking lot. He looked around in search of an officer. When he spotted a Marine with two silver bars on his collar, Walker grabbed him by the shirt.

"Captain," he shouted, "I'm the Ambassador. I —"

"Mr. Ambassador," said the Captain, startled, "you should be *inside*."

"No, I should be *outside*," Walker said. "Now you do just what I tell you. You tell these people not to panic. Tell them everyone will be evacuated. Tell them they have *my word*."

The Captain nodded.

Walker plunged toward the open hatch of the helicopter, under the spinning rotor-blades, and pushed aside a husky Marine who was shoving Vietnamese into the chopper. "I'm the Ambassador," Walker shouted. "You let me do that."

The Marine, surprised, backed off, and Walker began pulling Vietnamese by their arms and propelling them forward. He scooped up children and handed them to Vietnamese already inside the chopper. He moved swiftly, snapping orders, jamming as many Vietnamese as possible into the helicopter.

Tony, from the window of his office, could not take his eyes off the Ambassador.

Suzanne burst into the room, Thi in one arm, Thach in the other, each child carrying a small bag.

"They're coming with us, right?" Tony asked.

Suzanne nodded.

"Come here."

Suzanne set the two children on the couch and hurried to the window.

"Look at him down there," Tony said. "Fucking unbelievable! All alone he's America — *his* America. He sees every Vietnamese he shoves into the chopper as an extra statistic of U.S. integrity."

Their faces against the window, they watched silently as Walker kept piling Vietnamese into the choppers, an empty one landing as soon as a loaded one had lifted off the ground and spun away in the direction of the U.S. Fleet off the coast of South Viet Nam.

"Down there, Suzanne," Tony went on, ". . . the debris of U.S. policy." His mind echoed with all the old shibboleths of the Pentagon. " 'Light at the end of the tunnel.' Remember that one, Suzanne? Well, *that*" — he pointed to the frantic scene below — "is what is at the end of the tunnel. The end of the American journey . . . from conceit to defeat. Hard to believe, but it took defeat for him to learn there was more than *Realpolitik* at stake here. It's *people*. Crazy, crazy, crazy. It took *this* for him to finally make contact with the Vietnamese."

Tony scanned the crowd, inside and outside the compound. Suddenly he froze. A green cloth, mounted on a bamboo pole, was being waved back and forth. "Oh, God," he muttered. "I never got to call her." His eyes went down the pole, and he could make out Anh, Duc, their father.

Tony raced out of the office, and Suzanne could spot him a few moments later, below, pushing his way through the crowd inside the compound. He reached the wall, and a couple of American civilians in the crowd boosted him to the top. Close up, the roar of the crowd broke into pieces, individual voices.

"Take him, take him, please," Tony heard a young Vietnamese woman begging, holding up a boy of about six. "He's half American. The Viet Cong will kill him."

Tony turned away only to find himself trapped by the eyes of a middle-aged man who was desperately waving his arms. "My children are on the other side of the wall. *Help me over!*"

Tony picked out terrified faces, discarded them, searching for Anh. Then he spotted the green cloth edging closer. "Anh!" he shouted, motioning her to push through the crowd. She fought her way to the base of the wall. He leaned over, reaching for her hand. Their fingers locked. "Hold on, hold on!" he shouted. Suddenly, he felt a hard jab in his ribs.

"No more!" shouted a Marine. "Our orders are no more gooks come over the wall."

"Fuck your orders!" Tony turned back to Anh, but the Marine's M-16 again dug into his ribs. Tony's hand slipped from Anh's. He stood up, but the Marine slammed him in the hip with the butt of the rifle. Tony teetered on top of the wall, almost dropping to the outside. With a powerful effort, he thrust himself in the direction of the compound and fell ten feet to the ground. The Marine, still on top, stared down at him.

"Motherfucker!" the Marine screamed. "Try that again and I'll put a bullet in your head."

Tony lay sprawled on the ground, bruised, stunned. He could hear Anh shouting "Tony, Tony!" on the other side of the wall. He tried to claw up the wall but the Marine fired a bullet that hit within a few inches of his feet.

"Motherfucker, I mean it!" shouted the Marine. "I'll kill you next time! We've got enough whores inside the compound! No more!"

From below, Tony glared up at the Marine, at his baby face under the rim of the steel helmet — blue eyes, button nose, wide mouth, freckles. A cornflakes-ad face, the face of a kid who would give his seat to an old lady on a crowded bus. Now a monster's face, severing Tony from Anh. Suddenly the Marine's face was his own face, the Marine's rifle his own rifle at Nha Trang, clubbing Vietnamese off the C-47. Viet Nam fucking Viet Nam again testing for courage, honesty, cowardice, and Tony knew he could not fail again. Nha Trang already was unbearable. As if the future were compressed into an instant, he knew that if he did not bring Anh over the wall now, he'd be a cripple forever chained to this moment. He pushed himself off the ground, cursing the excruciating pain in his hip. He leaped up, trying to hook his fingers on the top of the wall. Suddenly the Marine dropped onto him like a bag of cement and they both fell to the ground, grappling with each other. "Cut it out, for Chrissakes," a voice shouted. Tony forced his eyes open. It was another half-face jutting out from under a helmet asking what the hell is going on and Tony asked who are you and the voice said Captain Smith — CO of the Marine security force — and Tony told the Captain there were some Vietnamese people on the other side of the wall who had been an invaluable help to the CIA during the war and that he'd promised to get them out and if it was the last thing in the world he did even if it meant that he would have to kill that young fucking punk Marine he was going to get them over the wall and the voice laughed and said okay who are they and Tony stood up and the Captain helped him to the top of the wall and he could see Anh and Duc and their father and he reached down and pulled them up one after the other even as other Vietnamese were tearing at their clothes trying to hitch a piggyback ride over the wall and when Anh and Duc and their father were all down on the ground inside the compound Anh began crying and Duc his crutches smashed put his arm around her and Tony said you'll be all right now Anh come with me and he led them to the parking lot compound and pushed the three of them into the waiting line and watched them herded aboard a chopper just before the hatch closed.

29

Midnight. Headlights of parked automobiles streak the LZ on the Embassy parking lot with garish, crisscrossed beams. A Jolly Green Giant touches down, its blades cutting blurred circles in the air. Ragtag lines of Vietnamese, hunched over, fight the blasts of the rotors and leap into the open belly of the helicopter. Marines in full battle-dress keep the refugees from stampeding toward the chopper. Embassy civilians, armed with knives, pistols, rifles, dart back and forth, trying to keep the evacuation moving swiftly and to reassure the waiting Vietnamese that they will not be abandoned. The Jolly Green Giant is now fully loaded. It lifts slowly off the ground, just clearing the treetops, and disappears into the darkened sky. Another big chopper touches down. Seven floors up, on the roof of the Embassy building, smaller helicopters set down on the helipad one after the other and fly out a steady stream of Americans.

On the Embassy's third floor, in his office, Walker was again on the telephone with the White House. "Mr. President, we need more chopper flights. Desperately. The compound outside my window is still jammed with Vietnamese."

"Hadden, we are doing all we can but the Pentagon tells me

they can handle only twenty more chopper flights in and out of the compound. Twenty."

"Twenty?" It was as much an expletive as a question.

"Twenty," the President reiterated. "They say the choppers need servicing, the pilots have been at it nonstop now for more hours than are safe, they're exhausted, the risk factor has increased. . . ."

"Mr. President —"

"Let me finish, Hadden. *Please.* We've already taken out several thousand — I repeat, several *thousand* — Vietnamese from the DAO. That part of the evacuation has now been closed down. You know that. All that's left is your Embassy evacuation. Twenty."

Walker moved to the window, pushed open one of the glass panels, and pointed the telephone receiver at the screaming crowd.

"Hadden, do we have a bad connection?" The President's voice came through thinly. "I'm suddenly hearing a lot of static."

"That's not static, Mr. President. That's panic!" Walker shouted. "I held the telephone outside my window so that *you* could hear what *I* am hearing. The Vietnamese out there are people we — *the United States* — have pledged to evacuate."

"Well, we *are* getting them out."

"We are getting *some* of them out. Twenty choppers are not enough! It will mean that we will have to abandon hundreds of Vietnamese already inside the compound. We need at least FORTY chopper sorties to get out these Vietnamese. EVERY LAST ONE OF THEM!"

"And another thing, Hadden," the President continued, ignoring Walker's outburst. "We must get *our* people out. I want you to understand that *these last twenty chopper sorties are for Americans only.* If there are still empty seats, fine, load up Vietnamese."

"Do I hear you right, Mr. President? Abandon the Vietnamese already inside the compound?"

261

"*Americans only!* We're already pushing our luck."

"*No!* We can't simply leave these last few hundred Vietnamese behind. We can't —"

"Twenty-five sorties, Hadden. That's it. *Twenty-five.*"

"I will not allow you to do that!"

"Hadden" — a presidential pause — "I'm going to overlook that last remark of yours. I know you're under terrible pressure. Now listen to me carefully. I want you to be on the last chopper. No time for heroics."

"Dammit, I'm not talking about heroics. I'm talking about throwing people away like stinking garbage. You're sitting there in Washington. You can't see what's going on here. Will this be the final proof of America's 'honor'?"

"Look, Hadden, I understand the hell you're going through, believe me. But don't give me a lecture on honor."

Walker could hear the President clearing his throat.

"Twenty-five, Hadden. And you be on the twenty-fifth. That's an order. A presidential order. You've got your work cut out for you. Now get on with it. And . . . good luck!"

The line was disconnected.

Over the intercom, Walker told Helen to telephone Madame de Clery at the French Embassy and tell her to come over at once. To his surprise, Helen said she had just heard from the Marine on duty in the lobby that Madame de Clery was on her way up; she had come through the hole in the wall between the U.S. and French compounds.

A moment later, Jeanne entered the office, breathless, her delicately flowered dress streaked with perspiration from the sprint up the three flights of stairs. She held out her arms, but then stopped short, staring at the shards of porcelain that littered the room. She looked up at Walker.

He searched her face for a glimmer of guilt but he could find no clues; he wondered whether the face that had so tantalized him, that mix of Asia and Europe, could be a mask — the Vietnamese conspirator behind the French veneer.

"Hadden? What is it?"

"Betrayal, Jeanne. That's the word. Did you know that the Swatow vase, *even* the Swatow vase, betrayed me? Did you know that a 'bug' in its repaired loop sent every word from this room — to *them?* Did you know that, Jeanne? Did you know?"

She moved toward him. Instinctively he drew back.

"Hadden . . ." She looked at him, puzzled. Then her eyes widened. "Surely you don't think that I . . . ?"

"Remember? It was you, at Bodard's party, who first told me about Hoan's new porcelain pieces."

"Hadden, Hadden." Her voice was desperate. "Listen to me. Please. Hoan *used* me, the way he must have used others who visited the Nguyen Dynasty. In order to reach you. I never suspected him."

Walker stood motionless.

"Hadden. Now . . . at this moment . . . what would I gain by deceiving you? If I had done this thing . . . would I come to you? How can I prove it to you? There is *no* time — and so you *must* believe *me. Please!*"

For a moment, the two of them stared at each other, the shattered porcelain a no-man's-land between them. Again, he searched her face. *A mask, or the anguish of innocence?* He could hear the boom of the artillery sounding closer and closer to the Embassy. She was right — there would be no time to know, even if it were possible to know. He would have to *decide.* To his amazement, the decision came easily. He smiled, moved toward her, and took her in his arms. "I believe you," he said.

In the silence that followed, the whine of the choppers and the shouts from the courtyard drew them to the window, and they stood there, numbly, watching the nightmarish scene below.

"Hadden," Jeanne said softly, as though she were trying to

find a way to soothe him, "just try to remember . . . you did what you could."

"But for it to end . . . this way. . . ."

"It was doomed from the start. Why? Because the foreigner has always been doomed in Viet Nam. The Chinese, the Portuguese, the French, the Japanese, now the Americans . . . they were all driven out." She put her finger to Walker's lips. "Did you think America would be exempt? Because you felt you were *protecting* the Vietnamese against the Communists?"

"Jeanne," he said, "you —"

She cut him off. "That Vietnamese *idée fixe*, Hadden . . . expelling the foreigner, adding Communist indoctrination, whipping it into some kind of holy war. Well, how can you fight all that? I have heard it called 'a collision with nationalism.' "

"I call it a collision with Communism . . . a failure on America's part to stick it out."

"Why should America stick it out? So as not to 'lose face'? But it's Asians who are supposed to be worried about that. Hadden, I'm trying to say this in a way that won't hurt you. For America, its involvement here was a terrible trauma. But for the Vietnamese, in their sweep of history, America's involvement was just another . . . foreign interlude."

Walker shook his head.

"Yes, Hadden. I *know* the Vietnamese."

The sounds from below echoed through the office. Walker took her arm and turned her away from the window.

She smiled warmly and took his hands in hers. "Hadden, you want to talk about . . . what will happen with us, don't you? We have been very good for each other. But 'us' could only have come together in some kind of . . . Saigon pressure cooker. Away from here . . . ?"

"It will be even better . . . ."

"No. Better to say *au revoir* . . . for now. Before we start hating each other. To you, I would always be a reminder of defeat. To me, you would always be a reminder of what America did to Viet Nam . . . where I was born."

"After a while, Jeanne, you would forget. . . ."

He pushed away the thought that she might be right, that, outside of Saigon, they'd find themselves strangers, Viet Nam forever pursuing them, locking them into the past, each a reminder for the other.

"Later, Jeanne, we can talk about that later," Walker said softly. "Listen to me now. Carefully. In five minutes, I'm going to slip out of the Embassy. I need to use your house, for the last time. Please see to it that your servant is gone, that the house is empty."

"But you must go with the Americans. From *here*."

"I am not going until every one of the Vietnamese in the compound is flown out."

"Hadden, that's not up to you." She touched his face. "It's time to go. It's over. These last few hundred Vietnamese? Why are they more important to you than the thousands on the other side of the wall? Or the millions in the countryside?"

"Call it personal honor," Walker said. He had the feeling that he was running out of words, patience, time.

"Honor? After all this time . . . and you still talk about 'honor'? 'Honor,' my dear Hadden, never got a visa to Viet Nam."

"Jeanne, no use. I'm not going until . . ." He pointed to the window.

She stared at him. He pulled her close, kissed her, and then he searched her face as if to record a final ineradicable imprint. "Please, Jeanne," he said in a low voice as he led her toward the door and opened it. "Not a word to anyone."

She seemed about to answer but changed her mind. Instead, she kissed him again, and left.

He walked to the window and spent the next minute or two looking out. Then, he picked up his portfolio and left the office, stopping at Helen's desk to tell her he would be in touch. Ignoring her look of surprise, he stepped into his private elevator and descended to the lobby.

What will the President do when word reaches him at the White House: "Sorry, sir, the Ambassador has vanished"?

Swiftly, Walker let himself into Jeanne's house the same way he had so often before — through the rear door. "Hello?" he called out. "Anybody home?" No answer.

Once in the living room, he poured himself a brandy. *Was it only last night that he had met with Stankiewicz? Here?* Restless, he paced the room. He looked at his watch. Fifteen minutes since he'd left the Embassy. He stared at the phone. Suppose the lines had been cut? He'd give it another five minutes, then call.

But three minutes was all he could manage. He dialed his direct number at the Embassy, and heard the ring at the other end. So far, so good.

Helen answered.

"Walker here," he said.

"For God's sake, where are you?"

"Never mind. Is Sommers there?"

"Yes. Right here."

"Hello, Mr. Ambassador?" Sommers's voice was frantic. "Where the hell are you?"

"Forget that. Have you heard from the President again?"

"*Three* times. He asked to talk to you but nobody could find you. The calls were switched to me. He couldn't believe nobody knew where you were. He had a few choice words to say about you . . . deserting your post."

A smile flickered across Walker's face. "Did the President say anything about chopper flights?"

"Yes. 'Twenty-five and no more and the Ambassador must be on the last chopper out,' was what he said."

Walker stared at the telephone.

"Hadden, can you at least tell me where you are?"

Walker gently put down the receiver.

That sonofabitch wants to play hardball. Okay. But he'll cave. How will it look if his Ambassador is taken prisoner by the NVA? A couple thousand Vietnamese left behind, a country betrayed, promises broken — all that can be explained away. But an Ambassador? He'll never let it happen. I am a weapon. It's forty choppers and me — or I get captured and it's his ass. His Presidential ass. Uncovered. For the whole world to see.

There was nothing to do but wait. Sweat it out. Give them another half hour or so. Hope the telephone lines would still be working. He sipped the brandy but it tasted bitter. He kept pacing the room, feeling the seconds tick by. He stopped in front of the photograph. Jeanne's parents. French father, Vietnamese mother. What would Jeanne do — once Hanoi took over Saigon? She had a French passport. It would be easy for her to leave. Or to stay. Somehow he would convince her that their feelings for each other did not have to be nourished by upheaval and violence. She'd see. . . .

Suddenly, a loud bang. Cracking wood. He spun around. The door was hanging on a hinge.

Suzanne!

She rushed to him. He backed away.

Behind her were Sommers, Tony, the Embassy doctor, two Marines, all closing in. How the hell had they found him?

"Please — come with us!" Suzanne tugged at him. "Don't make them —"

"I'M NOT GOING!"

"PLEASE!"

"NO!"

And then it happened very swiftly. The Marines rushed him. He could hear Sommers shouting that the President had ordered them to take this step — if necessary. The Marines now had him pinned to the floor. They were pushing up his jacket sleeve, his shirt sleeve. The doctor jabbed a hypo into his arm. Walker tried to shove them away, but his arms went limp, a sudden drowsiness overwhelmed him. He heard Suzanne screaming, Tony yelling, "Don't worry, this'll just knock him

out for a little while." And then, a voice saying, "His portfolio
. . . in the chair . . . let's not forget it."

The Jolly Green Giant lifted slowly off the Embassy parking
lot, cleared the tamarind's mangled foliage, and slashed into the
black sky.

Tony looked at Walker: the gray patrician head resting against
the cabin wall. Sleeping volcano, Tony thought. Eruption guaranteed. His eyes moved to Suzanne, hugging Thi and Thach.
Sommers was staring through the porthole of the chopper. He
tapped Tony on the shoulder and pointed down; they could
make out the last flickerings of the capital, like ten-watt bulbs
in a dark room. The lights grew dimmer and dimmer, finally
disappearing. Unreal, all this, Tony thought. Walker had reassigned him out of Saigon only a few days ago; now Hanoi was
reassigning them all. Nobody talked. The engines were too
noisy, and everyone was caught up in private memories. A burst
of antiaircraft fire exploded about a thousand feet away, a couple of hundred feet below. ARVN's farewell.

It took only forty minutes to fly out of America's two decades
in Viet Nam. As their chopper approached the deck of the USS
Midway — by now it was about four-thirty A.M., dawn just beginning to filter through — they could see through the mist a
macabre regatta on the surrounding waters: sampans, rafts, fish-
ing boats, all filled with Vietnamese; a floating population,
trying to nestle up against the hull of the carrier. The Jolly
Green Giant touched down on the deck and shuddered to a
stop. The Marines aboard the chopper carefully lowered Walker
to the deck; two husky sailors kept him on his feet. They slipped
their arms around him, half-carrying, half-dragging him to the
nearest cabin, where they stretched him out on a bunk. Only
Suzanne remained with him; she had asked Tony to look after
Thi and Thach. She studied her father's face, now drained,
cadaverous, and she recalled the way he had looked, so ener-
getic and hopeful, on his arrival in Saigon just a year ago.

After a half-hour, his eyelids began to flutter. His eyes

opened, closed, reopened, then focused on Suzanne; she could see him struggling to sort out what had happened during the last two hours.

"It was all over," Suzanne whispered. "Nothing more anyone could do. Nothing more even *you* could do. The President had ordered us all out."

"Yes . . . the President . . . ," Walker murmured. He rolled to his side, then suddenly sat upright on the edge of the bunk. "My portfolio!"

"Right next to you," Suzanne reassured him.

He reached for the portfolio and clutched it to his chest, as though it were some kind of protective armor. "Suzanne . . . maybe I could be alone for a while. . . ."

She leaned over, kissed him, and turned quickly to the door. She did not want him to see the tears streaming down her face.

On the flight deck, picking her way among the clusters of Vietnamese, Suzanne finally found Tony. Thi and Thach ran for her and looped their arms around her waist.

"How is he?" Tony asked quietly.

"What you'd expect."

"Wish I could get a moment with him."

"Hardly the ideal time — now."

Tony smiled. "Not everything I would say would be negative."

Suzanne looked up sharply.

"I'd tell him two things," Tony went on. "That I admired his piling those Vietnamese into the chopper. And that I wanted to apologize for what we had to do back there" — he waved his hand in the direction of the South Vietnamese coast, somewhere in the semidarkness — "in those last few minutes."

"That all?"

Tony ran his fingers through Thi's long black hair. "Then . . . *if* I had the courage . . . I'd tell him that if only he hadn't been so fucking pig-headed, so fucking stubborn, we might have had a negotiating crack at 'the other side' and . . ."

"You can't let go, can you?"

". . . and that we might, just might, have avoided all this." He pointed to the Vietnamese huddled everywhere on the deck. "If only he had told Washington the truth. How fucked-up ARVN was. How Saigon was beyond saving. Washington might have opted for a switch in policy. Maybe, just maybe, we could have worked out a coalition — which is still better than losing it all."

"Even now, Tony, you can't stop."

Tony shook his head. "We had our chance. We even blew that one."

Suzanne put her arms around Thi and Thach. "I guess the arguments, the second-guessing, the ifs . . . and whens . . . and buts of what happened will go on forever," she said. "Right now, I'm not thinking about that. But there is one little thing . . . more personal."

He reached out to take her hand. She pulled back.

"How did you find out my father was at Madame de Clery's house?"

"She telephoned. To Sommers. Said she'd promised to keep his secret. But she was terrified of what would happen to him if he were left behind." Tony crossed his arms over his chest. "But we'd have found him anyway. The Agency knew all about him and Madame de Clery. Did *you* know?"

Suzanne looked away for a moment, then nodded. "It was the only good thing that ever happened to him — in Saigon."

"I suppose."

All around them they could hear Vietnamese voices.

He moved closer to her. "Suzanne . . . ," he said softly.

"Tony . . . the struggle, the agony I felt about being caught between the two of you, you and my father — all that's over. Gone. Excess baggage thrown away before I jumped into the chopper. I could say I feel 'free' — but that's not it. I feel nothing . . . right now."

"And later?"

Suzanne shook her head. "We're survivors, Tony." She

looked around at the dazed faces of the Vietnamese on the deck. "All of us. It can take a long, long time to recover from survival." She turned from him, took the children by the hand. "Meantime, I'm going to look for the mess hall to see if I can get these kids something to eat." She glanced over her shoulder. "See you later."

"Tony?" It was Sommers. He had spotted Tony leaning up against the rail near the stern of the ship, looking out at the Vietnamese refugee boats scattered over the South China Sea. "How are you?"

"Disaster," said Tony. "Whole fucking thing is a disaster."

"Fits right in with the Hanoi scenario."

"What do you mean? If the 'old man' hadn't been sending all that ARVN-can-hack-it bullshit back to Washington, we might have had negotia—"

"No."

"What do you mean, no?"

"No."

"No *what?*"

"No!"

"Can you prove it?"

"Yeah."

"Prove it." Tony looked at Sommers with defiance.

"Yesterday. Four P.M. Walker had a secret meeting set with Hanoi. Twenty-two Hong Thap Tu."

"WHAT!"

"I won't go into the details now. Walker was there . . . *ordered* there by Washington . . . to negotiate. Subject: 'coalition.' "

"AND?"

"Hanoi's man didn't show."

"GOD!"

"Four P.M. When the shit hit the fan. Remember?"

"Well, what the fuck did he expect? Cheese and wine? When they had it *all?*"

---

*　*　*

The sun smashed through the porthole of his cabin. Walker glanced at his watch. Six A.M. He slowly opened the door. Vietnamese were everywhere, filling the passageways, crowding the stairs. He climbed to the flight deck. The sky was flawlessly blue; when he lowered his eyes just a few inches, he could see the final debris of the war sparkling in the sunshine: junks, tubs, trawlers, barges, tramp steamers, rowboats, tenders, all jammed with Vietnamese. In the distance, TF 76 — American warships, carriers, destroyers, support vessels. The silent U.S. Fleet, the motley Vietnamese flotilla, Walker thought. A floating obituary.

He walked past the parked helicopters, the bare-chested sailors, the murmuring Vietnamese; he felt oddly detached from everything, all alone, severed.

Suddenly the sirens began wailing. The *Midway*'s PA system blared an announcement that a South Vietnamese Air Force helicopter was approaching. Walker looked up. There it was, a small, olive-drab Huey, "934" painted on its narrow fuselage, the skids bumping down heavily on the deck. The chopper was obviously overloaded. The door swung open, and out tumbled four VNAF officers and eleven ARVN generals. Their faces were haggard, exhausted. They watched, silently, as a detail of sailors quickly pushed the Huey overboard; the *Midway* had simply run out of storage space. The helicopter made an eerie little splash as it knifed into the sea and disappeared in an eruption of foam.

A U.S. Navy officer quickly waved the new arrivals to the side, and they passed by, one after the other, within a few yards of Walker. He tried not to look at their faces; he half-lowered his eyes and focused on their names, embroidered into their military shirts just above the right breast pocket. TRUONG. MINH. TOAN. PHU. VIEN. THIEN. DINH. Dinh? General *Dinh*? Walker raised his eyes and recognized his old friend, whom he had last seen in the corridor at Doc Lap. Dinh here? Just another fleeing general? Walker would have bet his last dollar that Dinh was

272

the sort of military man who would have fought to the end, died in the field. But here he was lifted to the safety of a U.S. warship, again dependent on the Americans whom he must now despise. Maybe later, this afternoon, tomorrow, Walker thought, he'd get a moment with Dinh. For a fraction of a second, as Walker looked up, he thought Dinh noticed him. But it was all too fast; the generals and VNAF officers were waved on, moving through the anonymous Vietnamese on the deck.

Walker felt a tap on his shoulder. He turned around.

"Meeting more frequently than usual, aren't we?" Bill Starnes of the *Post* said with a smile.

Walker couldn't suppress a tiny, bitter laugh.

"Turns out we're all in the same boat," Starnes added.

" '. . . all in the same boat,' " Walker repeated. "A good image. Maybe someday somebody will believe it."

"Just out of curiosity," Starnes said as he fumbled for a cigarette in his khaki jacket, "did you really think conning me into writing that B-fifty-two story would have an effect on Washington? Or Hanoi?"

"Look, it's all over now — though it never had to end this way. It's finished." He looked up at Starnes. "I've got better stories."

Starnes shook his head. "No, thanks."

"The whole story."

Starnes's face now showed a wary interest.

Walker stared at the sky. "Maybe I'll see you in Washington," he said. "It's a small town."

The Ambassador threaded his way through hundreds of Vietnamese refugees. He recognized no one he knew. No Cabinet ministers, no politicians, no VIPs; they must have already created an elite corner of their own in another part of the ship. All these were the faces of ordinary Vietnamese: clerks, translators, secretaries — people who had worked for the U.S. mission; others with no American connection but who had managed to make it into the DAO or into the Embassy compound: shopkeepers, bargirls, café intellectuals, the list was endless. The lucky ones, yet they did not look joyful. Walker felt they were staring at him with silent accusation. He smiled, weakly, as if in self-defense. He found himself pushing past the faces in a semitrance. Suddenly he bumped into someone.

"Mr. Ambassador."

He recognized the voice.

"Didn't want to bother you," Sommers said. "But I want to apologize for . . ."

Walker nodded.

They stood silently for a few moments, watching a Vietnamese woman open a paper bag and dig out some cold rice. She formed the rice into little balls and handed them to three children.

"How many did we leave behind?" Walker asked, his eyes fixed on the rice.

"About four hundred or so. Inside the compound, that is."

Cold rice. How does cold rice taste? Walker wondered.

Sommers glanced at his watch. "The President's going to be speaking from the Oval Office," he said. "Within the next couple of minutes, matter of fact."

"Oh."

"Live. Going to be short-waved around the world. *Midway*'s going to pick it up. Put it on the PA. Pipe it into all the cabins."

Walker finally turned to look at Sommers. "We've got a lot to talk about, you and I."

"Yes, we do," Sommers answered.

"Not now," Walker said. He went back to his cabin, sat down on his bunk, and switched on the wall speaker. All he could hear was static. After a couple of minutes, the familiar voice of the President filled the small room.

"My fellow Americans, ladies and gentlemen, members of the armed forces. The last of the Marine security force at the U.S. Embassy in Saigon has been airlifted out of South Viet

Nam, and I can therefore now report to you that the evacuation has been completed. Thousands of Americans and Vietnamese, in one of the great rescue operations in history, have been helicoptered to safety. The long sad chapter of America in Viet Nam has come to an end. American integrity has been safeguarded, and in a saga filled with heroism, the American commitment to justice and honesty and decency was perhaps best exemplified by the behavior of our Ambassador, Hadden Walker. Operating under the most hostile of conditions, when panic was always a possibility, Ambassador Walker demonstrated true gallantry in the finest American tradition. Ambassador Walker would not leave the American Embassy in Saigon — and I concurred in his judgment — until he was sure that the people he had worked with, both American and Vietnamese, had all been evacuated."

Walker smashed his fist against the wall.

"The Ambassador departed only on the very last helicopter carrying American civilians from Saigon. The Ambassador is now aboard the USS *Midway* off South Viet Nam. As for additional details on the evacuation, let me say that the American helicopters never stopped flying until . . ."

Walker leaped from his bunk and switched off the speaker. He sat quietly, for a moment, then switched it on again.

". . . our country, tested in fire, emerges from the war stronger than ever. Our honor has survived Communist aggression. . . ."

Walker switched off the speaker again. *The President as pitchman, still mouthing words, selling shame as triumph, defeat as victory, projecting himself as the hero who had rescued the U.S. from Viet Nam, now sitting before the microphones, trying to induce national hypnosis. In the nonpolitical world, they'd haul you to court for that, for coast-to-coast perjury; at the White House, you toot your own horn and check the polls.*

He could not resist switching on the speaker once more.

". . . and now we can look to the future with —"

He switched the speaker off again. He could write the rest of the speech himself. Peace at last, all's well, America. Hallelujah!

Walker felt closed in, suffocated. He opened the door, stepped into the passageway, stopped short. Directly in front of him, a thin Vietnamese in Army uniform stood leaning against the bulkhead, arms crossed, as though he had been waiting.

"General Dinh!" Walker said, reaching out to shake his hand.

As Dinh raised his hand, Walker spotted the glint of metal, heard the shot, felt his chest explode. Then, nothing.

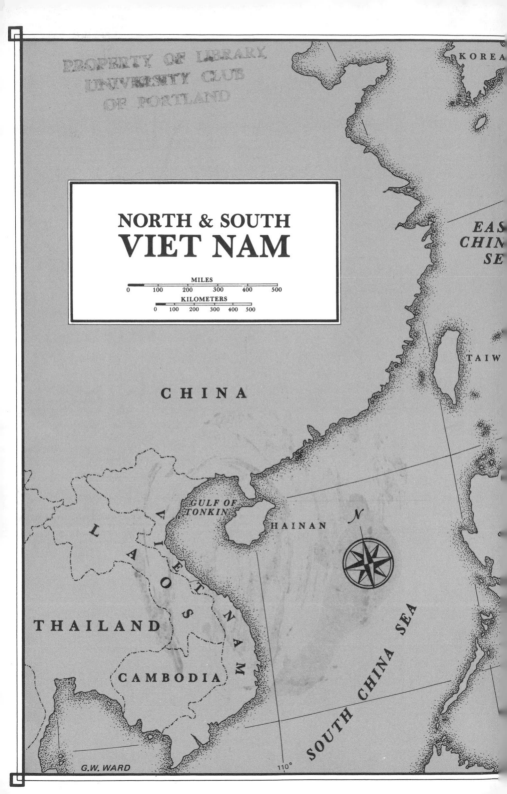

NORTH & SOUTH
VIET NAM

MILES

0   100   200   300   400   500

KILOMETERS

0   100   200   300   400   500

KOREA

EAS
CHIN
SE

TAIW

CHINA

GULF OF
TONKIN

HAINAN

N

L A O S

V I E T N A M

THAILAND

CAMBODIA

SOUTH CHINA SEA

110°

G.W. WARD